DEATH
AT
THE COLLECTIVE

ANOTHER
DAVID GOODHART
MYSTERY

Graham Cawley

About the Author

Graham Cawley joined Lloyds Bank in South Devon and eventually retired as senior manager of the St James's Street branch in London's West End. He then took up writing as a hobby and has had numerous articles and short stories published. These then led to his self-publishing three banking crime novels. CHAIN OF EVENTS and FATAL RETRIBUTION feature South Devon bank manager, David Goodhart, while AVARICE chronicles his advancement to branch inspector in the South East of England. DEATH AT THE COLLECTIVE continues the series. Each book depicts little-known-about financial crimes and also features Graham's love of football and jazz.

DEATH

AT

THE COLLECTIVE

First published in Great Britain as a softback original in 2020

Copyright © Graham Cawley

The moral right of this author has been asserted.

Typeset in Palatino

Design, typesetting and publishing by UK Book Publishing

www.ukbookpublishing.com

ISBN: 978-1-913179-54-0

To *Lisa*, *Katie* and *Lucy*, together with *Shelagh*, *Ian* and my great friend, *Mike Murray*, for their support and encouragement

Chapter 1

David Goodhart now knew that this had been a terrible mistake. Why, oh why had he accepted the invitation? Not that he had a valid reason to turn it down. A prior engagement? Not a chance. More pressing work to complete? Hardly a plausible alternative. As for trying to wriggle and squirm to get out of it . . .

And now that he was here, he had no choice but to remain in this dingy hotel banqueting suite, surrounded by men in grey suits. What was worse, those behind him effectively barred any escape by way of the glass-panelled swing doors through which they had just entered.

"Come on, David," David's companion and host, Frank Windsor, said, elbowing his way through the throng. His urging themselves forward now completely thwarted any thoughts David might have had about making a hasty about-turn. "Everyone wants to meet you."

It was not the obvious impression being made on David. Overt close scrutiny seemed to be touched with cynicism and no little suspicion. Anyone would think he were a police inspector, rather than a bank inspector.

He tried to smile, but his lips seemed to be fixed, slightly open, rather like ventriloquist, Peter Brough, when he attempted to make his dummy, Archie Andrews, do the talking. Only, in this instance, David was the one feeling like a dummy.

"Ah, there you are, Derek," Frank Windsor then said, as they came face to face with a remarkably gaunt six-footer who, to David's mind, would make a stick insect appear over-fed. "Let me introduce my colleague, David Goodhart."

Colleague?

Really? Yes, David and Windsor both worked for National Counties Bank, but they were hardly colleagues. David was in the middle of inspecting Windsor's branch, here in Crowborough, and from what he had discovered so far, he would not want to associate himself as being one of his colleagues.

Stick-insect's sunken grey eyes took in David warily and he seemed reluctant to extend his hand. David had no alternative but to take the lead and thrust his own hand forward.

"Pleased to meet you," he said, hoping that any insincerity would go unnoticed. He tried to widen his smile, but he could feel it turning into a grimace as he grasped a hand which lacked any meaningful flesh on its fingers. "Derek ...?"

"Herretson," stick-insect replied, a slight lisp making it difficult for David to decipher the spelling of his name. The man's thin lips did their best to shield any hint of a returned smile and his eyes continued to view David guardedly.

"Derek's the most successful investment consultant in town," Windsor interjected, clearly currying favour with the man. That was odd. Why would he do that? After all, stick-insect in his formative years was probably only a failed accountant - or banker? Or was David being unfair? It was hardly the man's fault that he had come into David's firing line when he was still smarting about having to be here.

"Come on, Frank," Herretson protested, though, to David's mind, not convincingly, "that's only because of the splendid introductions you put my way."

Windsor positively beamed at such flattery, his blue eyes sparkling; and had David imagined that fluttering of his eyelashes? He was not sure, but he was starting to feel distinctly uneasy. Giving away business which should be better domiciled under the roof of National Counties? In years gone by, it might have been appropriate to spread business around, subject to quid pro quos, of course. But now, in 1960, the bank should be able to provide customers with as good a return as might be available through some back-street investment consultant. Perhaps, despite David's misgivings about being here, he might actually gain something from being Frank Windsor's guest at this ghastly Crowborough Collective lunch.

Until three years ago when David had first inspected Crowborough branch, he had not heard of such an organization. Round Table, yes; Rotary, yes; but a Collective? To him, its very name conjured up the antithesis of a group of which he would wish to be a member. To his mind, cliques of any description needed to be avoided at all costs - apart from Crystal Palace Supporters' Club. As if in competition to the worthwhile Rotary Club, Crowborough Collective had been founded a few years ago by a group of local businessmen. David had been told that the members had originally wanted to call it Crowborough Cooperative, but they had been put off by grocery and political connotations. Some members might have felt that their new club did indeed equate to Rotary. But how could that be? Rotary was so different. That organization was all about fellowship and society, always seeking to do good in the community. Quite the opposite of Crowborough Collective which appeared to be entirely self-serving - for the sole benefit of its members, carefully chosen from their perceived elite within the business community.

3

No wonder David had abhorred the thought of attending today. But his main worry was how could Frank Windsor have become a member of such a group?

As for this stick insect . . . For a man whose business needed to thrive on new introductions and sales, his appearance was bordering on being unkempt. His three-piece charcoal suit hung limply around his spare frame and its pin stripes only emphasized his lanky stature. At least the waistcoat did its best to provide some much needed extra bulk. The suit tried vainly to hide a badly ironed white shirt, but Herretson had no need to worry about its soiled, detached stiff collar chafing his neck; it was a couple of sizes too large to cause such a problem. The collar also highlighted his Adam's apple which appeared way out of proportion to his slender throat. David appreciated that first impressions could be misleading, but a man in Herretson's position ought to be duty-bound to try and make the best possible impact when dealing with new and existing clients - never mind with a bank inspector who was already finding it difficult to understand why this man was 'the most successful investment consultant in town'.

"Frank! Who've you got here?"

Oh, no! Stick-insect had suddenly metamorphosed into a roly-poly businessman, clad in a garish primrose and tan check suit, its jacket protecting a canary yellow and blue ill-matching waistcoat. This vest reminded David of Torquay United's changed strip from their traditional white shirts and black shorts. The man must have only been about five foot six, but seemed even shorter because of his girth. It somehow reminded David of blues singer, Jimmy Rushing, known as Mr Five-by-Five, being five foot tall and five foot wide.

"My guest, Henry. David Goodhart."

"Ah, the famous inspector, what? Or infamous, Frank?"

Roly-poly chortled at his apparent witticism. David could only groan inwardly. As for this 'what?' business . . . A few months ago, David had encountered this quirk at Tunbridge Wells branch. Colonel Fawkes-William was the manager - 'was' being the operative word. After dreadful events at his branch, early retirement had been forced upon him. Such an indignity must have been chastening for an upper-crust ex-army officer who punctuated many of his utterances with the adjunct 'what?'. Could Mr Roly-poly also be an army man?

"Now, now, Henry," Windsor answered, "don't be flippant. David, this is Henry Purcell. We call him HP. You can already see he's a bit saucy."

Oh dear, oh dear. Oh my, oh my. Things really were going from bad to worse. And it was less than five minutes since they had come through the hotel's entrance.

"Actually, David," Windsor continued, before HP could get in a rejoinder, one which must have been on the tip of his tongue, "Henry runs a seriously good residential home. And his residents certainly appreciate his sense of humour. At their time of life, they don't have a lot to laugh about. Poor souls."

Poor souls? What about poor bank inspectors having to suffer this twaddle?

David had met HP's equivalent before. It had not been a sobering experience. Back in his time in Devon, this particular individual had run a chain of amusement arcades in Torquay and Paignton. Once again, this man had been the life and soul - one of the best known personalities in town, not least because of the ostentatious Cadillac in which he toured the area. He was generous, too; he always supported good causes with large dollops of cash. Always cash. It continued until the forces of law and order caught up with him for rigging his multitude of slot machines.

But, now, relief was at hand: HP turned his attention to a man who looked to be a likely candidate for his residential home, someone in his eighties, at least. Yet still a member of the Collective? On the other hand, like David, he could be a guest. In which case, not only would he be the recipient of HP's *joie de vivre*, but also, probably, of a sales pitch.

David's host moved to join them. Perhaps he thought HP to be better company than a bank inspector. David could hardly blame him. But David was suddenly on his own and immediately felt liberated. Where was the bar? And his other concern was whom, apart from Frank Windsor, would he be sitting alongside at lunch - when it was finally served? There were already two candidates who would not feature on his short list.

But his liberation was short-lived. He could see himself being eyed up by someone who looked to have no right to be here: he was suit-less. A sports jacket and flannels was his order of the day, accompanied by brown brogues. He looked to be anything but a businessman. His jacket was bulging at the seams and not, probably, from having had too many a business lunch. It looked to David as if his coat was filled with brawn and there was no evidence of a paunch. In his prime, some years ago, he could easily have been a boxer and this impression was enhanced by a nose which had certainly seen better days. But his eyes did not reflect stick-insect's suspicion, nor HP's schoolboy jollity. Instead, they twinkled rather wryly, making David feel that this individual might be a kindred spirit.

"On your own?" the man asked, thrusting forward a ham-sized hand which enveloped David's as if it were a child's. His fingers felt rough-hewn and were clearly not used to wielding a fountain pen.

David nodded. "At the moment. Seem to have lost my host."

The man grinned. "A guest, eh? Very brave of you."

It would seem that David was not alone in his feelings about Crowborough Collective and its lunches. "You too?"

"You must be joking! No one would invite me as a guest."

David frowned. "So ...?"

"You might call me the black sheep of the family. This particular family, anyway. That's what they are, after all. One big happy family - seemingly. All boys, though. No women allowed. Can't stand it, really. All the back slapping and schoolboy humour."

Definitely a kindred spirit.

"But you're a member?"

"Surprise you? Me, too, when they invited me to join. I'm Ted Callard, by the way. Don't worry, I've just twigged who you are. Can I call you David?"

David was certainly warming to the man, but another person who knew whom he was? As he nodded, Ted Callard clearly discerned David's bemusement.

"Word gets around."

"But you're making me curious," David answered. "From what you've just said, it doesn't sound as if this Collective business is your cup of tea."

"This part of it isn't," he said, waving his arms around and almost giving a nearby businessman a forearm smash. "But a year ago, they heard about my son. He'd been knocked down by a car - five years ago. He's twenty now. But apart from physical problems, he's got brain damage. Spends all his time in a wheelchair. And they've been great with him. Some of them, anyhow. Day Centre help, outings, that sort of thing. Then they asked me to join. Couldn't refuse, could I?"

Perhaps David had got it wrong. Perhaps there was a good side to Crowborough Collective. But he had winced when he heard the words brain damage. Memories flooded back about his own father's car crash many years ago and the devastating effects of brain injury. Dad had not been physically harmed, unlike Ted Callard's son, and no head injury had been diagnosed at the time. But as each year passed, Dad's increasing irrational behaviour had led to further investigation which categorically confirmed incurable brain injury. For David's family, it had almost been a merciful release when he had eventually died of a heart attack two years ago.

"But the other big problem is my wife," Ted Callard continued, even before David could express any sympathy. "She's finding it impossible to cope. Peter's our only child and, before the accident, he'd been doing well at school. Passed his eleven-plus and got to the grammar. Just about to start his 'O' levels when wham - his life effectively gone in an instant. Since then, it's worn Barbara down to a frazzle. I don't know what she'd do if anything happened to me."

This was getting rather too close for comfort for David. He and Sarah also only had one boy and Mark was at grammar school in Tunbridge Wells, not far off preparing for his own 'O' levels. God forbid the same thing happening to him. How would he and Sarah cope with another head injury in the family?

"Anyway," Ted Callard said, shrugging his shoulders, "you don't want to hear about my domestic problems. But there is something else . . ."

David groaned inwardly as Callard looked around, as if seeking out prying ears. He then drew himself closer to David, almost conspiratorially.

". . . something bad's going on. Really bad. I've made it known I might spill the beans, but I don't want to go to the police. I was just wondering . . . with you being a bank inspector. I appreciate you don't know me . . . but I do bank with National Counties. Could we meet up soon - away from here? I'd like to bend your ear."

Now this really was conspiratorial. David suppressed a grimace. It was not something he had expected to happen at this lunch. And it was certainly not something he wanted to happen.

"If it's as bad as you imply," he said, hoping to stave off any involvement on his part, "and you mentioned the police . . ."

"No, no," Ted Callard interrupted, looking around again. David followed his gaze. Callard's eyes had fixed on three people in conversation a few yards away. Two of the men were short and stocky, but the third was well over six foot tall, his bearing being like that of a soldier. Or a policeman? Perhaps there was a police inspector here, as well as a bank inspector. "I can't go down that route," Callard then said, returning his attention to David. " My business is in scrap metal . . . nothing illegal, of course. But I've had the police nosing around before - cash business, you know. And . . . let's just say . . ."

But before he could continue, Frank Windsor was back at their side.

"You've met our Ted, then," he said, eyeing him up and down surreptitiously and then rather hastily leading David away towards another (more appropriately dressed?) member. David would normally have preferred to remain with sports-jacketed 'our Ted', except that with 'something bad' hanging in the air, he was mightily relieved to be dragged away, though disconcerted by Ted Callard's parting mouthed words "I'll be in touch."

David had no time to ponder on this as he was immediately introduced to the Honourable Charlie Spencer O'Hara. Judging by Frank Windsor's overt fawning, it was a wonder David had not been paraded before the Honourable as soon as they had arrived at this wretched lunch. Our Charlie (not, of course, referred to as that by Windsor) seemed to be lapping up the attention he was getting from David's host. Perhaps, because David did not immediately follow suit, the Honourable seemed to eye him with some suspicion and not a little disdain. David immediately decided that there was unlikely to be much lightness and brightness in the company of such an apparently austere individual. Within seconds of meeting him, he was convinced that the man sheltered smugly under his hereditary title.

"Charlie's a big noise around here," Frank Windsor gushed. "And not just here in Crowborough, but throughout Kent and Sussex. We're most fortunate to have him as a member of our particular club. He'd have been welcome anywhere."

Except that Crowborough Collective was a one-off. Perhaps Windsor had other towns' Rotary clubs in mind. Anyway, David tried to look suitably impressed, though he had been given no indication as to why our Charlie's noise was big. His nose, yes, which was large and aquiline and out of proportion to a face which was manifestly landed gentry.

This impression continued elsewhere. Slicked-back black hair, much longer than the short back and sides so prevalent in this room, helped to distinguish himself from what he would probably describe as more mortal souls. He was also an inch or so taller than David's six foot, likely to give him a perceived physical advantage of looking down on others. In doing this with David, he still had his chin raised, his aquiline appendage giving the impression of testing the air beneath him. It reminded David of his *bete noire* at Regional Office, Angus McPhoebe. The regional manager's deputy also put on similar highborn airs, the difference being that McPhoebe's were cultivated, whereas O'Hara's were clearly inherited.

"And your line of business?" David dutifully asked.

"Property," Windsor interjected, as though our Charlie might have difficulty in answering for himself. "Realty management and valuations, to be exact."

David groaned inwardly. An estate agent, then. He had never previously thought of that as being a big noise occupation. As for the way this lunch party was progressing, no wonder Ted Callard had reservations about attending such functions.

Without our Charlie having said a word, they were on the move again, but this now looked to be much more interesting: David was being propelled towards the bar. What a pity that this had turned out to be positioned on the far side of the room from the entrance. Be that as it may, he deemed it to be an oasis amid this barren mass of the Crowborough Collective and a pint of Harvey's would certainly make the occasion a mite more bearable.

But no. Not just yet, anyway. As they made their way forward, a hand was thrust towards him and David had no choice but to take it in his. It was quite the opposite of Ted Callard's - this one being slender-fingered, silky-smooth to the touch. It belonged to a 'typical pen-pusher', as a war-time square-bashing NCO had described David when he had learnt about his banking background.

Frank Windsor beamed as he proudly made the introductions, his pride seemingly addressed at 'silky-fingers', rather than at David. Yet that could be deemed short-sighted; it was David who was inspecting his branch.

"David, this is Julian Palfrow - solicitor extraordinaire."

Extraordinaire? What had the man done to deserve such an accolade? David smiled, hoping that any lack of awe on his part would go unnoticed. "How do you do?"

Like so many others here, Mr Extraordinaire was attired in a dark three-piece suit, but unlike Derek Herretson, it fitted snugly, much more Savile Row than the best that Crowborough, or even Tunbridge Wells, might produce. The man must be in his fifties and had a striking debonair resemblance to Cary Grant. It was as well that this Crowborough Collective was male-only, otherwise David could imagine the ladies being unable to leave him alone as they vied for his attention.

He eyed David up and down, then returned his smile, the lack of awe on his part being most noticeable. "So, you're the famous inspector."

Unlike HP, Mr Five-by-Five, he resisted adding the infamous bit, but David was getting a little unnerved that everyone here seemed to be aware of his apparent renown. Was this a deliberate ploy on Frank Windsor's part? If so, why?

"No doubt you could do with a drink," the solicitor continued, looking at his watch. "We'll be sitting down soon."

David felt an inner glow. It was strange how such a suggestion could suddenly warm one to someone who initially seemed to share our Charlie's arrogance. But any respite was short-lived. As soon as David had taken his first sip of Harvey's, a bell clanged and an announcement was made that lunch was about to be served. This was likely to pose the problem David had previously feared: his seated companions.

But there was some relief: he and Windsor were not on the top table. And it did not pass David's notice that their own table was nearest to the exit. How fortuitous was that? But only if Frank Windsor shared David's wish for 'an early bath'.

David was on Windsor's left-hand side and a ruddy-faced, middle-aged gentleman, not that dissimilar to Ted Callard, was David's other seated companion. This man was, though, attired in a suit.

"George Bathurst," he said, grasping David's hand. David could feel that 'first impressions' syndrome re-surfacing, but he was quietly confident that he could have picked a worse dining companion.

He soon established that George, according to him, was a major player (or big noise?) in domestic house building. He had also recently expanded into commercial property and he certainly had some grand ideas. But any question of David getting carried along with his enthusiasm foundered when George mentioned the name of his firm: GB Builders. Only this morning, David had not discouraged Frank Windsor from bouncing two of the firm's cheques. The business was clearly under-capitalized and over-borrowed. But returning the cheques could certainly have had an adverse effect at this lunch table. Bathurst was, however, chatting amiably with David and, across him with Frank Windsor. It would seem that he was, as yet, unaware of this latest development on his bank account. David decided to change the subject to football.

He had to admit that the actual meal was proving to be better than he had expected. The standard of cooking was not at all bad for a member of a small hotel chain and, once they started to talk about football - and Crystal Palace in particular - the conversation became free-flowing.

But all good things must come to an end and the dreaded speeches were soon upon them. The toast to Her Majesty was always mercifully brief, though a chorus of 'God bless hers' from around the room threatened to extend it. But then came the toasts to the guests, to Crowborough Collective and to Tom, Dick and Harry. And as with most toasts and speeches on such occasions, they went on for far too long.

But just when David thought the end of the world was nigh, a fearful crash resounded from the other side of the room. Crockery fell to the floor, glasses were sent flying and a pitcher of water drenched the people on the other side of the table from the figure now lying face down in his place setting.

Silence befell the room until everyone realized the seriousness of the situation. People then stood up, *en masse*, to get a better view of what had happened. A name was called out and a man who was quite clearly the Collective's doctor member rushed to the table. Another hush descended on the room as he made a quick examination. He then looked up at the club's president and shook his head sadly.

Chapter 2

D avid got back to the branch at about two-fifty.

It had only been a five-minute stroll from the hotel and he had welcomed the calming influence of fresh autumn air wafting into his face as he made his way down the hill to the bank. It had, in fact, been a relief simply to step outside the hotel's front door. When he had retrieved his coat from the cloakroom, his hands had actually shaken as he thrust them down the garment's sleeves. Yet, how should he expect to react to a sudden death in such close proximity? It always surprised him how his stomach churned on driving past a bad roadside accident - an accident in which he had no involvement. No wonder his angst on this occasion at the sudden death of someone with whom he had been speaking only an hour or so earlier?

He reached the traffic lights at Crowborough Cross and waited to cross the busy junction where the bank stood on one corner. He was on his own. Frank Windsor had remained behind with a small number of other diners to deal with the aftermath of Ted Callard's sudden demise.

The shock within the dining room had been palpable. Ted Callard had clearly been popular and well-liked. David fully understood the feeling. Only a brief encounter with the man had supported this view. But this did not lessen David's disquiet. Could it be that he had been the only one privy to the anxieties of the scrap metal dealer? If so, why had he made David his confidant? That, in itself, was worrying enough, but now, David would never know what it had been all about.

Before going into the branch, he glanced at the pub on the opposite side of the junction. In other circumstances, he could have been tempted to cross its threshold. But he cast aside any thoughts of the welcoming aroma of hops which would greet him upon stepping into the bar. That would hardly be fitting after what had happened to poor old Ted Callard. In any case, the doors were closed. No extended lunch hours there, then. Yet this pub was too close to the branch for a watering-hole. He would not want the staff to get the wrong impression of a visiting inspector. On the other hand, an imbibing inspector might make him appear more human. Branch staff could view such unwelcome visitors as ogres, as if from another planet. Seeing him enjoying a pint of Harvey's might just lessen their prevailing 'them and us' mentality.

The branch, itself, occupied the prominent site where Eridge Road joined London Road. The bank's oak front door was positioned on the actual corner of these two roads and, unlike the pub, it was still open for business. Not for long, though, with closing time of three o'clock fast approaching.

David entered the branch and found the banking hall devoid of customers. That would please the two cashiers who would be making the most of this free time to balance their tills. They would not relish the arrival of traders leaving it to the last minute to pay in their daily takings. Crowborough was one of the smaller branches of National Counties and, with only ten staff, the cashiers needed to balance up quickly so as to provide the back-office staff with support to finish off the day's work.

Without having a key to the pass door which would allow him entry into the back office, David caught the eye of the chief clerk who was working at a high desk behind the cashiers. Frank Scrivens could only be described as an old-school bank official. Straight out of Dickensian times. His pristine white shirt even sported a wing collar, almost unheard of in this day and age, unless you were a pupil at Eton or King's, Canterbury. He was in his late fifties, approaching retirement and from what Frank Windsor had told David, had never held any ambition to be a bank manager. He was simply a pen-pusher, though meticulous in the extreme, and was fortunate to have risen to second-in-command at this small branch of National Counties.

"Thank you, Mr Scrivens," David said, as the chief clerk opened the door for him. Mr Scrivens confined any acknowledgement to a simple nod which then extended into a discreet bow. David made a mental note to mention this to his dear wife, Sarah, should she ever deign to deny him such regal status at home.

He then made his way to a small room at the back of the building. This was the staff rest room which had been allocated to him and his assistant for the duration of their inspection of the branch. He had not enquired as to where the staff would now consume their lunchtime sandwiches.

When he entered the room, Trevor Smith looked up from his desk and grinned.

"So you survived it, sir?" David's assistant had been well aware of his boss's reluctance at having to attend the lunch, but he immediately looked puzzled when David did not respond to his levity and remained serious.

"You could say that," David said, taking off his raincoat, thankful that, despite autumnal threatening skies, it had not been needed to keep him dry coming back to the branch. He hung it on the coat stand adjacent to the door. "But not everyone did."

Trevor's grin turned to a frown as David described how the lunch had culminated in Ted Callard's death.

"But what was the cause?"

"Probably a heart attack. After it happened, I was told he'd been under stress. That could well be the case. Family problems. His son is severely handicapped. On the other hand, he didn't seem too stressed to me - not about that, anyway. Yet . . ."

"Sir?"

David pursed his lips and tried to re-run in his mind the conversation he had had with the man. "I'd met him before the lunch started. Thought it was going to be the usual pre-lunch chit-chat. But then he started confiding in me - even though we'd only just met. That's when he told me about his son. Five years ago, he'd been knocked down by a car. He's twenty now and confined to a wheelchair. Apart from physical problems, he's also got brain damage. Both parents are finding it difficult to cope. But especially his mother. Callard actually said he didn't know how she'd manage if something happened to him."

Trevor Smith's appalled expression indicated his awareness of the apparent prescience of these words.

"But that's not the confiding bit," David continued. "He was really bothered about something else. He even mentioned the police. But he didn't want to go to them. He made it clear he wanted my advice instead. Yet, why me? Especially as I've no idea what it was about. Before he could elaborate, we got called in to lunch."

"Doesn't sound good, sir. Mentioning the police, I mean."

David could only agree with that. And was Ted Callard's reluctance to involve the police really because his scrap metal business was cash-orientated?

"The thing is, Trevor, now we're never going to know. But he did say that he banked with us. I think we should have a look at his account. If something dodgy's going on . . ."

A tap on the door interrupted him. He looked up as Frank Windsor stepped into the room.

Chapter 3

D avid had first met Frank Windsor in 1957, just after having been appointed as a branch inspector. Crowborough was a good branch to launch his new role. The size of the branch meant that most of his tasks should have been manageable, with few complications. And that is how it had turned out. Windsor had only taken on the manager's position two months earlier, so they were effectively two novices in their new roles.

The outcome had been a rather bland inspection report. Any lending-related problems were essentially down to Windsor's predecessor. That manager had retired prematurely for reasons of ill-health. It was then up to Windsor to clear up any mess he had inherited. Any criticisms in David's report thus related more to historical matters than those that might have arisen during Windsor's short tenure at the branch. And because David was, himself, new to his job, he had trodden a rather conservative line. Now, three years later, he had matured into an inspector's role, fully prepared to be as hard-hitting as necessary when assessing a manager's capabilities and attitude. Just a week into this particular inspection, he was already experiencing reservations about the competency of Frank Windsor.

But he set aside any such thoughts when the manager, clearly grief-stricken from the lunchtime trauma, entered the room. Gone was the bonhomie he had shown when introducing David to his Collective pals. He was only about five foot six, but he now seemed even smaller as he sidled into the room, his shoulders almost sunk into his chest. Gone, also, was his usual ruddy complexion. His facial pallor and sunken eyes would have been disconcerting had David not been aware of what had happened at the hotel. A discernable tick touched his right eyelid, threatening to become a flutter. This was not the man of only a couple of hours ago. But how should he react to being present at such a sudden death? David knew only too well how he, himself, felt. And, unlike Frank Windsor, he had hardly known Ted Callard.

"I can't believe what's happened," Windsor said, as he eventually slumped into the spare chair in front of the two desks which David and Trevor occupied for their written work. "Ted Callard, of all people. For God's sake, he must have been the fittest person there. He should have been the last person to have had a heart attack."

David could only agree with that sentiment, still recalling the iron-clad grasp of Callard's handshake.

"And he seemed larger than life to me," David said. " I hardly knew him, of course. Just had a short conversation with him, but that's how he seemed to me."

"Couldn't agree more. And it wasn't just that. He was like a breath of fresh air. Among the rest of us. Professional members, I mean."

David nodded - just the one sports jacket among all those grey three-piece suits. But professionals? As far as he was concerned, retail banking had not yet been classified as a profession. Perhaps this was a bit of ego-boosting on Windsor's part.

"I gather he banks here," David said. "Been a customer for some time?"

"Almost three years. Just private accounts for the family. His business account's with Barclays. The accounts here mainly relate to his son's compensation monies following his accident. Did you know about that? A terrible thing," he continued as David nodded, "I really don't know how he and his wife have coped with it all."

Windsor then clasped a hand to his mouth. In other circumstances, it would have seemed over-dramatic, but he was clearly aghast at his latest thought.

"My God, how's Barbara going to manage - with Ted gone now?"

This thought was still exercising David's mind, having just made that very point to Trevor. Callard had been so concerned for his wife, should something happen to him. However strong his wife might be, this added tragedy would hit her hard.

"They've always looked after their son at home?" he asked. "By themselves?"

"Yes. Ted and Barbara didn't want it any other way. But Peter's so big now. He must be twenty and takes after his Dad. Ted could handle that all right. You could tell how strong he was. But what'll Barbara do? She'll have to have help. Otherwise, I can see the lad having to go into a home. That would break Barbara's heart. Never mind how she must feel after Ted dying so suddenly. What a mess . . ."

As his words tailed off, an uncomfortable air embraced the room and David could tell that Trevor was getting edgy. He was sitting quietly, taking it all in, but all this talk of people he knew nothing about was clearly making him feel uncomfortable. At 25, he was not much older than the boy who had suffered so badly. In contrast, Trevor had so much to look forward to: a promising career within the bank; furthering his outstanding talent on the tenor saxophone; and having Katie, his adoring girlfriend who must, surely, be destined to be Mrs Smith.

"What's happening at the hotel now?" David asked, breaking the silence.

Windsor raised his head and seemed to recover some equilibrium. "I left not long after you, so I'm not sure. Our doctor called an ambulance and Jack Saunders - he runs the Crowborough police station - took charge of clearing the room. Our president was going to break the news to Barbara. What a task! But she can be assured of our total support. As I said, we all thought the world of Ted - and Barbara, of course."

He then rose from his chair with a muttered, "I must let you get on," and left the room, quietly closing the door behind him.

Chapter 4

Before going to his unwanted lunch, Mr Goodhart had set Trevor Smith a specific task: to look into the account of GB Builders.

A singular event had occurred that morning: the manager had bounced two of the firm's cheques. He had been reluctant to do so; Mr Goodhart had been insistent. Trevor was aware that his boss had already been getting uncomfortable vibes about the manager. Nothing he could put his finger on, but his nose had been twitching, something Trevor knew should never be ignored. Would the account of GB Builders be the catalyst to Mr Goodhart's unease?

The overdraft on the account had exceeded £20,000. Far too high; the limit was only £5,000. Why had the manager allowed such an excess? Enough was enough.

Trevor had now been on the bank's inspection staff for nearly a year. He had already witnessed many weird goings-on with customers' accounts. Limits could certainly be exceeded for legitimate reasons. Such excesses were often only temporary, with nothing to worry about. But it was another matter for borrowing to increase dramatically over several months, with no redress by the manager. As with GB Builders.

At school, Trevor yearned to join the police. At five-foot-ten, he was certainly tall enough. What he sought was excitement. That's how it seemed on the wireless and on film. There was certainly plenty of excitement in Dixon of Dock Green, even if Jack Warner bought it in the end. But then he saw a copper on the beat yawning. He put two and two together. Perhaps it was like being a cricketer - occasionally having a good spell batting or bowling, but spending most of the match days in the pavilion or twiddling fingers deep in the field. He chose banking instead.

And now, on the bank's inspection staff, some of his tasks certainly had the investigative nature of police work. Yes, there were also boring duties. Such as spending hours checking documents to ledger records. But there was also excitement. Some months ago at Tunbridge Wells, they had even been drawn into a murder investigation. Why join the police force when such excitement could happen with National Counties? And a banking career was safe and secure, with a resultant good pension. What more could he wish for? What indeed. And thereby hung the nub of his present problem: should he give it all up for the alternative job opportunity which was now beckoning? Could the prospects of a jazz musician ever be so safe and secure?

He had played the tenor saxophone since he was fourteen. And he seemed to have a natural aptitude. He was soon playing in groups, just for fun. But that eventually developed into gigs at jazz clubs. The Walnut Grove club in Torquay then proved to be a perfect venue for him. Trevor shook his head as he recalled two particular gigs which he would never forget. The first had been acutely embarrassing, never mind potentially career-threatening. Not so the second. Pete King, Ronnie Scott's partner, was in the audience and introduced himself after the second set. Trevor was dumbstruck. Mr King actually invited him to sit in some time at their London club in Gerrard Street. How good was that?

It took three years for it to happen. Last April, Mr Goodhart gave him leave to play at the club. He was in the supporting group, opposite the great American tenor player, Sonny Stitt. Sonny Stitt? One of Trevor's all-time favourites. Some people originally thought Stitt was a clone of Charlie Parker, matching his tone and improvisatory approach on the alto sax to the great man. But such people soon came to their senses. And when Stitt played tenor, Trevor could only drool at the saxophone wizard whose sound and lines were much closer to those of Lester Young. To be at Ronnie Scott's each evening for a whole week listening to Sonny Stitt put Trevor in dreamland. But there was a downside: it gave him severe reservations about his own playing. To listen to Stitt's long, flowing phrases on *Easy Does It*, could only convince Trevor of his own limitations. It was like a good player in Torquay United's team trying to match the skills of the inside forward maestro, Don Mills.

It was, then, a huge fillip when, at the end of the week, Pete King assured him that he could make the grade professionally. With that accolade ringing in his ears, he returned to his day job of working with the bank's inspection staff. But with reluctance?

He forced his mind back to the case in hand: GB Builders.

He would have liked to have spread out the company's ledger sheets across the desk. But it was too small. Instead, he kept them in a pile in chronological order. The desk was small, because the room was small. It fitted in with the whole branch being small, as with the staff numbers. Even the manager was small. What was it about this branch? On the other hand, inspectors were always allocated the smallest room in any branch. Was it a conspiracy? Make life as difficult as possible for these unwanted visitors. Yet they were all working for the same bank. Weren't they? Trevor supposed it depended on how the inspection proceeded. If all went well within the branch, harmony existed between both sides. He had to accept there were two sides, even though they were all under the same banking umbrella. And a 'them and us' attitude could easily prevail. Especially when criticisms were levelled at managers and staff during the course of an inspection.

This particular room could only accommodate two small (again) desks: one for him and the other for Mr Goodhart. And two accompanying chairs. One further chair sat opposite Mr Goodhart's desk, to be used when staff were interviewed. To accommodate this meagre furniture, any easy chairs for use by the staff when they ate their sandwiches had been removed. Trevor had no idea where they ate now. Possibly at the pub across the road?

Now, GB Builders. Where should he start?

Chapter 5

David scrutinized Trevor for a reaction. A minute had passed since Frank Windsor had left the room. They had remained silent.

"Why was he so upset?" Trevor finally asked.

David had felt the same way. Yet, had he not been equally distressed?

"It's not easy being in the same room when someone has died."

"I appreciate that, but ..."

"You mean, it wasn't as if Ted Callard was a relation?"

Trevor nodded. "Perhaps not even a close friend. Just a customer."

"Just a customer? Had been for three years. Also a pal in Crowborough Collective."

Trevor frowned. "But the manager was ashen. He could hardly look you in the eye."

"People react in different ways. You must know that."

"Come on, sir. You're winding me up. You felt exactly the same way."

David did not respond. But he felt like clapping Trevor on the back. They were thinking as one; already proving to be a team working in perfect harmony. Yet Trevor had only been his assistant for less than a year. And David's insistence on Trevor's appointment had been vindicated in spades. It went back to their Barnmouth days in South Devon. David was branch manager; Trevor was his assistant, despite being only twenty-one. It had been the start of their effective teamwork. But it was not to last; David was promoted to be an inspector in the south-east, some 200 miles away. Three years on he needed a new assistant. He immediately thought of Trevor. Too young, the regional staff manager had insisted. At only twenty-four at the time, that would normally be so. But if he's good enough, he's old enough, David had equally insisted. After much argument, David's opinion had prevailed and Trevor had enthused about the move, despite the distance involved. Now, nearly a year on, they seemed always to be on the same wavelength. So often, David felt like clapping Trevor on the back. Just like now.

"But we don't have the answer, Trevor. Not yet, anyway. But let's get on. What about GB Builders?"

Trevor glanced down at the ledger sheets on his desk. "I've checked back to last October, sir. All seemed well until July. The maximum overdraft was £1,000 - against the limit of £5,000."

David pursed his lips. Unusual for a builder. In his experience, limits were there to be used. Especially by builders.

"Three months ago," Trevor continued, "the borrowing took off. By up to £2,000 a week."

"Even though the limit stayed at £5,000?"

Trevor nodded. "The way the account worked, the limit was meaningless."

"But why the change?"

"You mean, why did the manager let the debt get so high? It soon got up to £20,000."

David frowned. "With no questions asked?"

"Mr Windsor might have asked all the right questions. And got all the right answers."

"It didn't seem that way this morning when we bounced the cheques. He wanted to pay them. But he had no justifiable reason. Apart from avoiding an embarrassing confrontation with the customer."

Trevor now frowned and sat back in his chair.

"And ," David continued, "there's no security to cover the borrowing. Has that always been the case?"

"I dug around a bit. It used to be a limited company. With the guarantee of a Richard Bathurst. But it got wound up. That's when it became GB Builders. Run solely by George Bathurst."

"I met him at lunch today. Sat next to him."

"Really? What a coincidence!"

Trevor said this with a glint in his eye. He well-knew that his boss never believed in coincidences. Yet it appeared to be so on this occasion.

"I found him friendly enough," David replied, ignoring Trevor's inoffensive jibe, "but he couldn't have known about the bounced cheques."

Trevor again frowned. "But getting back to any security. Bathurst must be liable. Being a sole trader."

"But what's that worth if he hasn't any tangible assets behind him? Life assurance cover? Property? Stocks and shares? If he had any of these, Windsor would have got his hands on them. Surely?"

"What about the actual building business? If the bank's lending for this, we should have a charge over any houses under construction. And the land must be worth something."

David sighed. "This has the makings of a long interview with the manager. What's more, the overdraft is now knocking at the door of his personal discretion."

Every manager had a discretionary limit: the amount he could lend without reference to Regional Office. Windsor's was £25,000 and he was getting perilously near to having to refer any excess borrowing by GB Builders to the powers-that-be. That looked like an imminent case of rapped knuckles, unless he had justifiable reasons for paying the debt up to that level.

"And what about the bounced cheques, Trevor?"

"They could be trade cheques. They weren't made out in favour of individuals."

"Don't forget the amounts."

"Of course," Trevor exclaimed. "Both for exactly £1,000. Round amounts."

"Precisely."

"Big problems then. He might be paying off people in fixed instalments."

"So, debts elsewhere? Not just at the bank."

David pursed his lips. It now looked like a classic case of overtrading: not enough capital in the business.

"This doesn't augur well," he said. "He reckons he's a big player in domestic building. And he told me he wants to be the same in commercial property. No doubt with other people providing all of the finance."

Trevor now looked concerned. "Bouncing those cheques could bring the business down. Like a pack of cards."

"That's more likely to happen if we refuse to cash his next wages cheque."

"I think there's some more delving for me to do, sir."

"Yes, starting with digging out the other paid cheques in his file. Go back a few months. Check out the payees. Who's he been paying money to? And look at his credits. Is he getting in regular income? Or is it spasmodic? You might not be able to tell, but does it look trade-related? Finally, check out his PM card."

Private Memorandum Cards are held for all customers. Anything of note is recorded, particularly what is said at customer interviews. Questions and answers. Cards with only a few brief entries implied good news; those that resembled a full length novel invariably spelt trouble. David had no doubt as to which would apply to GB Builders.

One of his major tasks in any branch inspection was to check out the lending. Was the manager granting facilities to customers wisely and safely? He had not yet started his examination at Crowborough and would carry this out alphabetically. It meant that GB Builders would be approaching half-way in this respect, but he had already decided that it would be the first account he would investigate thoroughly.

Chapter 6

At about five-thirty, David's Ford Consul was approaching Eridge, home to the Nevill Crest and Gun, one of his favourite hostelries. It was about half-way between Crowborough and Tunbridge Wells, where both he and Trevor lived. Following his promotion to inspector, David had somehow acquired a three-bedroom detached house in Forest Road, one of the town's more salubrious addresses. Trevor, in his more humble position, rented a one-bedroom maisonette, yet less than half a mile from his boss. Because of this close proximity, and to save on costs, they normally shared a car for travelling to and from branches. David usually ensured that sharing meant using his own car. For many years, he had had his fill of small, under-powered cars. Trevor's ageing Austin A30 fell neatly within that bracket. Far better to use David's Consul, if only for the additional room to carry their inspectorial baggage.

Trevor, in his accustomed front passenger seat, now let out an audible gasp. His boss had failed to slow down and then actually drove past the Nevill Crest and Gun - without any explanation.

"Sir?"

David could understand Trevor's exclamation. But this was not the time even to contemplate the downing of a pint of best bitter. He could not rid his mind of the lunchtime trauma. And the shock of Ted Callard's sudden heart attack was compounded by it being preceded by Callard's concern that 'something bad was going on'. In Crowborough, of all places? Not that David had any reason to believe that this could relate to his inspection of the branch. On the other hand, why would Callard open up in such a way to a bank official he had only just met? Why not involve the police? Especially as the officer in charge of the local police station was a member of Crowborough Collective.

The borrowing by GB Builders was also exercising David's mind. What had possessed Frank Windsor to allow such an escalating overdraft? Was it indicative of his overall lending philosophy? If so, David could imagine his work turning into a hard slog during this inspection. So much for his original assumption that this visit to Crowborough would be something of a doddle.

David kept Trevor waiting a full half-minute before replying. "Simply not in the mood, Trevor. And I also need to get home. A family outing tonight."

"After today's events, I was sure we'd be stopping off for a pint."

Despite his current frame of mind, David smiled. Did Trevor really find him so transparent? More to the point, did he dare admit as to where he, Sarah and Mark were going tonight? For the moment, he would keep mum, while Trevor also remained quiet, apparently feigning any interest in what might be happening in David's social life.

They travelled for the next five or six minutes in companionable silence until they were approaching the Pantiles in Tunbridge Wells.

From the corner of his eye, David then discerned Trevor glancing to his left where a huge poster had been erected at the side of the road. It was positioned on the grass verge in front of a large pond, home to a variety of water fowl. Trevor turned back to David, wide-eyed. "You must be joking, sir."

David laughed, as if he had, indeed, uttered a rib-tickler.

"Yes, Trevor, that's where we're going tonight. Up on the common. Bertram Mills Circus. Not that I'm really in the mood to savour what they claim to be the greatest show on earth."

Trevor frowned. "It might be the greatest show on earth, but they ought to get their grammar right."

It was now David's turn to furrow his brow. But was he at last getting through to the lad? Was he now joining his boss as a stickler for good grammar? Over recent months, David had certainly put him wise in so many ways, particularly concerning misplaced apostrophes, especially those often favoured by grocers and greengrocers. Apple's and pear's were choice examples.

"Explain yourself, Trevor."

David could sense the lad licking his lips in anticipation of raising a little gem which his finicky boss might have missed.

"Surely, sir," Trevor said, giving these two short words undue preciseness, "there's a missing apostrophe. Shouldn't it be Bertram Mills's Circus?"

David shook his head. There was no answer to that - grammatically, anyway. Billy Smart's Circus always had an apostrophe. Why not Bertram Mills? He could only reflect that the problem was the final s in Mills. Some people considered that, in such circumstances, adding an apostrophe s made the end result look clumsy. Yet that should not stand in the way of correct grammar. That prestigious street in the West End was always spelt properly as St James's Street. On the other hand, Newcastle United's football team always played at St James' Park. It was all a bit of a nightmare, really.

"I'm afraid I don't have an answer to that, Trevor. Perhaps the exception to prove the rule?"

"You know, sir, I've never really understood what that particular saying actually means."

David could certainly sympathise with that, but in order not to lose face, he needed to provide Trevor with some form of explanation.

"Let's just say that an exception proves that there is such a rule in place. For instance, if most bank inspectors were middle-aged men and a 25-year-old woman then got the job, she would be the exception that proved the rule."

Trevor nodded, but did not appear to be too convinced. David decided to move on.

"Anyway," he said, "in my opinion the Mills circus, without the apostrophe is greater than Smart's, with one. It's all about what happens in the actual ring."

"But what makes you want to go to a circus?" Trevor asked.

It was a good question, because David did not claim to be a big circus fan. In particular, he always felt a mite uncomfortable where wild animals were concerned. But, here in Tunbridge Wells, the arrival of Bertram Mills gave him what was a rare opportunity of meeting up with his older brother, Robert, who actually worked on the circus. Whenever he mentioned this family connection to others, the usual response was whether Robert was a juggler or a clown. David could well-imagine that this would be Trevor's reaction in a few moments time when he put the lad in the picture.

No, Robert was neither juggler nor clown in the literal sense. His previous career had certainly given the appearance of hoops being tossed in the air, not all of them having been caught successfully on the way down. And he had also been called a clown for having thrown up a potential fine banking career by effectively running away to the circus. The perpetrator of this slur had been the National Counties manager of Wiveliscombe branch. The man had suffered the self-imposed indignity of receiving Robert's letter of resignation almost immediately after his arrival at this manager's precious branch. For some reason, Mr 'high and mighty' Threadgold deemed his branch to be the pinnacle of banking excellence and anyone having the temerity to disagree with such a sentiment needed his head examined. Especially when a career at his branch was being shunned for life on a circus.

For as long as David could remember, Robert had been circus mad, but having left school with the required 'O' levels, he had been persuaded to settle for a safe and secure banking career. He had hated it. And the bank had not helped by shunting him from branch to branch, usually involving a succession of uninspiring and depressing digs. If he was to suffer such a nomadic life, he might as well be living on a circus, something he had always dreamed about.

And then it happened. After months of pleading for such a job, Bertram Mills came up trumps. Not for him to become a juggler or a clown, but as a general dogsbody to learn the skills of tent-building, transportation and everything else to do with operating a circus. The job offer came within three days of his starting at Wiveliscombe branch. Mr Threadgold had gone berserk. It was as if he took it as a personal insult - circus life taking precedence over his cherished bank. He failed to speak to Robert during his entire one month's notice period.

This episode almost had repercussions for David. He, himself, had continued to pursue a career with National Counties and then, without warning, came face-to-face with the dreaded Mr Threadgold. Despite his questionable man-management skills, the man had subsequently been appointed as a staff manager at Head Office. One of his tasks was to interview applicants in line for managerial promotions and he actually saw David when he was put forward to be manager of Barnmouth branch. Robert had previously told David that Threadgold was a little man and tended to strut everywhere to make himself seem more purposeful. Now, in his office, he had tried to disguise his literal short-comings by choosing a chair behind his desk which was considerably higher than the one interviewees used in front of him. It gave the illusion of his towering over others, an option denied him in all other circumstances. He also had the habit of glaring over his half-moon glasses and David had some difficulty in not reacting to such ingrained pomposity.

It all made for an extremely frosty interview, made worse by David who seized an opportunity of saying how well Robert had done since he left the bank and that he was now general manager of Bertram Mills Circus. Through gritted teeth, Threadgold had opined that he knew Robert would always have done well. He had, though, half expected him to have been a clown and he could not resist a snide comment that he hoped there was not another one in the Goodhart family. David had felt really proud that he had managed to disguise his seething at such a slur and maybe this helped him to be actually given the managership of Barnmouth branch. This had looked decidedly doubtful during the course of the interview. One thing for certain, he sincerely hoped that his career path would not cross that of this Threadgold creature at any time in the future.

Now, back here in Tunbridge Wells, David took advantage of an approaching tricky roundabout at the Pantiles to give him time to formulate an appropriate reply to Trevor's question about why he would want to go to a circus. He stopped for a light blue Hillman Minx, almost a replica of the one he had owned before the Consul, and then turned right towards Forest Road.

"You might not believe this, Trevor," he eventually replied, "we're going to see my brother who actually works there."

There was a pregnant pause and instinctively David knew that Trevor was not going to disappoint him with his response.

"He's not a clown or a juggler?"

Bingo! It never failed. "No, Trevor. He actually runs the show. He's the general manager."

Trevor now showed his maturity by casting aside any thoughts of flippancy as he sought out the reasons for a sibling's unusual choice of occupation. He listened intently to David's potted version of Robert's career and gave David the impression that he, too, might now visit the circus while it was in Tunbridge Wells.

Despite the lunchtime trauma, the banter with Trevor had lifted David's spirits as he turned the Yale key in the lock of his front door. His improved mood was then enhanced when he entered the hall. The aroma of his favourite dish wafted through from the kitchen.

"Oh no," he groaned, just loud enough for Sarah to hear in the kitchen. "Not Lancashire hot-pot again."

Her response was to greet him in the hall, wielding a rolling pin in one hand, as she brushed a dusting of flour from her apron with the other.

"And, afterwards, you're going to have to make do again with apple pie and cream," she said, raising the rolling pin above her head.

"Okay, okay, I surrender," David said, embracing her so that her face nestled against his chest. Then, unusually, he continued to grasp her tightly, failing to let go of her.

"What's happened?" Sarah asked, as he eventually released his grasp and gave her a lingering kiss.

"It's not been a good day," he said. "Let's have a glass of sherry and I'll put you in the picture."

Sarah had always been a good listener, too good sometimes. A while ago, they had briefly employed a cleaner for a couple of hours each week. A big mistake. Each week, the woman's problems, many self-inflicted, were recounted *ad infinitum*. Sarah dutifully listened. The cleaning was put on hold, to be completed by Sarah when the cleaner had gone home. David failed to see this as value for money: payment for listening? Sarah duly stopped being an employer. Instead, she reminded David how to use the vacuum cleaner.

It also helped that Sarah was *au fait* with banking. Her latest position was as a part-time enquiries clerk and sometime cashier at the Tonbridge branch of National Counties. Her only complaint with this was that, compared to David's inspectorial tales, nothing exciting ever happened at Tonbridge.

Now, having heard about the lunchtime trauma and possible lending problems in Crowborough, she was clearly glad that Mark had remained upstairs doing his homework. She would not have wanted him to learn about Ted Callard's heart attack and the problems his widow would now be facing with her only son.

"It's just as well we're going out tonight," she said. "It'll do you good to see Robert again and the clowns will lighten you up."

David had to smile. Clowns once more! Not jugglers this time, but it jogged his mind back to Frank Windsor. Would he turn out to be a lender who tossed figurative overdraft hoops into the air, hoping that none fell to the floor by way of a bad debt?

Whatever, Sarah was right about their going out this evening. That should, surely, help set him up for whatever Crowborough branch might throw at him tomorrow.

Chapter 7

David could not believe what he was hearing. Gone was the exhilaration he had experienced with last night's thrills at the circus. Instead, he felt utterly dumbfounded, nonplussed as to how he should react.

Late morning and he was sitting opposite Frank Windsor in the manager's room. Compared to the rest room where David and Trevor were working, it was palatial, at least six times as large. Windsor sat behind a huge mahogany desk which only appeared smaller because of the size of the room. An ornate cupboard and Georgian chair sat alongside one wall which also included a frosted window looking out on to Eridge Road. The other three walls were mainly adorned with landscape paintings which David considered could well be originals, rather than prints. Had the bank supplied such works of art, or did they actually belong to the manager? Possibly the latter, because one additional mural was of a large portrait in oil of someone who could only be Frank Windsor, himself. This must be a man desperately seeking self-esteem, emphasised still further by his adoption of that dreadful Threadgold man's ruse of winding up the seat of his swivel chair to its highest level. For the moment, though, this elevated position to increase his stature was offset by his being slumped down in the chair, resulting in his eyes being on the same level as David's.

Earlier in the morning, Trevor had briefed David about the activity on the account of GB Builders. Neither of them could comprehend what Trevor had established. He had told David the previous day that borrowing had escalated on the account in recent months, but he had by then not yet looked more thoroughly at the actual entries. These were the specific credits paid into and cheques drawn from the account. Once processed, these vouchers were sorted into a filing drawer under the name of GB Builders, but Trevor had soon established that these transactions bore no relation to what would normally pass through a builder's account.

They had believed yesterday that the bounced cheques for £1,000 had been trade-related, but this now seemed unlikely. One payee was DH Finance, while Trevor had now established that the other bounced cheque had been in favour of DH Investments. These payees had featured regularly in recent months, while credits to the account had been of much smaller sums of around £50. This was hardly typical of a builder's account. Armed with this information, David had demanded an immediate interview with Frank Windsor.

And now, he could not believe what he was hearing.

"You mean to say, Mr Windsor, that GB Builders is a misnomer? It isn't really a builder's account?"

Windsor nodded dumbly. Any self-esteem had clearly been knocked out of him.

"But," David continued, staring at Windsor intently, "I sat next to George Bathurst at lunch yesterday. He told me he was a big player in domestic building. And that he was now going into commercial building, as well."

Windsor again nodded and gave the distinct impression of wanting to be anywhere other than sitting in his chair opposite a bank inspector.

"All that business is with the Midland," he eventually said. "When George's father left the business, there was a problem here with security. It was before my time and my predecessor insisted that George provide some collateral. But he took umbrage at that and he went to the Midland instead. Just left a more or less dormant account here, in case of need."

"But it's not dormant now."

Windsor's normal ruddy countenance had now long disappeared, just as it had yesterday after Ted Callard's demise.

"These last couple of years," he said, almost wistfully, "I've been doing my damnedest to get all his business back here. He's now the most successful builder in town."

David did not like the way this was developing. To allow increased unsecured borrowing hardly seemed to be the right way to obtain business from another bank. Was it a form of bribery? And although Bathurst might be the best builder in town, that did not necessarily mean that his actual banking business was good.

"That may be so," he said, "but what's happening on the account here? Quite apart from the recent hike in unsecured borrowing, we've had a look at the activity on the account. It doesn't seem to have any relevance to the building trade."

"No, it doesn't," Windsor accepted, with seeming reluctance. "It's really an account run by George in a personal capacity."

"Then why is it in the name of GB Builders?"

"Well, George is a sole trader, so it's as broad as it's long."

David could not believe that a bank manager could be talking in such a way. Soon after he had started his inspection here, he had been getting bad vibes about Frank Windsor. It had been nothing specific, nothing that he could put his finger on. Just his inspectorial nose twitching in a way that his experience told him he should not ignore. Now, he was getting some tangible evidence that his instincts had been far from wrong.

"Mr Windsor, in no way can an account in the name of GB Builders be construed as a private account for George Bathurst ."

Windsor nodded and eventually said, "Yes, you're probably right."

"Probably? Too damned well I'm right. But what's actually happening on the account? These payments to DH Finance and DH Investments? Who are they? And what are all the tiddly credits on the account?"

Windsor gulped several times before replying, his Adam's apple bobbing up and down like a yo-yo.

"It's all related to Derek Herretson. You met him at the lunch."

Stick-insect? The most successful investment consultant in town? Now linked to the most successful builder in town? What on earth was going on? David simply raised his eyebrows and his expression could leave no doubt that he was imploring Windsor to carry on.

"I told you that he was an investment consultant," Windsor duly obliged. " I don't know how he does it, but he's an investment genius. He manages to generate huge returns on funds put his way - far higher than the bank can offer. And word has got around. He's getting clients from all over the place."

Including GB Builders? Or George Bathurst in his private capacity? But that did not explain the regular lump sum payments - by way of an unsecured overdraft.

Whatever, crowing about the skills and merits of stick-insect seemed to have restored some of Windsor's equilibrium, as if taking pride at the investment consultant's achievements. David, on the other hand, was getting more and more concerned.

"Just hang on a minute," he said, pursing his lips before continuing. "Let me get this straight. Over recent months, you have been paying cheques issued at will by George Bathurst to DH Finance and DH Investments, resulting in an overdraft of some £20,000. For God's sake why? And why are they two separate companies?"

For some reason, Windsor had the gall to smile. "I don't know why Derek uses separate vehicles for his business, but it's all about the returns he gets. Derek's skills result in rates of about 10%. That's why many of the residents in Henry Purcell's residential home are using him. Derek's system is to pay out interest on a monthly basis and such a good return helps enormously with the fees. As for George Bathurst, he's making a nice profit out of the arrangement. The credits on his account are the regular interest payments and are much higher than the borrowing costs here. So that keeps things ticking over nicely."

David was now finding it difficult to maintain control of himself. "As far as I can see, the only thing that is ticking over nicely is the increasing bank overdraft. And how on earth is it going to be repaid? Thank goodness we bounced those cheques yesterday. At least that kept the debt down by another £2,000."

"No, no," Windsor hastily said, "there's no problem with repayment. At any time, George can withdraw his funds from Derek's investment schemes."

"In which case," David said, "he better do that right away. I want this borrowing repaid immediately."

Five minutes later, David was still seething as he recounted the interview to Trevor. Windsor was supposed to be a bank manager, for goodness' sake. Before his appointment he would have completed his bankers' exams and pre-management training courses, yet here he was throwing out all the cardinal rules of bank lending. The acronym PARTS summed those up nicely. In the case of this lending to George Bathurst, any justifiable Purpose was nonsensical; the Amount was ludicrous; getting Repayment, to David's mind, was highly questionable; the period of Time for the overdraft would appear to be open-ended; and any Security was non-existent. There was not one pukka factor in this borrowing arrangement.

"It makes you wonder what the rest of his lending is like," Trevor said, with complete justification.

"And what about Derek Herretson, Trevor? How can some back-street investment consultant manage to achieve such apparent high returns in this day and age? Your next task is to see if he banks here. If not, where? And can we somehow get any pertinent background information on his business activities?"

Chapter 8

This morning, for a change, Sarah had plaited her hair, causing the tresses to oscillate in her slipstream as she skipped down the Frant Road. She could not help but smile and feel exhilarated as she made for the railway station in the centre of Tunbridge Wells.

The trip to the circus last night had been a great success. Robert had done them proud by putting them in a front row box. However, when the galloping horses threw up sawdust into their faces, Sarah would have preferred to be a few rows back. Especially when she saw one of the ring-boys smirking at their predicament. His eyes also reflected contempt that such well-dressed people should occupy the best seats. It seemed almost as if he felt that they deserved all that might, literally, be thrown up at them. Perhaps he had a chip on his shoulder. Whatever, Sarah felt sure that Robert would not approve of his attitude.

Being so close to the ring threatened another drawback: they could have been the butt for some of the clowns' antics. Mercifully, though, the clowns had chosen other patrons instead.

After the show, they had, in fact, come face-to-face with the world-famous Coco the Clown. Robert had introduced them and then later explained that Coco's title was really a misnomer. Clowns who dressed up in funny clothes and, among other things, had water thrown at them, were really called augustes. Those with white faces and wore beautiful clothes and were never the victims of others' antics, could be properly called clowns. So, it should have been Coco the Auguste. But Sarah guessed that such a title would never have caught on with the paying public.

It had been such a good idea going to the circus - just the lift that David had needed. Although he was often able to hide his feelings from others, she could tell that the sudden lunchtime death had made a big impact on him. It was not as if there had been any warning of its happening, unlike with his father. Dad had been the only dead body he had previously seen, but he had been able to prepare for that particular eventuality. Even in his wartime experiences, he had managed to avoid witnessing the horror of death. Yesterday was, then, an experience for which he had had no prior readiness. Who knows how he might have reacted to such a happening, but he was bound to dwell upon it for some time to come. It was, therefore, good that he had been able to enjoy the circus so much last night.

Mark had, of course, particularly revelled in the clowns. Their schoolboy humour had suited him down to the ground. Now that he was a teenager, he did his best to exhibit an air of sophistication and adulthood, but at times like last night, he was still a child at heart. And Sarah loved him for that.

She was aiming for the 9.30 train to Tonbridge. The journey only took ten minutes, followed by a five-minute walk up the High Street to the branch of National Counties. Getting this particular train could cut things fine if there were any delays, but she was rarely late for her part-time job which started at ten o'clock.

She had first begun work with National Counties 25 years ago in 1935, straight after leaving school at sixteen. This was down in

Devon and she had a promising career ahead of her until Mark was born. Like most mothers who were able to at the time, she had made a conscious decision to stay at home with him until he went to school. Thereafter, she had only worked part-time, normally from ten to two. That way, she would always see him off to school and be at home when he returned. It had worked well in Devon, and for the last three years in Kent. This had followed David's promotion, but her transfer to Tonbridge branch had got off to a ticklish start.

"Welcome to the best branch of National Counties," Mr Herbert, the manager, had gushed on her first day. He might have said it in all sincerity, but Sarah could not dismiss from her mind the congruity of Robert's episode with his manager at Wiveliscombe branch. Could Mr Herbert be of the same ilk?

"What sort of experience have you had?" he continued, preening himself behind his oak-panelled desk. Sarah felt that he might be trying to make a good impression on her, rather than the other way round.

She had explained that her experience had included cashiering and dealing with customers' securities. She had then risen to be the manager's personal assistant. At that, the manager's face had fallen.

"Oh dear," he said, failing to hide his apparent concern. "I fear you're going to be too well-qualified for what we want you to do here. We need you to manage the enquiries counter, with some part-time cashiering thrown in."

"That's fine with me," Sarah quickly said. "Being a part-timer, I wouldn't expect anything else."

The manager had been frowning, but he now smiled. In relief? It was as if he had not been expecting Sarah's response. "That's the spirit," he said, visibly relaxing. "Good girl. Some people with your experience wouldn't say that. They'd find lesser jobs demeaning. Good girl," he repeated.

Good girl? Good girl? Now in her forties? How patronizing! Her previous managers had not been like this. Was it going to be a mistake coming to Tonbridge? She felt disinclined to respond, but there was no need.

"I'm sure we're going to get along famously," the manager continued, hardly drawing breath. "But what made you come to Kent? It's a far cry from Devon."

Sarah groaned inwardly. The staff manager must have given Mr Herbert her background information. But not everything? Such as the salient bits: that she was married to David; that her husband was an inspector in this manager's region; and that David could at some stage be inspecting his branch. Mr Herbert would have the inspector's wife working in that very same branch. It would not be beyond his thinking that he was about to have a mole in his camp.

She answered his question truthfully, but tried to play down David's role in the bank. Not totally successfully, apparently, because the manager's bonhomie quickly disappeared. But it did not take many days for him, and the other staff, to realize that Sarah was 'one of them' and that she had no airs and graces, whatsoever, in relation to her husband's position.

Three years on and she was still doing the same part-time job and she loved it. She did not mind that it was not too demanding and was rather humdrum at times. David was welcome to all the excitement that could attach to his own job. She would certainly not have wanted to have switched roles with him yesterday. And it did seem that he might be about to encounter further problems by way of the manager at Crowborough branch.

Chapter 9

At the small Crowborough branch, it would take David two to three days to examine the manager's lending. This was a major purpose of a branch inspection. As far as other staff were concerned, the sudden arrival of inspectors was seen as a taxing hindrance to carry out their jobs. They would perceive these unwanted outsiders to be peering over their shoulders to check that rules were being strictly observed. Staff would then be rightly censured over any laxity with keys and cash, together with all other lapses in branch security. Rules were there to be observed and woe betide a branch where they were openly flouted.

But inspectors were also part and parcel of the bank's auditing function. Lending, being a prime purpose of any banking operation, needed outside scrutiny to ensure that any potential risk situations came to light. Some managers could be extremely generous in the way they doled out their depositors' money. This could certainly be to the detriment of the bank's overall end of year profitability. The question for David was to establish whether or not Frank Windsor was one such manager.

In this respect, the omens were not good. Windsor had disregarded so many cardinal rules of lending in respect of GB Builders. David could only hope that this particular account was the exception; but he feared the worst.

Yet it was now nearing lunchtime and some three hours of examining overdrawn accounts had revealed little untoward. It was also becoming clear that the lending portfolio was proving to be quite extensive. Provided this did not reveal potential bad debts, branch profitability was likely to be enhanced above the norm for this size of branch. In which case, Frank Windsor would need to be commended; a far cry from David's reaction to the lending the manager had provided to GB Builders.

But lunch now beckoned. "What about the Nevill Crest and Gun?" David asked Trevor. He was still hesitant about going to the pub across the road, particularly if it was being used by branch staff who were being denied the use of their rest room. There were, of course, several cafes in Crowborough, but it would be unusual for inspection staff to visit such establishments; especially when there were perfectly good pubs in the vicinity.

Trevor agreed with the choice of venue and within minutes of jumping into David's Consul, they were sitting in the Eridge pub, taking their first sips from two pints of Harvey's. David exaggerated the smacking of his lips as he set down his tankard on the table. "That's better," he said. "Nothing like a pint of the local brew."

And he always did like to try out the local beer, rather than the national brands, particularly around Kent where so many hops were grown. Driving from branch to branch, they never failed to pass numerous hop fields. Although most people probably associated this 'Garden of England' with the growing of apples, pears and assorted vegetables - especially potatoes and cauliflowers in north east Kent - hops must be the most prevalent of all things grown in this county. It led to the rural scenery being enhanced by innumerable picturesque oast houses, some of which had been converted into private accommodation. All very well, David had often thought, but what sort of furniture would fit properly within their rounded walls?

As for those cauliflowers … David would never forget his trip to inspect Margate branch. He had driven past field after field of cauliflowers which threw up such an obnoxious stench. It had permeated the car, despite all windows being firmly closed. How could people living in the vicinity possibly put up with this?

"Now, Trevor," David said, as he eyed up the sandwich menu lying on the table between them, "what have you found out about Derek Herretson?"

"Not a lot, sir. He doesn't bank here, probably not at all in Crowborough. The cheques Bathurst issued were all paid into accounts at the Midland in Tunbridge Wells."

David frowned. "That's a pity. We won't get any information from that source. But where does he actually operate from? Just here in Crowborough? Or also in Tunbridge Wells? That'd be logical if he banks there."

"I don't know about Tunbridge Wells. But according to the phone book, he's got premises in Croft Road. That's down the High Street opposite the bank, then turn right."

"Must be only a few hundred yards away."

Trevor nodded. "Yes, sir. Should we go round and have a look?"

David shook his head. "Not me, anyway. Bearing in mind we've met, I wouldn't want Herretson to see me nosing around. In any case, what are we looking for? Frank Windsor says he's an excellent investment adviser and people are putting money his way to invest. What's wrong with that?"

"Putting it that way, probably nothing at all. But what about the returns he's managing to make? And GB Builders, sir? Those payments made by the company are unusual to say the least."

"On that we can certainly agree, Trevor. Tell you what, when we get back to the branch, you pop round to Croft Road yourself. See what the set-up looks like."

"Is it worth speaking to Mr Windsor, as well?"

David again shook his head. "No, I don't really want to quiz him on this any more. Not yet, anyway. I'd rather get some gen from elsewhere. But where?"

"We could do a search through the bank's information department."

That was good thinking. This department was a source of information on companies all over the country. "Another thing for you to do, Trevor," David said, grinning.

"And what about the residential home, sir? Mr Windsor said the residents are using Herretson for their investments. Should we ask Mr Windsor about that?"

"I don't think so. Not at this stage, anyway. I actually met the owner at lunch yesterday. Henry Purcell. Strange man. Would you believe it, they all call him HP. Yes, Trevor, because he's saucy."

Trevor shook his head. "No wonder you didn't want to go to that lunch. Reckon they had a name for you, sir?"

Just as well Trevor's eyes were twinkling when he asked that. "The Purcell man did actually call me infamous," David replied, now able to smile about it. "That's when I was told he was saucy."

Trevor returned his smile, but apparently chose not to pursue the matter of his boss's possible infamy. "We'll just have to put our thinking caps on," he said, instead. "You could, of course, contact Herretson as a potential investor."

"That might not be a bad idea, Trevor, if all else fails. But not me. Sounds like another job for my under-worked assistant. Now, what are we going to eat?"

Three quarters of an hour later, replenished, David returned to his lending examination. The branch's business borrowers were the usual bunch: retail shops; cafes; farmers; small-time builders; and the occasional entrepreneur. These were out-numbered by personal borrowers who needed the bank's help for houses, cars, home improvements and, even, holidays. This was where the acronym PARTS particularly came in.

In his days as a branch manager, David had often asked customers to provide some sort of plan, business or personal, to justify their request for bank funding. This was especially relevant concerning the proposed repayment of any borrowing. So often, customers would assure him that they could meet any monthly repayments, only for David to establish, through intensive questioning, that their existing outgoings already accounted for any available income. If such customers had only made a list of existing income and expenditure before approaching their bank manager, even on the back of a hand, it would save them any humiliation when their request for borrowing was rightly turned down.

Another acronym David and other lenders would use was the Three Cs: Character, Capital and Capability. A customer who failed this particular test would be unlikely to obtain bank finance. Good Character was essential: would anyone knowingly lend to a crook? Some Capital should be behind a customer: why should the bank lend 100% and thereby take all the risk? And is the customer Capable of carrying out what he or she is proposing, particularly in the case of repayment?

The availability of security, or collateral, as the Americans prefer, was a material factor. David was a firm believer that this was the last question a bank manager should ask of a potential borrower. If all other aspects of a borrowing request stacked up, security may still be needed, as a form of insurance should things eventually go wrong. This was one difference between banking and pawnbroking. David was certainly aware of some managers who always put the question of available security first

- before establishing whether a lending proposition was feasible. If security could not be provided at that stage, lending by those managers was an immediate non-starter. In other words, they were acting like pawnbrokers, not bankers.

But it was not just customers who were subject to providing security. Shortly after the war, when David was a lowly clerk, he needed £25 to complete the purchase of a £50 shiny black BSA motorcycle. He duly applied to the bank for a loan. Notwithstanding his fulfilment of all lending criteria, particularly the Three Cs, agreement was only granted upon his father signing a guarantee. It was a classic case of belt and braces. The guarantee was needed even though David was an upstanding member of the bank's own pensionable staff. It was there in case David, could not, or would not, repay the debt, unimaginable as that might seem. On the other hand, something else could go horribly wrong. Which it very nearly did. One morning, on the way to work, he skidded on wet leaves and the bike and David parted company. The bike smashed into an on-coming car, while David, with seeming prescience, steered a face-down slide between that car and the one following. He survived to repay the loan; Dad was not called upon under his guarantee.

It was David's current task to assess Frank Windsor's capability in all these aspects of bank lending. The manager had not got off to a good start with GB Builders, but, so far, David had not found much to query concerning other business customers. But, moving in alphabetical order, he had only examined those accounts up to the initial letter F.

Loans on half a dozen personal accounts were, however, exercising his mind. In each case, the loan stood at between £5-6,000, with no evidence of any repayment yet having been made. Each loan was certainly secured by a property, but the deeds were not deposited at the branch. They were still held by a firm of reputable local solicitors who had given the bank a good undertaking to hold those deeds to the bank's order. Good cover had been provided by a professional valuation of each property carried out on behalf of the bank, so there was no apparent risk with any of this borrowing. But none of the customers was local, all living in the Sussex and Surrey border area around Crawley and Horley. It did not seem that Frank Windsor had actually met any of these customers, all of whom had been introduced by the same Crowborough solicitors whom Head Office had properly authorized to act on behalf of the branch.

On that basis, David could see that this borrowing might well be above board, with no risk attached. But there was no evidence that the Three Cs had been covered, nor the constituent aspects of PARTS. Clearly, he needed to discuss these accounts with Frank Windsor. He was also mindful that the pattern of such accounts he had seen so far, could be repeated in the G to Z range of customers he had yet to examine.

Chapter 10

On their return from lunch, Trevor briefly popped into the branch to check the telephone directory for the property number of Herretson's address in Croft Road. Armed with this, he now stepped out of the front door and crossed the road into the High Street, home to a motley group of small retail establishments. His eyes were immediately drawn to the distinctive red and white cylindrical hanging sign of a barber's shop and he instinctively raised his right hand to the nape of his neck. Yes, feeling strands of hair touching his collar, he knew that it was getting time for his next haircut. Short back and sides was the normal order of the day for bank clerks, a far cry from the style he adopted in his RAF National Service days.

He had felt quite daring at the time. But orders were orders. "Get yer 'air cut" his square-bashing drill sergeant had barked on his arrival at his barracks in West Kirby, not far from Liverpool. And, with another couple of sprogs, he had done just that, all of them opting for severe crew cuts. He could never have contemplated doing this two weeks earlier, as a lowly bank clerk with National Counties. And he would always remember the look on his mother's face when he came home on his first leave. She did not say anything and did her utmost not to notice his newly-acquired shorn locks. But he had seen the look: a brief sense of realization that she had clearly lost her innocent little boy to the ravages of the wicked outside world.

Yet it had not been a wicked two years of National Service. An eye-opener, yes. He had joined the RAF as a naïve, eighteen-year-old Young Conservative bank clerk from Torquay, suddenly thrust into a world he could not have previously contemplated. Prior to work, he had been a cub and a scout, but his Akela and scout leader had certainly not prepared him for the metaphorical savagery of square-bashing corporals and sergeants. To this day, he was amazed that he had actually survived those eight weeks of initial training and there had been little immediate respite to come.

He was given the trade of fireman and was posted to Aldergrove aerodrome, just outside Belfast. He would eventually develop a great rapport with the other 40 firefighters, but initially? A bank clerk in their midst? From salubrious Torquay? And what was this? He had O levels to his name? Thank goodness he did not mention being a Young Conservative. At least, the crew cut helped. But as weeks followed days, the others started to accept him, their initial reaction to his credentials dissipating. Communal trips into the nearest town of Antrim also helped. There was nothing like a shared interest in beer and dance halls to cement camaraderie.

As for his naivety, after two years of National Service, it had all but disappeared. Except for one thing: an innate inability to chat up girls.

He had been 21 when Katie first came, nay bounded, into his life. They both worked at the Barnmouth branch of National Counties, under Mr Goodhart. Although two years younger than Trevor, Katie's sheer ebullience contrasted sharply with his in-built shyness with girls. How he had drummed up the courage to ask her out, he would never know. In the end, his saxophone was his master stroke. He played gigs at the Walnut Grove Club in Torquay and, if he dated her there, he would spend most of the time playing. That would cut down any time for the usual, stilted small-talk which had dogged him with previous girlfriends. Yet, with Katie? Small-talk was simply not on her agenda. Her natural high spirits would see to that. And that was how it had turned out. Her infectious personality had penetrated his psyche until he had become as animated as she.

It had been even better on their second date: at Torquay United's Plainmoor. Katie knew nothing about football, but had met him at the ground, actually wearing a United scarf. How prescient was that? And it had got better. When Torquay eventually scored, Katie had jumped up and down, flung her arms around him and planted a kiss on his lips. Their very first kiss. Bliss.

Their romance had then flourished, but, now, over 200 miles away, Trevor saw little of her. She had come up to London to see him play at Ronnie's, but, since then, he had only been able to get down to Barnmouth once - several months ago. His feelings for her had not changed. But was it the same for her? Absence had certainly made his heart grow fonder, but it also harboured doubts. Katie, so pretty and perky, could not help but pick up admirers, but was she able to shun them in favour of himself - so far away on the other side of the country?

He forced himself out of his reverie and decided that, yes, he must get his hair cut, probably this coming Saturday in Tunbridge Wells. He turned right off the High Street and into Croft Road, seeking out a shop number. Why was it that so many shops these days failed to display street numbers alongside their names? Eventually, he came across one and it was clear that Herretson's abode was at the other end of the road, well past the supermarket and its adjacent car park.

It turned out to be a substantial residential property on the left hand side. It had probably been built early in the century and was double-fronted, a large oak-panelled front door sitting between prominent bow windows. It looked as though there would be three upstairs front rooms and Trevor guessed that the layout would be similar in the rear. A garage, big enough for two cars, sat alongside the property and there was parking space for a further four cars. Trevor was already drooling over one of the two cars which were parked there. Next to a Ford Prefect was a sparkling-bright-red Aston Martin DB4. It looked brand new and must have cost a bomb. Trevor had only ever seen one before, this model not having been long on the market. Did it belong to a client, or was business so good that Herretson could afford such a beast?

But Trevor was now curious about the matter of clients. There was no business sign on the front of the building to indicate that it was the home of a thriving investment business. Not even a small plaque next to the front door bell push. Had Trevor found the right building? Or had he taken the number down wrongly from the telephone directory?

He was just about to turn round and return to the branch when the front door opened. Out stepped a remarkably thin man, wearing the most ill-fitting suit Trevor had ever seen. The way Mr Goodhart had previously described such a man, it could only be Herretson himself. He immediately answered Trevor's question as to whom might own the DB4, by opening the boot and placing in it a suitcase he was carrying. He then returned to the house, closing the front door behind him.

After arriving at the property and while giving it the once-over, Trevor had made himself inconspicuous by sheltering behind the hedge which was growing between the front garden and the pavement. He did not want to be seen loitering, in case his motives might be questioned and he was mightily relieved at such forethought when Herretson had made his appearance. The whole situation was now giving him some concern. Yet he had not seen anything which might not be readily explained. But he felt certain that something was amiss. Was he developing Mr Goodhart's inspectorial nose? He certainly hoped so; in having such a boss, he could not have wished for a better role model.

He now turned on his heels and made his way back to the branch. What would Mr Goodhart make of it all?

Chapter 11

"All very odd," David said, after Trevor had recounted his findings. "But I like the sound of that car."

David had always yearned to own an Aston Martin, ever since he had managed to arrange a trip to Le Mans in 1949 and saw a DB2 racing there. At the time, this particular model was only a prototype, but it distinguished itself so well that it went into production in 1950. Apart from its sleek good looks, it had impeccable road behaviour, plus an effortless 100mph-plus performance. But, at the time, David actually owning one? On a bank clerk's meagre salary? It could only be a pipe dream. Even when the DB4 was introduced in 1958, with David now a manager, it was as much as he could do to afford a Hillman Minx. At least, that had now been upgraded to a Ford Consul.

"You're not the only one liking the sound of it," Trevor replied. "Just you wait until I'm a world-renowned saxophonist. I'll give you a ride in mine."

"World-renowned? Busking in a tube station, more likely."

But David found any such levity on this particular subject disquieting. Lurking just below the surface was the distinct possibility that Trevor might well give up his promising banking career for the not inconsiderable risk of becoming an itinerant jazz musician.

Yes, Trevor was an extraordinarily talented saxophone player. David had first seen him play at Torquay's Walnut Grove club. As a jazz aficionado, David was a regular patron, mainly because the house piano trio played the bluesy, soulful music that sent shivers down his spine.

Only occasionally did a horn player sit in and David could not believe his eyes one Saturday night when Trevor strode on to the bandstand to join the trio for their second set of the evening. Bank clerk Trevor playing the saxophone? He had kept that particular skill secret from his boss. Possibly because moonlighting was strictly forbidden by National Counties. But David, in Trevor's particular case, was prepared to turn a blind eye. A case of jazz fans united? In any case, Trevor might not be getting paid; he could have been playing just for fun. David decided not to question him on that. In that way, he would have a clear conscience.

Whatever, Trevor had played like a professional and this had eventually led him to appear at Ronnie Scott's club earlier this year. The only possible downside for National Counties was that Trevor had told David afterwards that Ronnie Scott's partner, Pete King, had declared that Trevor was, indeed, good enough to play professionally. Just the sort of comment to turn a young man's mind. But was he really good enough to make a living out of his hobby? David remembered reading of the reaction of Oscar Peterson's father when his son said he wanted to play full-time. Father agreed provided he first practised hard enough to become the best jazz pianist in the world. Otherwise, back to the day job.

It was a philosophy which David could well understand. To be at the top of your field, you have to work so hard to have that little bit extra over others. That applied to those such as actors, footballers or tennis players. You might be by far the best player at your tennis club, but in the outside world, you could well be an also-ran. So often, disillusionment would then set in. Oscar Peterson had a wise father. And Oscar duly obliged. But where would Trevor stand in such a scenario?

And David was finding it hard to conjure up a dispassionate viewpoint. He felt almost ashamed at harbouring selfish motives. Trevor was already becoming his best ever assistant. He did not want to lose him - to jazz or to anywhere else.

But should another factor come into consideration about a possible career change for Trevor? Probably not, but David was becoming a mite concerned about events around the world. Since the debacle of Suez, he felt that the flexing of muscles was increasing, particularly regarding the Soviet Union. And changes were afoot in the States. Two young pretenders were vying to take over from Eisenhower and prior to the presidential election next month, Nixon and Kennedy were holding a series of televised debates. Neither had, so far, impressed David and he worried about what might happen if the chosen one became gung-ho. Pitted against Khrushchev, he feared there might be only one winner. God forbid that this might be by way of World War 3.

He realized that such thoughts should not affect whether or not Trevor chose to change his career, but he was, nevertheless, still worried.

But what about this Herretson man? Why were they getting interested in him, never mind launching some form of investigation?

"Now, Trevor, let's decide what we're trying to do here."

"Sir?"

"With our Mr Herretson. Why are we actually thinking about him at all? He's not even a customer."

"But what about George Bathurst? He's been investing thousands with him."

"In a private capacity. Why shouldn't he invest his money in any way he wants?"

A loaded question? But David was confident about Trevor's response.

"Hardly his money, sir," Trevor replied, confirming David's faith in him. "Not by way of a £20,000 unsecured overdraft."

Good lad. He was absolutely right. But that was as much to do with Frank Windsor as George Bathurst. And the funds could always be got back to clear the overdraft. Even if realizing the investments resulted in a short-term loss, the bulk of the overdraft should be covered.

"But we've now got round to talking about George Bathurst, Trevor. I know we're concerned about him, but, at the moment, I'm trying to get my head round Herretson. Why are we getting involved with him?"

"Because something doesn't seem quite right, sir. And having now seen his property, it's just like a private house. There's no signage that he's running a thriving investment business there."

"Perhaps he doesn't think it's necessary. Perhaps he doesn't need to advertise the services he offers. Maybe it's all about word-of-mouth introductions. We know he gets those from Frank Windsor. And that could apply to other bank managers here, or in other towns. Like Tunbridge Wells? And what about those residents in HP's residential home? We know they use him and they must have heard about him by word-of-mouth. Presumably HP's mouth?"

"And there's also that DB4."

"If I were as successful as we're told Herretson is, I'd certainly buy myself a DB4."

"But what about that nose of yours, sir?"

David grinned. "It's still there, Trevor. And after what you've been saying, I think yours is twitching, as well."

Trevor pursed his lips and nodded, as though appreciating the implied compliment from his boss. "So, what's next, sir?"

"I think we'll leave it at that for the moment. Let's see what else might crop up. And when I'm next with Frank Windsor, I'll talk to him about it. In fact, I'm planning to see him in the morning about the lending. But I want to sound you out first."

"But you haven't finished the lending, have you?"

David shook his head. "No. But while you were up the road, I looked at some more accounts. And a definite pattern's developing."

"In what way, sir?"

David drew towards him the securities register covering accounts in the A-L category. The register set out all items of security for each borrowing customer. These would include details of life insurance policies, stocks and shares and deeds of properties charged to the bank to cover any lending. He opened the register for the account of William Crickhaven and then found the customer's private memorandum card. Leaning down to the floor area beside his desk, he extracted Crickhaven's ledger sheet from a can designated for customers with the initials A-C. This branch had four such cans containing individual ledger sheets for each customer, a far cry from not so long ago in the days of pre-mechanization. Then, every transaction, covering cheques issued and credits paid in, would have been meticulously recorded in huge, bound ledgers, in best copper-plate writing. David could imagine Mr Scrivens doing this scrupulously, prior to his chief clerk days. He would have been sitting on a high stool at one of the tall desks at the back of the office, probably with an angle-poise lamp to hand in order to provide more light to aid the intricacies of his calligraphy. Wielding a steel-nib pen, he would constantly dip this into an adjacent ink well, ensuring that drops should neither tarnish the surrounding area nor, heaven forbid, the actual ledger pages. Those were the days when copious sheets of yellow blotting paper would feature in any stationery order, something that had drastically diminished following the increasing use of ballpoint pens. Then came mechanization. All staff must now thank the powers-that-be for the introduction of machines to do all this work for them, especially as the handwriting of some of the younger staff left much to be desired.

"Just have a look at this account, Trevor," David replied, motioning him to come and stand next to him at his desk. Trevor first looked at the securities register which gave details of the property which Mr Crickhaven had apparently purchased in Crawley, back in June. It was clear that the branch had not yet received the actual deeds of the property. These, for the time being, were still being held by solicitors who had given an undertaking to hold them to the order of the bank.

Trevor then turned his attention to Crickhaven's ledger sheet. This was for a £5,000 loan account, opened in June at the time the property had been bought.

"No repayments yet?" Trevor said, turning towards David.

David shook his head and handed the private memorandum card to Trevor. "And it looks as though no specific repayment arrangements have yet been made. In fact, you'll see from the PM card that it doesn't tell us much at all about the customer. Just that he was introduced to Frank Windsor by the solicitors who gave him a first-class reference."

Trevor turned back to the securities register. "At least this shows that we hold a professional valuation of the property. And with that coming out at £8,000, we've got plenty of cover."

"And at £8,000, it must be quite a property." David felt quite envious. His own detached house in Tunbridge Wells had cost far less, at £5,000, although that had been three years ago. Nevertheless, he had always felt that Tunbridge Wells was a more salubrious area than Crawley where a house valued at £8,000 must be something of a mansion.

"It seems to me, sir," Trevor then said, "that we just need a bit more information. Everything looks safe enough and a one-off loan like this shouldn't be much of a worry."

"But it isn't quite like that," David replied. "It's not a one-off. I'm not yet halfway through the lending, but I've already come across half a dozen similar cases. And all these customers live in the Crawley and Horley areas. What's more, there's no indication that the manager has actually met any of them."

"That's daft, sir. 'Course he must have met them."

David shook his head. "Nope. Not one of them. Unless the meetings were simply not recorded on the PM cards. But I can't believe that."

"And have no repayments been made on these other loans?"

"Not on any of them."

"How very odd, sir. So, first we had George Bathurst's dodgy lending and now these?"

"We can't actually say that, not yet, anyway. Bathurst's borrowing is totally unsecured. In all these other cases, there's a property involved and a valuation giving the bank plenty of cover."

"But we haven't got the actual deeds yet. Just a solicitor's undertaking."

"Yes, but it's from Walsgrove and Lithgow and they're properly authorised to act for the bank. It's not as if there's a rogue element here."

"But no repayments yet, sir?"

"That's certainly a bit odd, especially as there's no indication as to the background of these customers. What do they do? What do they earn?"

Trevor frowned. "But Mr Windsor must know that. Perhaps it's just in his head. For the moment, anyhow."

"Maybe for just one customer. But for half-a-dozen? And more to come in the second half of the alphabet?"

Could Trevor be right and this was further dodgy lending by the manager? Maybe not necessarily risky lending, but with no apparent repayments arrangements in hand, how would the loans be actually cleared? Simply by the eventual sale of the properties? On the other hand, these loans might just be bridging arrangements, prior to planned sales. Yet, in such cases, the loans would have been styled as bridging loans. But David was also bothered that all the properties were in the Crawley and Horley areas. What was going on there? And why were these customers banking in Crowborough, of all places?

Chapter 12

S arah arrived at Tonbridge branch a few minutes before her ten o'clock start. The train was usually on time and she always found a seat. Not so with earlier ones, choked with commuters and boys making their way to Tonbridge School.

This week, her duties were primarily to serve customers at the enquiries counter, while providing lunchtime relief as a cashier, should this be required. She loved helping out on enquiries, simply because each day could be so different. Some people might think that banking was just a matter of taking in credits and paying out money, but the range of customers' enquiries was far-reaching. Mr Herbert had originally feared that she might be too well-qualified for what he had in mind for her, but her deep knowledge was put to good use on the enquiries counter.

By late morning, she had dealt with customers wishing to stop cheques, to arrange standing orders and two who had wanted to transfer their accounts from the Midland Bank. That was always good news. It was never the case when accounts were lost to the opposition. On the rare occasions when this did happen, Regional Office demanded a full-scale inquisition as to the whys and wherefores. Woe betide should this be because of poor service provided by their branch.

Sarah suddenly found Tracey at her side. That was unusual in itself; Tracey never sidled up to anyone. An ebullient East Ender, her arrival was normally presaged by incessant chatter. Sarah loved her for that and, when Tracey had arrived at the branch from Leytonstone, she had been like a breath of fresh air. Bank staff might have a reputation for being conservative - even stuffy - but that could never be said of Tracey.

"I've got a geezer at my till," Tracey said. "Says 'e's from Walsall. 'E wants to cash a cheque. But 'e ain't got an account here. 'E banks at Coutts. And 'e ain't signed 'is cheque proper - just 'is surname. I can't make 'ead nor tail out of 'im. Will you 'ave a word with 'im, Sarah?"

A geezer? From Walsall? Yet banking at Coutts? Sarah grinned at Tracey. Geezer and Coutts certainly seemed like strange bed-fellows.

"All right, Tracey. 'Course I'll see him. Just send him down to me."

Tracey's till was one of four, the furthest from Sarah's enquiries position and Sarah could see a tall, rather distinguished-looking man standing there. When Tracey spoke to him, he smiled, said something and turned to walk across to Sarah.

"Good morning, sir," she said, when he reached her. "How can I help?"

The man was the spitting image of Clark Gable, even down to his pencil-slim moustache. He was well over six foot tall and was immaculately clad in a full-length, navy overcoat, open at the front to reveal a double-breasted, dark business suit. To set his appearance off, the collar of his pristine white shirt held in place a military-style red and blue striped tie. Crow's feet indicated that the smile he flashed Sarah was not uncommon. She could imagine that his voice would match this overall impression, in which case, she wondered how he had responded to Tracey's broad cockney.

"That nice young lady," he said, glancing across at Tracey, "said that you'd be able to help me. All I'd like to do is cash a cheque."

Sarah smiled, she hoped, sympathetically. "But I gather you don't bank here."

"No, I don't. But I can't get to my own bank. It's Coutts, in London. In the Strand. You see, I've just flown in from Warsaw. I'm the High Commissioner there. And I've come straight from the airport to attend a lunch at the castle, across the road. It's with the High Sheriff of Kent."

So much for the 'geezer from Walsall'. It would seem that such an assessment could not be further from the truth. Even so, the man had not made a prior arrangement to cash a cheque, so Sarah would normally telephone his bank for authorization. But for a High Commissioner? Unless he wanted to cash a significant amount. In which case, Sarah would need to remember that the best con men were the most plausible.

"I only want a tenner," the High Commissioner continued. "I just need to have some pound notes on me for tips."

Sarah made an instant decision. Definitely not a risk; certainly not a con man.

"I'm sure we can do that for you, sir," she said. "If you'd just let me have your cheque, I'll take it along to Tracey. Just pound notes?"

"Please," the man confirmed, handing over his cheque.

He then smiled at her as she examined it, taking note of his one-name signature. "Don't worry," he said. "That's how people like me sign our cheques. One of those typical British quirks. I'm Lord Chilstone, you see."

Sarah blushed, now not entirely sure how she should address him. As she asked him for some form of identification, she ducked the decision by smiling and simply calling him 'sir'. She then went to get the ten pound notes from Tracey.

After tucking the notes into his wallet, Lord Chilstone thanked Sarah for her help and, before leaving the branch, even went across the banking hall to thank Tracey, as well. Sarah slowly shook her head. She would relish telling David this evening about the geezer from Walsall.

It was now approaching the busy lunch period and Sarah could tell that she was likely to be asked to open her part-time till. This would enable the regular cashiers to stagger their lunch hours, yet with each till position remaining open. There was little worse for customers than to use their own lunch hours in order to get to the bank, only to suffer long queues because tills were closed.

After opening her till, her first customer was a schoolboy of no more than thirteen, clearly a pupil of Tonbridge School, situated only a couple of hundred yards away at the top of the High Street. Before she could speak to him, one of the other enquiries clerks came up behind her to get her attention.

"I've just seen this boy," she said. "He doesn't bank here, but wants some cash."

Not another geezer from Walsall? "So?" Sarah replied.

"He only wants a pound. Out of his savings bank account. But he can't identify himself. So I said we can't help. And now he's come up to see you."

"Only a pound? Is that really a problem?"

"But we don't know him. I don't want us to get into trouble."

Get into trouble? For a pound? This boy was at Tonbridge School. At enormous cost to his parents. People like Lord Chilstone?

"All right," Sarah said. "Leave it to me."

She turned round to face the young boy who was not much taller than the bank counter. He must only have been in his first term at the school and Sarah almost wilted when a pair of pleading blue eyes confronted her.

"I only want a pound," the boy said. "I just want to get some tuck, like the other boys. I've got my passbook here."

His plea was so heartfelt. How could Sarah refuse? That would mean two handsome men having twisted her around their little fingers in one morning. But this boy could even become a High Commissioner one day. Maybe he would remember her act of kindness if that happened.

"The thing is," she said, "we must have some form of identification. We need to be sure you're who you say you are."

"I've got my passbook."

He was clearly too innocent to realize that someone else might have picked up his passbook and then tried it on with the bank.

"Yes, but we need something more. Tell you what, just lean over the counter here towards me. No, come on, a little nearer."

With that, Sarah stretched out her arm and took hold of the boy's tie, gently turning it around. Sure enough, it revealed the familiar sewn-in Cash's tape showing the boy's name which coincided with the name on the passbook. What better identification could she get than that?

Another satisfied customer.

And Sarah, herself, felt great satisfaction with her morning's work. Her tasks as a cashier and enquiries clerk might not be as demanding and exciting as those of her dear husband, but a job well done at any level was just cause for satisfaction. And she could get all the excitement she needed from listening to David's tales, particularly when they had involved the police in Tunbridge Wells last April. That was unlikely to be repeated, but his time in Crowborough branch did not seem to be turning out to be the straightforward inspection he had been anticipating.

The remainder of the lunch period consisted of the usual motley group of customers, paying in money and cashing cheques. The only customer she could have done without was the man from Mac Fisheries. His weekly arrival was abhorred by every one of the cashiers, all of them taking their time with whichever customers were at their tills in the hope that the fishmonger would join someone else's queue. This time, Sarah had drawn the short straw and her till now contained a bundle of pound and ten shilling notes which, not only reeked of the shop's merchandise, but were also soiled by the scales from a variety of fish. Ugh!

Despite this, she had enjoyed her day, but as she was about to lock up her till box and take it to the strong room before making for home, she was aware of another customer standing at her till. She looked up and was horrified to see a man wearing a black Balaclava, with a scarf drawn up over his nose and mouth, leaving only his eyes visible. He had his hand in the pocket of his raincoat and he was clearly holding something which bulged through the garment. He did not say a word; he had no need to. His instructions were set out clearly on a scruffy piece of paper which he thrust across the counter: 'Dont say nothin. I got a gun. Just hand over your note's'.

Chapter 13

D avid received the telephone call at four o'clock. From Regional Office. From his *bete noire*: Angus McPhoebe. David had been about to speak to Frank Windsor to arrange a time in the morning to discuss the Crawley and Horley loans. And he would have much preferred to speak to Frank Windsor on any subject, rather than be on the receiving end of what was bound to be a diatribe from the deputy regional manager.

Angus McPhoebe was the antithesis of his regional manager. Whereas Reginald Porter was an experienced, knowledgeable banker and, above all, a good man-manager and gentleman, David considered McPhoebe to be an arrogant upstart, who should have no part in National Counties Bank, never mind its Regional Office. The big conundrum was how Mr Porter had chosen him to be his deputy in the first place. More than likely, McPhoebe had been forced on him by some old-boy network in Head Office. And another potential problem now faced David: Mr Porter had suffered ill-health for many months and was now retiring early. McPhoebe, surely, was not now in line for the top job?

"Ah, Goodhart," McPhoebe snapped over the telephone, eschewing any form of salutation. "There's been a hold-up. At Tonbridge. Get over there straight away."

At Tonbridge? Dear God, no. Not at Tonbridge. David could not stifle an involuntary gasp. But hang on a minute, it was four o'clock. Sarah would have left the branch at two. She should be at home by now, awaiting Mark coming back from school.

Even so, other staff must have been involved and he could only hope that the hold-up had failed, with staff neither hurt nor, even, traumatically affected. The only person David had known to have been subject to a raid was poor old Trevor. About four years ago, he had been a cashier, on relief at Chagford branch in Devon. While there, an armed raider had vaulted the bank's counter, almost into Trevor's actual till. The man had got away with some cash and although Trevor had not been hurt, it had taken him months to get over the experience. Heaven forbid this situation having occurred at Tonbridge.

"What actually happened?" David asked McPhoebe, not really expecting to be given any meaningful details. It would be up to David, as an inspector, to establish all the nitty-gritty. "Has anyone been hurt?"

"I don't know any of the details," McPhoebe replied, confirming David's prognosis. "That's why I want you to get over there."

"But if it's only just happened, the branch would have been closed for up to an hour?"

"What do you mean, just happened?"

"Well, it's now four o'clock. You must have been told straightaway. Any branch would have done that. As well as getting the police involved."

And the branch would have given McPhoebe full details of what had happened. Why would they not do this? It must simply be McPhoebe being obtuse in not passing on the facts to David.

"It happened just before two."

"But it's now four o'clock!" David had not meant to raise his voice. He had always tried to be equable in his dealings with McPhoebe, despite outrageous provocation. But this was serious. A two-hour delay? And he was now getting really bothered. Had Sarah just been handling enquiries today? Or had she opened her relief till?

"I've been trying to get another inspector to attend. It's taken time. But I haven't managed it."

"But why? Here in Crowborough, I must be the nearest inspector to Tonbridge."

"That's why I'm ringing you now. As I said, I couldn't get anyone else. But I thought another inspector would be able to handle it more dispassionately."

Oh, my God! He does know something. And he certainly knows that Sarah works at Tonbridge; he had originally sanctioned the arrangement. And any thought of McPhoebe trying to get another inspector for compassionate reasons was groundless.

"Anyway," McPhoebe continued, before David could express his concern, "you're wasting time. Get on your bike".

David slammed the phone down. His wasting time? Who wasted those two hours between two and four?

Trevor had been out of the room when the call came through. When he walked back in, he found David clearing the desks and stuffing papers and files into their inspectorial bag.

"What's going on, sir?"

"We've got to go. I've packed up most things. But this ledger can and securities register . . . just pop them back to the staff, will you? I need to make a call before we go."

He was thankful that there was a telephone extension in the staff rest room, which was not normally the case. He must phone home before they left. But there was no answer. That certainly failed to ease his mind.

"But where are we off to?" Trevor asked, when he returned to the room.

"Tonbridge. There's been an armed raid."

Trevor immediately blanched. That could only be because of one of two things: his mind had either returned to Chagford, or, more likely, it being Trevor, he was fully cognisant that his boss's wife worked at Tonbridge. He did not say anything. He did not have to. David knew that Trevor would, consciously and literally, be by his side, whatever they were about to discover.

The journey to Tonbridge should take about 40 minutes, but at this time of the afternoon, getting through Tunbridge Wells might be a problem. As it happened, that part of the journey was not too bad, but there was a snarl-up in the suburb of Southborough. A broken down lorry was causing long queues in both directions.

They finally reached the branch just before five and immediately saw that the front of the branch had been cordoned off with police tape. It was not possible to park the car outside, but David managed to find a space about a hundred yards away. They then hurried to the branch, Trevor carting their heavy bag, in case it was needed.

Having first been properly identified, they were allowed into the branch. Apart from the presence in the banking hall of a solitary policeman, everything seemed normal. David asked to be shown to the manager's room. George Herbert was sitting with his elbows on his desk, chin resting on clasped hands, as if in prayer. When he saw David and Trevor, he stood up, crossed the room and shook hands with them both.

David knew Herbert, but not well, and he had not yet inspected his branch. He was quietly pleased about that, what with Sarah working there. But the manager had a sound reputation, the only possible blight having been made by Sarah when she had felt patronized on her first day. Since then, though, he had been fine and most supportive of her. The big question was whether such support had been needed today.

"It was just before two," Mr Herbert said, after David had asked what had happened. He then confirmed David's worst fears. "I'm afraid it was at Sarah's till . . . but she's fine," he hastily added.

Despair, quickly followed by relief. But where was Sarah? She was certainly not in the outer office. In fact, apart from the policeman, the branch was virtually devoid of staff.

"I've sent Sarah home . . . and most of the other staff," Mr Herbert said, as if reading David's thoughts. "You'll be proud to hear that Sarah was a hero, or should I say heroine. The man was wearing a raincoat and had one hand in his pocket, clearly holding something. He passed across a note saying it was a gun and demanded that Sarah handed over her cash. She didn't dare move to press the alarm button and simply thrust some ten shilling notes across the counter."

David was now feeling prouder by the minute. Sarah had clearly not panicked and had done what was needed if faced with such a situation: hand over cash, but starting with the lowest denomination notes.

"But the man demanded more," the manager continued, "and Sarah handed over a bundle of pound notes. He was becoming more agitated and Sarah then heard what she thought was a click from his pocket. It was enough to make her faint. Flat down on the floor. At that, the man panicked and fled from the branch. Sarah recovered immediately, thank God. So quickly that Tracey, the cashier next to her, thought she'd been acting. But no, Sarah really had passed out briefly at the sound of that click. Quite understandable, of course. But you've got a brave wife there, Mr Goodhart. No doubt about it. And she kept her head . . . apart from when she fainted," he added, grinning. "And the man got away with hardly anything."

"And she's now gone home?"

"Yes, about half an hour ago. After the raid, we shut the branch immediately and called the police. They came right away and wanted statements. But I told them they'd have to wait to speak to Sarah. I'd got her lying down in the rest room. Although she said she was feeling fine, I was concerned about a possible delayed reaction. So I made the police wait. They weren't best pleased. But Tracey had seen the man and gave them a reasonable description right away, despite his wearing a Balaclava and having a mask over his face. And that description was confirmed by Sarah, when I let them see her."

"So, no one was hurt," David said, much relieved for everyone, not just Sarah.

"That's right," the manager replied. "But it's been a sobering experience for all of us. I'm just pleased that our previous training came up trumps."

David had already got the impression from Sarah that this branch was running smoothly and efficiently. This unfortunate episode clearly confirmed this view and he was also impressed with how Mr Herbert had handled everything. In particular, he had been extremely caring with Sarah and David would be forever grateful for that. But there was still one point which was bothering him.

"What about Regional Office?" he asked. "You rightly called the police straight away, but . . ."

"My very next call," Mr Herbert interjected.

"So what time would that have been?"

The manager pursed his lips and was clearly thinking back to the chain of events. "It must have been about two-fifteen. I must say I'm surprised it took you so long to get here."

David was now quietly seething. Not only had it taken Angus McPhoebe about two hours to contact him, but he could tell that Mr Herbert was putting any tarrying down to David, himself.

"And it was Angus McPhoebe you spoke to?"

The manager nodded. "I thought I'd better speak to him directly, rather than one of his underlings."

"And you were able to give him full details of what had happened?"

"Of course. And by the time I spoke to him, Sarah had come to . . . after her fainting."

That confirmed it then. McPhoebe knew very well what had happened to Sarah. Why on earth had he not said so on the telephone? Had the man no compassion?

"Then I'll report to him tomorrow," David simply said, keeping his thoughts to himself. He nodded to Trevor and they both got to their feet. David then thrust his hand forward to grasp the manager's own hand. "Many thanks, Mr Herbert. You've done really well. As have all your staff. But I must get off home to see Sarah. Thank you so much for all you did for her. I only hope I can carry on your good work," he added, smiling.

David remained quiet about McPhoebe as he drove home, ready to drop Trevor off on the way. Trevor was well aware of the running animosity between the two men and he must know how his boss would be feeling about this latest spat. A spat David feared would only worsen tomorrow.

As soon as he opened the front door, Sarah rushed into the hall, almost tripping over the rather dog-eared rug that they had been threatening to replace for over a year. She threw her arms around him and they remained clasped together for what seemed like minutes, but, in reality, was only a few seconds. She then drew back from him and looked him directly in the eye. "I do love you, David," she said, then kissing him gently on the lips. "Mr Herbert phoned to say you were on your way home. And you know something? This afternoon made me realize even more what you and Mark mean to me."

"But let me look at you properly," David replied, drawing away from her. "Are you all right? Really all right? Mr Herbert said you were fine. And he was so proud of you. But, really, are you all right?"

Sarah smiled. "David! You realize you've just asked that question three times? But, yes, I'm fine. My main concern was what you'd be thinking when you heard. And I was worried about Mark . . ."

"Mark, of course. What happened when you weren't at home? Was he all right? And where is he now?"

"Have you forgotten? Remember when I made arrangements with next door? That he should go there if something held me up? Oh dear, that phrase sounds rather apposite now. Anyway, we agreed to do the same with their daughter - if she was ever in a similar situation."

"So, he's next door now?"

Sarah nodded. "When I got home, I told Sally what had happened and she offered to give Mark his tea. He should be back soon."

"In that case, before he returns, it's high time we had a drink and you can tell me all about it. Sure you can do that? You feel up to it?"

"David! You know me. I'm as strong as an ox."

David shook his head. "Don't I just know that. I certainly wouldn't have been brave enough to try and hold you up. Even with a gun in my pocket."

David poured them both a gin and tonic and Sarah recounted the whole story. It made him feel even more proud of her. He could only ponder on how he might have coped with a raider pointing a gun at him.

"Do you think it was a real gun," he asked, when she had finished.

"We'll never know," Sarah said, "but I did hear a click. And that's when I really let the side down. Actually fainting. How stupid of me! You know I never faint."

"It did the trick, though. It made the man scarper."

"But you know the best thing about it all, darling? I'd just had Mac Fisheries in, with all their smelly, fish-scaled notes. Guess who's got them now?"

David grinned. It was good to hear Sarah find some humour out of such a serious episode. He feared there would be no humour at all when he made his report to Angus McPhoebe. And he had now decided that he would submit his report in person, tomorrow, rather than on the telephone.

Chapter 14

David picked Trevor up the next morning and they then made their way to Crowborough. Once he had dropped Trevor off at the branch, David would go immediately to the Regional Office which was domiciled in Haywards Heath. He had no idea why that town had been chosen. This particular region of the bank stretched from the eastern edge of Surrey to the far reaches of East Kent. This meant that Haywards Heath was at the extremity of the region. Tunbridge Wells or Maidstone would have made a much better central location. But who was David to question the logic of those in Head Office?

He had decided to present himself in person to Angus McPhoebe, believing that a telephoned report would prove acrimonious. Far better to be able to look the man in the eye. This was not a question of who might blink first should any confrontation arise. David simply believed that a face-to-face discussion with McPhoebe would be far more preferable.

He had chosen not to ring McPhoebe first. He feared that the deputy regional manager would try and put off his visit, preferring, instead, to shield himself by way of the comparative anonymity of the telephone. If, for some reason, he was not available, David could always present his report to one of his underlings for passing on.

It was a fine, late October morning and the foliage on the trees had already started to turn. In a couple of weeks, the vivid yellow and golden leaves would be displayed in all their glory. David felt it was just a pity that red foliage, so prevalent in North America, would be missing. He had not yet been to New England in the fall, but he hoped he could make it there one day with Mark and Sarah.

He decided to make the most of this upcoming picturesque scene by choosing the country route through Ashdown Forest. This would also take him through the pretty village of Horsted Keynes. Whenever he drove down its main street in the morning, he always wound down the car's window to savour the aroma of freshly-baked loaves wafting from the popular baker's shop. To aid his mood still further, the next village of Lindfield boasted a large, centrally-located pond. Its wildfowl occupants always put a smile on his face as they squawked and flitted around their habitat.

All in all, this route should put him in a better frame of mind to face Angus McPhoebe, rather than the more direct, but busier, option of the A272.

He arrived at the Regional Office just before ten o'clock. It was a detached, three-storey, Victorian building, a few hundred yards from the centre of town. Three vehicles occupied part of the car park, including a dark blue Rover 90. Good. Angus McPhoebe was in residence. Whether he would be prepared to see David was another matter.

Having parked his car, he presented himself at reception and asked if he could see the deputy regional manager. The young lady asked him to take a seat and then picked up her telephone. David could not decipher what she actually said, but she soon confirmed that Mr McPhoebe would see him in a few moments.

David immediately opened his briefcase and withdrew a copy of The Times. It always accompanied him on his visits to see Angus McPhoebe. He had never yet been kept waiting for less than 30 minutes.

Whether such delaying tactics were the man's normal practice, David would never know. He could, however, quite understand being kept waiting today, having not first made a prior appointment. But David considered it to be the height of bad manners to be always late for timed appointments.

After 35 minutes, McPhoebe's door eventually opened. David glanced up and saw this rather imposing man, some six foot tall, clad in an immaculate three-piece, charcoal-grey suit. As usual, he made himself appear taller by stretching his neck and pointing his chin forward, giving the impression that some noxious air was infiltrating his nostrils. " Ah, Goodhart," he said. "You'd better come in."

David carefully folded his Times, returned it to his briefcase and followed McPhoebe into the room.

"Good morning, Mr McPhoebe," he said, doing his best not to stress the first two words, even though he wanted to ensure that his own use of a salutation would not go unnoticed.

McPhoebe waved him to the chair on the opposite side of his desk and David dutifully sat down, deliberately not opening his briefcase. He had all the information needed in his head. If necessary, McPhoebe could always take notes from what he said, although his desk was clear of anything, never mind a pad of paper and pens. What on earth could have been occupying his time during the 35 minutes he had kept David waiting?

"A bad business," McPhoebe simply said, as an opening gambit.

David nodded and waited to be questioned.

McPhoebe frowned. "Well?"

"Well, what?"

McPhoebe sighed. "What have you got to report?"

"Not a great deal more than you already know. I gather that Mr Herbert gave you all the facts when he rang you. So, I'm curious. When you phoned me, why didn't you put me fully in the picture?"

"I gave you all you needed to know. I wanted you to look into everything with fresh eyes. You didn't expect to be spoon-fed, did you?"

No wonder David did not like dealing with this man. And he was glad that, as an inspector, he did not come under his direct command. His own boss was the chief inspector who was based in London. Inspectors, such as David, were allocated to the bank's various regions around the country to make independent assessments of what was going on in those regions. They were not actually part of those regions' staff. Yes, they had to keep the regional managers informed of what was happening, but not necessarily to be at their beck and call. Having said that, the regional manager and his deputy, in this case McPhoebe, could make life awkward for a visiting inspector should they so wish. The submission of an unfavourable report on an inspector to the chief inspector in London was certainly best avoided, if at all possible.

"But what about my wife?" David countered. "Couldn't you have told me? That she was the cashier involved?"

McPhoebe looked out of the room's solitary window. Not that there was much to see, apart from a patch of blue sky peeping out from behind some recently-arrived scudding clouds. So much for eye-to-eye contact. Was the man embarrassed by David's questions?

"I didn't want you to be worried," he eventually answered, still looking out of the window. "On your journey to Tonbridge, I mean. And Mr Herbert told me she was all right."

David pursed his lips. Did McPhoebe have a point? No, of course not. The fact that Mr Herbert had told McPhoebe that Sarah had not been hurt was just the sort of information he should have passed on to David. And any worry David might have had would then, surely, have been dispelled.

David decided not to pursue the point and, instead, recounted all that he had learnt about the raid. He particularly dwelt on how well Mr Herbert had handled everything.

By then, McPhoebe had seen enough out of his window and was giving David his full attention, especially on hearing about his praise of Mr Herbert. "Just what I would have expected from one of my managers," he gushed. "They're all the same. Know exactly what they're doing. You must be finding that with Windsor in Crowborough."

David could not prevent a fleeting dropping of his eyelids. He could foresee another pending battle with McPhoebe. But he was not going to be drawn on events at Crowborough. Not yet, anyway. And there was one thing about the Tonbridge raid which had been exercising his mind since yesterday.

"I'm just wondering if this was a one-off hold-up," he said. "And if the man actually did have a gun, I'm bothered that he might try again."

"Yes, I think he might well try again," McPhoebe replied, astonishing David by actually agreeing with something he had said. There had to be a first time for everything, David surmised. "I don't think this is a one-off," McPhoebe continued. "It's certainly the first raid we've had for some time in our region, but similar ones have been happening elsewhere."

This was news to David, but he would not necessarily know of what might be happening in other regions within the bank. Certainly not if such raids had been recent. Several times a year, inspectors from all over the country would meet up to discuss problems which might have occurred, but the last such meeting had been in August. On the other hand, if something serious had been going on, the chief inspector would normally have circulated his inspectors by way of warning.

"In that case," he replied, pleased that McPhoebe was continuing to give him more attention than the sky outside, "I'm surprised I haven't been warned by the chief inspector."

"That's possibly because they've been very recent. They've also been very amateurish, with nothing actually taken. And this is the first time a gun has been used."

"If it was a gun."

McPhoebe nodded. "It could have been anything in his pocket."

"But Sarah did hear a click. As if it were being cocked."

"Could have been a toy gun."

"Especially if the perpetrator was an amateur in such things."

David was getting a bit disconcerted. Not about the matter under discussion. But that he and McPhoebe were actually having a discussion which had not (yet?) turned acrimonious. Perhaps, on reflection, McPhoebe now believed he had caused David an injustice in not properly informing him about Sarah's involvement in the raid.

"Where did these other raids take place?" he asked.

"There have been just two, in the last three weeks. Both in the southern region. One was in a small branch just outside Guildford and the other was at a sub-branch near Portsmouth."

"But not in the big towns themselves?"

McPhoebe shook his head. "That's why we think the man's probably an amateur. And it sounds like the same man. But the police could do with a more positive description. Difficult, I know, with his face covered. Just the same at Tonbridge. But do you think you could ask your wife to put her thinking cap on? There could be a small detail she might remember."

This was getting better by the minute; McPhoebe actually asking for some help?

"Anyway, report back to me," he snapped, reverting to his normal self. "As soon as possible. Come and see me next week. I can then introduce you to Mr Porter's successor. He starts on Monday."

Ah, that was interesting. McPhoebe was clearly not going to get the top job. David wondered how he must be feeling about that. Had someone actually twigged that he did not have the qualities for further promotion? Anyway, it was certainly a relief for David. Perhaps he could somehow engineer future meetings to be with the new man, rather than with McPhoebe. But his relief was short-lived when he was told whom it was. McPhoebe might be David's *bete noire*, but the new regional manager was his brother's old *bete noire* from his Wiveliscombe days: none other than the dreaded Mr Threadgold.

Chapter 15

David got into his Consul for the drive back to Crowborough. Before turning on the ignition, he remained sitting behind the wheel and reflected on what he had just been told. Mr Threadgold? Of all people? The new regional manager? With Angus McPhoebe as his second-in-command? What kind of team was that? It was as if Hitler and Goebbels had been put in charge of the Salvation Army. All right, that was being rather fanciful, but it did not stop David from smiling at such a whimsical analogy.

On the other hand, it might not be so bad. It was all of six years since he had seen Mr Threadgold. He might well have changed. He could have mellowed in these intervening years. And David had learnt how to handle Angus McPhoebe, by simply not rising to his bait. Although he had to admit that he was not always successful with that. But he still had great sympathy for the managers and staff in this south-east region. Both brother Robert and he had been on the receiving end of Threadgold's questionable characteristics. As for McPhoebe, it could not only be David who had suffered at the hands of the man's arrogance. So it was unlikely that managers and staff in this region would enjoy much empathy with these two men at the helm of Regional Office.

He started up the car and pulled out of the car park. He would return to Crowborough via the A272 and he should be back in time for lunch. A pint and a chinwag with Trevor would be just the ticket. After that, he must get to meet Frank Windsor.

The manager was able to see him at 2.30 and David now sat in his room, still curious about the landscapes which adorned three of the four walls. Frank Windsor noticed his roving eyes.

"A hobby of mine." he said, smiling, as if in pride, then taking in one picture after another. "I started collecting them a couple of years ago. Several more at home. So I swap them around. Gives the room a different perspective. The portrait isn't me, you know. Many people think it is. But it's my father. Anyway, they all help me to concentrate when I'm faced with tricky situations."

Tricky situations? In that case, the paintings might well bear the manager's scrutiny during this afternoon's session. Unless, of course, he had logical explanations to David's exploratory questions.

"But enough about that," Windsor continued. "What a week it's been. First, poor old Ted Callard . . . and I still can't get over that . . . then your poor wife. I was so sorry to hear what had happened at Tonbridge yesterday. I really felt for you both. I must say, I didn't know she worked there. But what a shock for her, and for you, of course."

Now, that was nice. David felt himself warming to a man whom he now hoped would have some feasible answers to the lending questions he was about to pose.

"Thank you," he answered. "And thank goodness no real harm was done. I've just been to Regional Office and they told me that a couple of similar raids have just taken place in the southern region. I just hope it's not going to be a spate."

"I'll certainly second that," Windsor said. "I called all our staff together this morning. It wasn't to put the fear of God into them. But if we do ever get a hold-up here, they're all aware of what they should and shouldn't do."

"That's good to hear," David said, "but I'm sure there's one thing that could help in such cases. I really can't see why the bank doesn't install some sort of bandit screens on the counter. Poor old Trevor was a victim of such a raid some . . ."

"Your Trevor, with you now?"

David nodded. "Yes, it was some four years ago. I was manager at Barnmouth branch. We'd sent him on relief to Chagford. Only for a week. But it turned out to be the wrong week. An armed raider scaled the counter and made off with most of the contents of his till. Fortunately, he wasn't hurt. But it took him months to get over it. Anyway, after it happened, I wrote to Head Office to suggest the introduction of bandit screens. That was all those years ago. And? Zilch. Maybe they'll get round to it one day."

Frank Windsor shook his head, no doubt in sympathy about the workings of Head Office. "I just hope that nothing like that ever happens here. Yesterday must also have been a shock for your Trevor."

David waited a moment or two as they both reflected on this. He then decided to set about the purpose of this afternoon's meeting.

"I've started to look at your lending here," he said, "but I'm nowhere near finished. You've certainly been hard at it, haven't you?"

Frank Windsor smiled and seemed to rise a few inches behind his desk. "Yes, I've really been able to build things up these last couple of years. There's a lot of untapped business here in Crowborough. And I've made some good connections. Particularly through Crowborough Collective. So much so that time's becoming a problem. Poor old Scrivens. I'm putting more and more of the other work his way."

David could see that this could be a problem with an old-school chief clerk. "Can he cope?"

"At the moment all is well. But I think he was anticipating a gentle passage towards his retirement. That's the last thing he's getting now."

"Anyway," David continued, "apart from GB Builders, which we've already talked about, I'm quietly impressed with what I'm seeing."

Windsor seemed to grow another couple of inches.

"But I'm really curious about some particular loans," David continued. "What's going on at Crawley and Horley? I've already come across half a dozen loans for customers living there."

Windsor smiled and nodded, as though knowing full well as to where this was leading. But he said nothing, just raising his eyebrows, as an encouragement for David to continue.

David duly obliged. "For instance, take your customer William Crickhaven. It seems he bought a house in Crawley last June. You gave him a loan of £5,000 and the property was professionally valued at £8,000. That doesn't seem to be a problem, then. But there've been no repayments yet. And I'm not sure you've ever met Mr Crickhaven. Not according to the PM card, anyway. And the same applies to the other five loans."

Windsor smiled again. A rather indulgent smile to David's thinking.

"You've found my hidden gem," he said, actually rubbing his hands together. "No, it's not hidden . . . couldn't be more open. But it's a big one for me . . . and for the bank. And I can see it growing and growing."

This was not meaning much to David. But he was getting an uncomfortable feeling that he might not be going to share Frank

Windsor's enthusiasm. He simply raised his hands for Windsor to elaborate.

"It's all about Gatwick Airport," Windsor said. "As you probably know, there are big expansion plans there. And British United Airways and Dan-Air are dramatically increasing their charter flights. I reckon there's going to be a huge rise in overseas holidays and Gatwick's going to be at the heart of it."

David was certainly aware of what was happening at Gatwick, but what had that to do with Mr Crickhaven and those other loans?

"I understand all that," he said, " but what has Gatwick got to do with things happening here in Crowborough?"

"That's down to my contacts," Windsor replied. "And Crowborough Collective, specifically. I'm so pleased I was invited to join. You know, I'm their only bank manager member. It certainly gives me an edge over the other banks here. The man at Lloyds is itching to get invited. Anyway, it means I'm closely involved with so many of the town's influential businessmen."

David suppressed a wince. Like the most successful investment consultant in town? Like the most successful builder in town? Or was this being a little unfair?

"So who's put this Gatwick business your way?" he asked.

Windsor smiled, preening himself still further.

"Julian Palfrow, no less."

The solicitor extraordinaire?

"He's the senior partner with Walsgrove and Lithgow," Windsor continued. "One of his biggest clients is the British Pilots' Association. And that's where Gatwick comes in. British United pilots and those of Dan-Air need to live near the airport. As do other airport personnel. So there's a great demand for houses in the area. At Crawley and Horley especially."

David pursed his lips. Walsgrove and Lithgow were the bank's well-respected authorised solicitors. It was they who had given their undertaking to hold the deeds of the properties to the bank's order. And Julian Palfrow - solicitor extraordinaire - was their senior partner. Interesting.

"So," he said, "Mr Palfrow introduced these pilots to you, despite your not being in the Crawley area?"

"But it makes sense," Windsor replied. "With Julian acting for the pilots, he can handle all their requirements here in Crowborough."

"So, all your dealings are with him? Not with the pilots, themselves?"

"But that's not a problem. Julian deals with all the paperwork. And he's given us impeccable references for all the pilots."

"And what about loan repayments?"

"I agreed that these could be deferred. Only for the time being. It all depends on the coming flight schedules . . . with the airlines. Everything should be finalized in the next few months. Then it'll be take-off, literally," Windsor added, smiling at his witticism.

"And the actual properties? They all seem to be quite expensive."

"Only what such high-fliers, in all senses of the word, deserve."

Another witticism. Windsor was clearly enjoying this little exchange.

"Have you seen them - the properties, not the high-fliers?"

Windsor shook his head. "No need. They've all been professionally valued. By Charlie Spencer O'Hara."

Ah, the Honourable Charlie Spencer O'Hara. But this was all beginning to look somewhat incestuous. Or was that also being unfair? Was David's natural antipathy towards Crowborough Collective doing an injustice to this particular honourable gentleman? As for Julian Palfrow . . . it seemed that he was equally honourable, even if not bearing an honourable title.

"It looks as if I'm going to come across more of these loans," David said. "I'm still only halfway through the alphabet."

Windsor hesitated in replying, appearing to make a mental calculation. "Another dozen, I'd say. At the moment, that is. I'm expecting many more introductions. And it's such good business for the bank. I'm charging a 1% arrangement fee, plus a good rate of interest."

This was all starting to sound too good to be true. Yet David was beginning to feel increasingly nervous. But why should that be? Reputable people were involved in the introductions and valuations, while airline pilots with all the right introductory references, should make most satisfactory customers. The lending did not seem to be at risk and the business looked extremely profitable for the bank. But his nose was twitching. And David knew that this would meet with Trevor's approval. In this particular case, though, he wondered if his nose was letting him down.

Chapter 16

What a relief for David. To wake up on Saturday morning, knowing that he would have two days of respite from the goings-on at National Counties.

He had now been an inspector for three years. During much of that time, his inspections of branches had been perfectly straightforward. Examination of the managers' lending was always a major task, while branch security was another prime issue. Not security by way of collateral relating to borrowing propositions; no, the protective security of bank premises, cash and valuables and, especially, branch staff.

David's inspectorial visit always started by the ring of the front door bell, shortly after the branch had closed at three o'clock. Staff were never forewarned of the coming of bank inspectors, although they were aware that such visits took place every couple of years. They must always be alert to security measures, but any lapses around the time of an expected inspection would be careless in the extreme. Gone should be any impulse to throw open the front door to see who might be awaiting entry. Instead, the built-in spyglass should be squinted through, then the door opened with the security chain still in place. Once the inspector's identity card had been scrutinized, these unwelcome visitors could be let in. Woe betide should this rigmarole be ignored. The inspectors would immediately chalk up a black mark for the branch. They would also then be on high alert for other misdemeanours they might find. Slackness in one area could well be duplicated elsewhere.

Crowborough branch had, fortunately, got off to a good start by dealing impeccably with the front door opening procedure.

Once an inspection was underway, it would be Trevor's duties, primarily, to check out other aspects of security. In particular, strict control of keys was vital. Strongrooms were always locked under dual control and no member of staff should ever have the opportunity of holding both keys. Cashiers must have sole control of their cash and must never relinquish their keys which must be kept on their person at all times. Even the drawer holding postage stamps was the sole responsibility of that particular keyholder.

Last April, at Tunbridge Wells branch, Trevor had found a bunch of keys lying idly on the sub-manager's desk. It was a typical case of such laxity then being reflected in other areas within the branch. David had never known such an inspection. Poor security procedures had contributed to a murder, a kidnapping and the branch messenger being shot by a gunman at point-blank range. The messenger had, fortunately, since made a full recovery, but the manager was no longer in charge. If he had not taken early retirement, he would have been sacked. What an end to some forty years of loyal service.

Despite this experience, David found most inspections to be humdrum affairs. That had to be a good thing. Goodness knows how Crowborough would turn out. But there had certainly been a questionable start. He could still not understand how Frank Windsor had allowed George Bathurst such a large overdraft facility to invest with Derek Herretson. What had that been all about? Especially as the activities of stick-insect looked to be decidedly questionable. The most successful investment consultant in town? Pertinent evidence would be needed to support such a fulsome laudation. As for all those loans to airline pilots . . . Yet there did not seem to be any risk with these and it appeared to be profitable lending on the manager's part. At least none of these matters could be linked to Ted Callard's heart attack, yet why had he said that something bad was going on? God forbid that this inspection at Crowborough might have echoes of what had gone on in Tunbridge Wells.

But it was now Saturday. Time to dwell on another matter: Crystal Palace football club to be precise.

David accepted that the Glaziers was his second love in football. Until three years ago, he had spent most of his life in South Devon and Torquay United had been his one and only team. Transferring his affections had not been easy. And he would have been shocked at any accusation of infidelity. But what could he do? Being so far away from his beloved Plainmoor? And, in his defence, he would always seek out United's results before all others.

But he still needed his footballing fix. Of all the professional clubs in the area, Crystal Palace was the nearest and he had genuinely come to love the club. Yet, even being a famous London club, it was actually a step down from Torquay. That was, perhaps, no bad thing. Until a couple of years ago, both teams had languished in the 3rd Division (South). Then the powers-that-be had altered the North and South format into Divisions 3 and 4. Torquay had made it into Division 3, while Palace had to make do with the lowest tier of English football. Oh, well . . .

Yet, was there a change afoot?

Last April, the legendary Arthur Rowe had been appointed manager; he who had introduced the famous 'push and run' football of the wonderful Spurs team in the fifties. Now he was at

Palace. And excitement was in the air. David could not believe the first game of this season when Accrington Stanley were thrashed 9-2. Then last week, a 2-1 win at Gillingham took Palace to the top of the table.

Could promotion this year be a possibility? Could Palace be playing United next season in Division 3?

Match days on Saturday meant no breakfast for David. That was the bad news. The good news was that it was now eleven o'clock and brunch was about to be served.

For the last ten minutes, the aroma from sizzling bacon had permeated the whole house and David was already licking his lips. He had avoided stepping into the kitchen in case Sarah had demanded some help and he just hoped that the bacon would be accompanied by a couple of fried eggs, a sausage and two slices of fried bread. Just perfect. And the helpings would be doubled up today; not for him, but to include Mark who would be accompanying him to the match.

Yet until an hour ago, David had shunned any thought of going to the match. It had been less than 48 hours since Sarah had faced an apparently-armed gunman. It had been typical of her to make light of the fact. But a fact it certainly was. David had been determined that he would give her his whole attention this weekend. And Mark, recently promoted to the school's second eleven, had immediately cried off from playing this afternoon.

But Sarah would have none of it. She was absolutely fine and insisted that her two boys should attend the match together. Especially as the bank's chief inspector had given David two tickets for the directors' box. The chief was not, apparently, a fan of football and no other inspector was interested in a trip to Selhurst Park. When told this, David had shaken his head. More fools them.

Yet David knew that Mark had some reservations about this 'treat'. The last time he had accompanied David in a directors' box had been at Torquay. It had been a grave disappointment. Normally, he liked to arrive at the ground early. He would then devour the contents of the programme, while waiting on the terraces for the game to start. At the same time, he would soak up the pre-match atmosphere, even though crowds could be sparse. But on that day in the directors' box, he had been forced, instead, to attend pre-match drinks with people who only went to their seats when the players were already out on the pitch, ready to kick off. For Mark, it was definitely not the way to prepare for a football match.

Today, they bought a programme and took their seats. They sat alone. All the directors and their guests were clearly happy to swill their gins and tonics, or cups of tea, rather than sit outside in the cold.

The opponents today were Bradford and the crowd was likely to be bigger than that at Torquay. Especially as Palace were now top of the table. And especially as Palace now had a player destined for high honours. Johnny Byrne had joined the club in 1956 and was a great international player in the making. The only snag was that he would not achieve such success with a 4th Division club. David, along with all other Palace supporters, accepted that he would move eventually to a bigger club. In the meantime, he was scoring goals for Palace; 13 this season, so far, including four in a 5-0 win over Southport. David was already dreaming of a repeat performance today.

As it happened. David and Mark did see four home goals, but only one scored by Byrne in a 4-1 win. Mark could hardly contain himself and David hoped his sole allegiance to Torquay might now waiver. Whatever, they made their way to the directors' bar with a spring in their steps.

Despite shunning the pre-match drinks, they were made most welcome. The room was crowded and everyone was buoyant from the convincing win. And Palace still topped the table. David could then hardly believe his eyes. He saw a familiar face in a crowd of strangers. He could not, at first, put a name to the face. It was a case of seeing someone out of context; in unfamiliar surroundings. The man then crossed the room and offered his hand.

"The famous inspector," he said, smiling broadly. Got it! There was no doubting it now: he of the Crowborough residential home.

"Mr Purcell," David answered, grasping HP's hand which was surprisingly firm. "What are you doing here?"

"I might ask the same of you. But I think we might have one thing in common."

"Palace?"

"Of course. Been a fan for many years. And you?"

David was suddenly warming to a man of whom he had harboured severe reservations at the Crowborough Collective lunch.

"Only three years for me. Since I came up here from Torquay. I'm a firm United fan, really. But I have a feeling I'm going to become a Palace fan through and through. And you're a director?"

Henry Purcell looked shocked. "Goodness no. Don't know enough about the game for that. Just a fan."

"A guest, then?"

Purcell nodded. "And you?"

"Not exactly a guest. I was given two tickets for the directors' box. I've brought my son. This is Mark," he added, pushing the lad forward.

"Good to meet you, young man," HP said, shaking Mark's hand. At least he did not ruffle Mark's hair, something he hated. It had happened in the directors' bar at Torquay, but he was, of course, much younger and smaller then.

"So you know the right people?" David asked. "Being a guest, I mean."

David had first likened HP to Jimmy Rushing's 'Mr Five-by-Five' and he seemed to swell even more as he prepared to answer the question.

"The chairman, no less," he replied, looking behind him and beckoning to a man who then moved towards them.

"Arthur," he said, "may I introduce someone else from Crowborough. This is Mr Goodhart, a bank inspector, no less. He then paused, looking questionably at David. "It's David, isn't it?"

David nodded.

"Please meet Arthur Wait, David, chairman of the Club."

This was certainly a big moment for David. He knew that Arthur Wait ran a successful building empire and he had a high regard for what the chairman had done for Palace. At the very least, it was he who had appointed the great Arthur Rowe as manager. But how were Arthur Wait and HP connected?

"We're very privileged to be here," David said, shaking the chairman's hand and again pushing Mark forward.

"Glad to meet you both," Arthur Wait replied. "But you'll soon have more important people than me to meet. Some of the players will be here in a moment."

David was impressed with that. A humble chairman was no bad thing.

"Including Johnny Byrne?" Mark asked, much surprising David. Mark was normally most reticent on such occasions.

Arthur Wait nodded. "And Roy Summersby. He didn't get one today, but he's a great goalscorer."

David could now imagine that Mark would soon become a committed Palace supporter. In the meantime, Arthur Wait excused himself to talk to other people and David raised his eyebrows at Henry Purcell.

HP understood immediately. "I've been business friends with Arthur for many years. So I couldn't support any other team. I come to all the home games, but I'm not always a guest. I normally stand behind the goal on the Holmesdale terrace."

David was definitely starting to get a different impression of the man he had met at the Crowborough Collective lunch. And it was not just because they were fellow Palace supporters. For one thing, HP had resisted uttering any witticisms or schoolboy rejoinders. He had also made the point that he was a business friend of Arthur Wait, though probably also personal friends. But if they were primarily business acquaintances, it might say much about his acumen in running his own residential home. At the Collective lunch, Frank Windsor had indicated as such; maybe he was right.

"I prefer to stand alongside the half-way line," David answered, then grinning. "And I do like to stand. You can't get so animated sitting in the grandstand."

HP returned his grin. " I believe all proper supporters think that way. Anyway, now that we're better acquainted, why don't you pop over some time and have a look at my place. I'm quietly proud of my little residential home. And you'll be able to see all the work Arthur put into it. He's a great builder. Just the sort of business you should have at your bank. I'll put in a good word for you, if you'd like."

David smiled and nodded, as if in appreciation of the offer. But, as an inspector, this was not his role, at all. Branch managers were the business getters. He wondered if HP had made a similar offer to Frank Windsor. Or had he made the suggestion simply because of the Palace connection? It was also not David's brief to visit customers at their places of business. Again, that was Frank Windsor's job, particularly if HP banked with him. And if he did not, the residential home must be a target for the manager to acquire such a business from a competitor.

"Both those offers are very kind of you," he replied. "But it's really not my role to play. And I wouldn't want to tread on Frank Windsor's toes. Perhaps I could . . .?"

David was pleased not to be able to finish his sentence. Arthur Wait had appeared at their side and apologized that that there was someone else whom he wanted HP to meet.

When they had gone, David looked at Mark. "Had enough?"

Mark nodded. "I think we'd better get back to Mum."

"Not bothered about missing the players?"

Mark shook his head. "Not really. And they might be some time yet. The main thing is we saw a good match. And I'd rather get home to see how Mum is."

David could only agree with that. Despite the excitement of the afternoon, he had frequently wondered how Sarah had been coping on her own.

"Good," he said. "Let's get on our way, then. I just hope she's been all right without us being around."

Chapter 17

Trevor decided to lie in on Saturday. Neither sleeping nor dozing. His mind was gyrating like the turntable of his record player. It was always thus on the day of an important gig.

Tonight he was playing at the Old Vine in the hamlet of Cousley Wood which bisected the towns of Wadhurst and Lamberhurst. He was fronting a trio comprising piano, bass and drums, his favourite format. He had played with the others before and they always left him to decide the programme. No sheet music was needed, often the case with jazz. Musicians of tonight's calibre would know hundreds of tunes, including all the ones which Trevor had chosen for this evening. All he had to do would be to give the others the running order when they arrived and they would then simply follow his lead. The joy of improvised jazz.

He chose *Stomping at the Savoy* as his opener. Played as a blues, at medium tempo, it should get the punters on his side from the very first note. He would then try and match Sonny Stitt's version of *Easy Does It,* before launching into his first ballad. Now, what should that be? The whole point of ballads was to create feeling and empathy with the listeners. Gershwin and Rogers and Hart were composers who did this admirably in their writing. When selecting their tunes, Trevor would always subliminally have in mind a particular person to whom he would direct his playing. Much better than to play to the audience as a whole. He had once been told about Duke Ellington's master saxophonist, Paul Gonsalves, doing just that, in fact taking it to the next extreme. A very young schoolgirl was sitting in a club with her parents at a table immediately in front of him. To her astonishment and awe, he bent down in front of her and played a whole solo effectively just for her.

Now, who should be the recipient of Trevor's playing tonight?

There was only one answer: Katie, of course. She might be over 200 miles away, but playing with his eyes closed, he could imagine her sitting in the pub right there in front of him.

He needed something to remind him of Katie, because he had not yet received her weekly letter. He had, in fact, written to her twice this week, sending his second missive yesterday. He needed to tell her about Mrs Goodhart, rather than for her to hear about the raid at Tonbridge from elsewhere. In particular, he wanted her to know that Mrs Goodhart had assured everyone that she was perfectly all right after her traumatic experience.

Trevor hoped that this was not a case of bravado on her part. It had taken him so long to get over his own experience at Chagford and this week's raid had brought it all back to him. Would Mrs Goodhart suffer from a delayed reaction? Her experience had not been as physical as his own; his armed raider had actually jumped over the counter into the cashier's run. But, even so, she had been on the receiving end of someone holding a possible gun in his pocket. How frightening must that have been?

But Mrs Goodhart was Mrs Goodhart. Mr Goodhart had always said of her, in the nicest possible way, that she was as strong as an ox. He must have been talking mentally, because her petite, five-foot-twoish would be no match physically against her six-foot husband.

Back in Devon, Trevor often felt that this lovely lady had a soft spot for him. He was Mr Goodhart's personal assistant at the time and she seemed to appreciate the way the two men worked together. She was also a keen advocate of Trevor's relationship with Katie. It was not a case of her trying her hand at matchmaking; there was no necessity for that. Trevor had already staked his case with Katie. And Mrs Goodhart could see that they were made for each other. Since then, during the last year here in Kent, Trevor had not seen too much of his boss's wife, but he definitely reciprocated any fondness she felt for him.

So, thinking back to the trauma of the raid, he could only hope that Mrs Goodhart was, genuinely, 'perfectly all right'.

He also hoped it was the same for Katie, down there in South Devon. Had he made a mistake by coming up to the London area? Had he been selfish in accepting his promotion? It might have happened anyway, if he had remained in the south west. No, promotion would not have occurred down there, not at his age. Becoming an inspector's assistant was unheard of at only twenty-four. It was only Mr Goodhart's influence that had made it happen. But Trevor could still have turned down the promotion to be with Katie. If he turned the clock back, would he make the same decision again?

What he did know for certain was that he missed her terribly and seeing her only three or four times a year was not enough. But was he still too young to marry? Would Katie, indeed, say 'yes' if he asked her? But just thinking of her had enabled him to choose his first ballad of the evening: *My One and Only Love.*

He then settled back to thinking about the rest of his programme, eventually rising from his bed to transcribe the numbers on to paper. He made four copies, one for himself and the other three for his accompanists. He then decided to have some breakfast. Fifteen minutes later, as he was about to wash up his cereal bowl, he heard the letter box clatter and there on the mat was what he had been yearning for: Katie's long-awaited letter.

He tore open the envelope and tossed it into his wicker wastepaper basket. He then plonked down on the sofa, his feet drawn up under him, and smiled in anticipation of what must be the highlight of his week.

A few moments later, his eyes moistening, he knew the answers to the questions he had posed to himself earlier: yes, he had made a mistake in coming up here; yes, he had been selfish; and yes, he could have turned down his promotion and stayed with Katie. She would then, surely, not have cast her eyes elsewhere.

Then, despair turned to rage which seared his damp eyes. He flung the letter to the floor, slammed his fist into an adjacent cushion and yelled "why?" at the room's mute walls. But his fury was not directed at Katie; he could never be angry with her. No, it was this other man. Who was he? Katie had not said. But he must have known that Katie was spoken for. Katie would never have kept that from him. Did he have no scruples? Was he taking advantage of darling Katie, simply because Trevor was so far away? What a mess! And what could he possibly do about it?

Calming down somewhat, he picked up the letter and re-read Katie's words. Were there any hidden clues? In fact, having first scanned the letter quickly, with increasing blurred eyes, he now decided that he may have read too much into what she had written. In his haste to gobble up her words, had he assumed the worst - unjustifiably? She had not actually said that she had met, and was going out with, another man; just that she had seen someone else. But that, surely, meant the same thing. Met? Seen? Yet not going out together? And she did say that she was missing Trevor. Was it just that she needed some company, with his being so far away? She also finished her letter with all her love. Would she do that if she had fallen for someone else? Surely, not.

Questions, questions, questions. And doubts and more doubts.

He found it difficult to get through the day. He had never known hours drag by so slowly. He tried to immerse himself in his music, working on tonight's programme and practising his scales, but his heart was not in it.

Yet he was certainly relieved that the gig had been arranged for that evening. Even if he wanted to, there was no getting out of it. And, despite all the turmoil in his head, once he started playing, he would be absorbed in his music. If, instead, he had been without a gig and at a loose end, he would have just moped around, feeling sorry for himself. Doing something positive must be a good thing.

Without undue delay, he must also take some further action. At the very least, he needed to telephone Katie. Neither of them was on the phone at home, so ringing during the day, at work, was the only option. He just hoped that Mr Goodhart would agree to this. And depending on how the call went, he needed to get down to Devon and see Katie as soon as possible. Surely, that would sort matters out between them? But when could he make such a trip? The inspection at Crowborough had the makings of difficulties ahead. Mr Goodhart was having reservations about Mr Windsor and there seemed to be something odd about the manager's relationship with that investment consultant. Why would he point his own customers in that man's direction when he was effectively a member of the opposition? If further developments arose with the inspection, particularly in respect of the manager's lending, Mr Goodhart was hardly likely to think favourably about allowing Trevor to have time off. Particularly if this was simply to sort out matters with his girlfriend. What a mess it all was.

When he arrived at the Old Vine in the early evening, a reasonable crowd was already in attendance. That was good. There was nothing worse than playing to a sparse audience. The other three musicians arrived at about the same time and Trevor gave each of them his proposed programme for the two sets they planned to play. The pianist queried the soloing arrangements on a couple of numbers and then they were all ready to start.

How appropriate it was that Trevor had opted to start with a blues. But it was when he launched into *My One and only Love* that his emotion almost overwhelmed him. He effectively felt he was doing a Paul Gonsalves. With eyes closed, he breathed into his saxophone for the opening chorus and imagined Katie sitting right there in front of him. Towards the end of the number, he felt tears tumbling down his cheeks, their saltiness searching out the mouthpiece of his instrument. When he ended the number, their was a brief pause before the audience erupted in applause. It was as if they had witnessed unexpected raw emotion on the bandstand. But only Trevor knew the reason behind it.

Chapter 18

Sarah watched David and Mark going off to their match with mixed emotions. Neither of them had wanted to go - because of her. But she had insisted; it would be good for them both and she enjoyed seeing them do things together. They had reluctantly agreed and there had been no need for them to know about her niggling anxiety at being alone in the house for some six to eight hours.

She had felt fine immediately after the raid. Yet 48 hours later, her equanimity had most certainly waned. Bad dreams during the last two nights had not helped. She had not told David about them. In fact, once awakened, and apart from the depiction of the gunman himself, she could not exactly remember what they had been about. They just gnawed away at her normal composure. But they would, surely, go away in the course of time. Far better, then, not to worry David, if that were to be the case.

But it was not like it had been after Mark's birth. Then, she had been in the depths of despair for over three months. Having craved a child for so long, no one had said that Mark's arrival could cause her so much suffering. She had almost been suicidal. Yet she later learned that her condition was far from uncommon:

post-natal depression. If she had been forewarned, it might have made all the difference. Motherhood had, instead, been painted with rose-hued brushes and ne'er a thorn in sight. She shook her head as she recalled those baby blues, then smiled. On reflection, that expression was more like a number for Trevor to play on his saxophone.

No, her present anxiety bore no relation to those dark days and she knew she would be soon over it.

She decided to do some housework and, it being a raw day, laid a fire which she would light an hour or so before the boys returned. She had already prepared the fish pie which was her menu choice for tonight. All right, David would have preferred a hot-pot - yet again - but fish would make a nutritious change. Mark's favourite of apple and blackberry crumble would follow; she had picked the blackberries that morning from the brambles at the end of their garden.

At five o'clock she must remember to tune in the wireless for Sports Report. Forewarned of the result at Selhurst Park, she would be able to anticipate the boys' mood when they got home. Whatever the outcome she would ensure that they would have an enjoyable evening together.

But now, on her own, she could not rid her mind of the raid. Would it ever go away? Each bad dream had featured the same man, unkempt, just as on the day itself. That dirty raincoat, with its bulging pocket had not changed, nor had that black Balaclava, pulled down over his forehead. His face mask then meant that his eyes were the only possible distinguishing feature. Those eyes. What was it about them? She could not recall their colour, but they certainly held a hint of recognition. Had she seen this man before?

Yet how could that be so? He was not the sort of person she would come across in everyday life. Not only was he scruffy, but his scribbled note and juvenile handwriting had questioned his literacy. Despite the horror of her ordeal she had even noticed a misplaced apostrophe. Apart from anything else, David would be proud of her for that.

But where could she have met someone like this gunman? Then it came to her: those travellers. Just down the road from Tonbridge branch, a motley group of caravans was parked in one corner of the car park behind the cinema. Sarah had never seen the women and children, but the men often loitered near the High Street. Just being there they managed to create an air of intimidation and she always hurried past, avoiding eye contact. Except for one occasion: a man had deliberately blocked her way and she had no alternative but to look at him before hurrying by. Were those the eyes which held some recognition for her? And that man was not only the same height as her gunman, but also similarly dressed.

This was something she must definitely discuss with David when he got home.

In the meantime, she settled down on their Greaves and Thomas saffron sofa, having first scoured the bookshelves for a suitable book to read. Definitely not a crime novel today, nor a thriller in any shape or form. But Jane Austen sounded about right and she had not read Emma for years.

The next thing she knew was the front door being opened and then slammed shut. She sat bolt upright, her foot then kicking Emma as she rested gently on their Wilton lounge carpet. What on earth was going on?

"Hello", a familiar voice called out. "We're home."

Oh my goodness! Not only had she failed to light the fire, but she had also missed Sports Report.

"Ah, there you are," David said, as he entered the lounge. "We were worried as we drove up. No lights on anywhere."

He bent down to give her a kiss; Mark then did the same.

"Are you all right, Mum?" Mark asked.

"Of course I am," Sarah replied, feeling more and more guilty. "I'm so sorry about the lights. I just lost track of time. You know, I found it strangely comforting sitting here watching the dusk settling in. But now you're here, I'll put the fish pie in the oven. Perhaps you'll light the fire, Mark." Then, avoiding David's eyes which had previously looked rather quizzical, she asked, "and how was the game."

"Haven't you heard?" Mark answered. " We won 4-1."

"We? I thought Torquay was still your team."

"Mum! I'm allowed two teams, aren't I?"

"We had the chance of meeting some of the players," David then said. "That would certainly have sealed it for Mark. But we left before they arrived. We wanted to get back to you."

"You mean to say you put me before the players," Sarah asked, feigning incredulity and then rising to do the tasks she should have done long ago.

Two hours later, their meal having been much enjoyed and with the washing-up done, Sarah was grateful that Mark had gone upstairs to study his football programmes and Charles Buchan magazines. She could now draw David into her deliberations over her bank raider.

"You're sure you want to talk about it now?" David asked, knowing that she had previously been rather reticent about discussing her experience.

Sarah nodded. "But before we do that, I forgot to tell you about my geezer from Walsall and my Tonbridge schoolboy."

Sarah felt herself relax as David clearly enjoyed her anecdotes. In fact, with their sitting closely together in the lounge, the fire glowing warmly, she sensed that her worst fears were getting behind her. The brandy which David had poured for them both was also helping.

"There's something about the man which is bothering me," she said. "Something about his eyes. It's almost as though I've seen him before."

David drew away from her, his own eyes betraying understandable scepticism.

"I know it's ridiculous," Sarah quickly added, "but I'm wondering about the travellers camped in the car park behind the cinema. They often spill out on to the High Street. One, in particular, could have been the same man."

"A bit close to home, isn't it? Would they carry out a raid just round the corner? On the other hand . . ."

Sarah frowned as David paused, something clearly having jogged his mind. "Darling?"

"I was just thinking back to my visit to Regional Office. McPhoebe told me there'd been a couple of similar raids in the southern region. And what do travellers do?"

Sarah pursed her lips. "Travel?"

"Exactly. Travelling around they could easily pick out likely targets. In this case, in the south and south-east, moving on to different towns when the job's done. What do you think?"

"It's certainly possible."

"Anyway," David continued, "McPhoebe asked me to get you to think more about the man's description. If that then ties in with the raiders in those other towns, we might be on to something. And if they used threatening notes each time, the handwriting might well coincide. And there could be fingerprints."

"That rogue apostrophe could well come back to haunt the gunman," Sarah said, grinning.

"Pardon?"

"Oh sorry, I forgot to tell you. There was a greengrocer's apostrophe on the note he thrust at me."

"And you spotted it?" David asked. "I am impressed. But I also forgot to tell you something yesterday. Guess who's just been appointed to take over from Mr Porter as regional manager?"

Chapter 19

David could not help but smile as he drove to pick up Trevor. Sarah's response at hearing about Mr Threadgold's appointment still floated around his mind: "Well, there's no hope for you now, David. You'd better take Trevor's lead. Take up the saxophone."

Two ex-bank saxophonists? Just a couple more and they could then vie with Woody Herman's famous reed section, known as the 'four brothers'. Not that David could contemplate going down this route. Especially as Mr Threadgold should have little influence over his career prospects. Not like the man's managers. They faced having a new boss with no man-management credentials to his name. There would be no future with that. The only harm the man could do to David would be by being awkward, even objectionable, when he had to make reports to Regional Office. But David could handle that. In any case, his immediate reporting would continue to be with Angus McPhoebe. Although he could never develop a rapport with Threadgold's deputy, he tried not to let their sparring get out of hand. He just hoped this situation would continue. Especially after their latest clash, following the raid.

Trevor was unusually quiet after David had picked him up. He simply looked ahead through the Consul's windscreen, seemingly miles away with his thoughts.

"You all right, Trevor?" David eventually asked.

Trevor nodded. "I'm fine, sir."

David frowned, ran his tongue over his lips, but then decided to bide his time before continuing the conversation.

As they approached Eridge, he found himself concentrating more on what might be going on with Trevor than his actual driving. How dangerous might that be? So he decided to press the lad further.

"How was your gig on Saturday? Did the punters like it?"

Trevor now turned to him, for the first time on the journey. "Yes, sir. It was great. Very receptive audience. And it's a good trio I'm with. The landlord wants us to go back next month."

"That's fantastic," David replied, but he now had an inkling as to Trevor's reticence. Was he harbouring further thoughts about his banking future? The more accolades he received with his playing, the more his mind might be turned towards a musical career. Although David abhorred the thought of Trevor giving up banking, what would he, himself, do if their roles were reversed? The thrill of playing before an enthusiastic audience must be awe-inspiring. And, if good enough, a jazz saxophonist's career would not stop at playing at the likes of Ronnie Scott's club. The world could be waiting with outstretched arms; the world effectively being 52nd Street in New York City. David could only dream of walking along this home to a profusion of magnificent jazz clubs. Birdland might be featuring Miles Davis, while Dizzy Gillespie could be playing at the 3 Deuces. As for saxophonists, the patrons would be spoilt for choice: Coleman Hawkins could well be vying with John Coltrane at the Hickory House, while Dexter Gordon might be blowing his horn further along the street at the Spotlight. The major problem for any fan would be choosing which club to enter. But what if it was not just a case of being a fan walking down this awesome thoroughfare? What would it be like to be actually playing in one of these clubs? David could well-imagine such a scenario far outshining anything National Counties might have to offer. But he still did not want Trevor to give up banking.

"Then," David added, in the wake of Trevor's continuing silence, "what's troubling you, Trevor? I mean, if all went well at your gig . . ."

Trevor smiled rather pensively. "I'm fine, sir. Really I am."

David pursed his lips. It still did not ring true, but there was no time to pursue the matter further; they had reached Crowborough. David parked the car around the corner from the bank and they made their way to the front door. Once they were ensconced in the rest room, he prepared himself to continue with his examination of the manager's lending. Trevor's 'problem' could wait. They must both get on with their inspection of the branch.

Trevor's task today was to examine the boxes and parcels which had been left by customers for safekeeping. The largest branches might have private safe deposits where customers could deposit valuables in individual repositories. But at smaller branches, such as Crowborough, individual boxes and parcels were stored collectively on shelves within the confines of the main strongroom. It was Trevor's job to match these items with the register to ensure that nothing was missing. It would take him the morning to do this, after which David had decided to share his increasing concern at the manager's lending to all these Gatwick pilots.

By lunchtime, he had completed his assessment of all the lending and he reckoned there were some dozen and a half of these property loans. Plenty to discuss with Trevor this afternoon.

They changed their venue for lunch, choosing the Dorset Arms in Withyham, some four miles away from Crowborough. David had passed this small country pub on several occasions, wondering what it might be like inside. Working in Crowborough was an ideal time to try it out.

First impressions were excellent. The front door led directly into the bar area where a crackling log fire greeted them, despite it only being just past mid-October. The aroma from what must be apple logs permeated the whole bar. David then immediately noticed that, like all good Sussex pubs, Harvey's was on tap. Getting a nod from Trevor, he ordered two pints and asked for the sandwich menu.

Fifteen minutes later, the fine ale washing down ham and tomato sandwiches, David again broached his concern for Trevor's wellbeing. If a good pint could not get the lad talking, nothing would.

"It's about Katie," Trevor eventually said.

"Not your career, then," David blurted out, but seeing Trevor's eyes widen, he immediately regretted the impulsiveness of his reply.

"My career, sir?"

David grinned, hoping it might lighten the prevailing mood. "Not your banking career - not directly, anyway. No, it was when you said your gig had gone so well. I just had the horrible feeling that . . ."

Trevor now returned his grin; the atmosphere was definitely getting back to normal. "Don't worry, sir. Ronnie Scott's isn't beckoning, not just yet, anyway."

"I was thinking more further afield. 52nd Street to be exact."

"And wouldn't I just love to go there," Trevor replied, his eyes glowing. "As a fan, I mean."

"Perhaps we should go together. On the other hand, I'm sure you'd rather be there with Katie. Anyway, what's this about Katie?"

Trevor took a swig from his tankard, wiped his lips with the back of his hand and looked hard at David.

"I think she might have found someone else."

David involuntarily put a hand to his mouth. That was impossible. Trevor and Katie were made for each other. Katie Tibbs was never a two-timer. Her utter loyalty and keen sense of duty had been instrumental in his decision to make her his secretary, back in Barnmouth. Only nineteen at the time, she should have been far too young to handle such an appointment. But she had maturity beyond her years. Being also vivacious and sociable, however, it was not just David whom she had impressed. She turned the heads of boys who had queued up to date her. But they were always kept at arm's length. And then, she started going out with Trevor.

"It's the distance," Trevor continued. "My being up here. Being so far away from Devon."

"But you've never had any inkling of this before," David said, still not believing what he was hearing. "And when Katie came up to see you playing at Ronnie's, she seemed even more besotted with you."

"That was six months ago. I've only seen her twice since then. And writing weekly letters isn't the answer. All in all, it's not enough. She deserves more from me than that."

"It's not your fault, Trevor. But I still don't believe it. She'd never go out with anyone else. You might not agree, but I think I know Katie as well as you do. In different ways, of course. Don't forget, it was before you started dating her that I made her my secretary. Why did I do that? Loyalty for one thing. She has it in spades. For me, then, and for you, now."

"But I got her weekly letter on Saturday," Trevor said, looking increasingly glum. "What she said was a bit ambiguous, I have to admit. But she said she'd seen someone else. Isn't that enough to make me worried?"

David was not sure how to play this. He was still convinced that Katie would not desert Trevor. And 'seeing someone' was a bit nebulous, to say the least. Trevor was clearly worried sick. But was he reading too much into whatever she had written in her letter?

"Have you spoken to her?" he asked.

Trevor shook his head. " No. I'm not on the phone at home and neither is she. I was just wondering, sir, if . . ."

David did not need to know the rest of the question to give him the answer he was seeking.

"Of course. Just what you need to do. Ring as soon as we get back to the branch. I'll have a word with Mr Scrivens. We'll need to pay for the call . . ."

"We'll pay, sir? You mean I will."

"Trevor, if there's any way I can help to ensure that you and Katie stay together, then I'll do it. And the cost of a telephone call to Barnmouth is the least I can do."

Trevor slumped back in his chair. Yet in a positive way. He at last seemed relaxed. He finished the rest of his beer and raised his eyebrows.

"No, Trevor, one's enough. We've got work to do this afternoon. When we get back I want to bend your ear about these Gatwick loans."

"Just one thing, sir. Depending on how the phone call goes, I really must get down to Devon to see Katie. I can go at the weekend, but Friday afternoon would be much better. Any chance of my having that afternoon off? I'd rather not drive, but I can get a fast train from Paddington. And then come back on Sunday."

David pursed his lips and gave himself a moment to think about Trevor's request.

"We've a busy week ahead of us," he then said. "And I've got a specific task for you to do tomorrow. But Friday afternoon's fine. Anything to get things sorted out between you and Katie. But let's first see how your phone call goes. Do it as soon as we get there. As I said, I'll square it with Mr Scrivens."

Private telephone calls were always frowned upon by the bank. It was not just a question of cost; reimbursement was always insisted upon. But time was a factor, time which would be better spent on bank work. An odd short phone call would not be a problem, but it had been known for staff at some branches to take advantage of any laxity in the ruling. And David certainly did not want those at Crowborough to witness inspectors flouting the rules. But he felt that Trevor's was a special case and he was confident he would get the chief clerk on board.

And so it was. Mr Scrivens was most understanding. Trevor rang from the staff rest room and David made a tactical retreat into the general office. No way did he want to appear prying.

After only a short while, Trevor beckoned him back into the room.

"And?" David asked, fearful that the brevity of the call heralded bad news.

Trevor nodded and smiled. "It was okay, sir. But it had to be quick. Katie was in the middle of taking down the manager's dictation. And you know what? She sounded pleased that I'd rung."

"Thank goodness for that," David said, encouraged that any brevity had not equated to negativity.

"You're still sure I can get a train on Friday afternoon?".

David pursed his lips and sighed. "I suppose so. I'll just have to learn how to cope on my own."

"Sir!"

"Anyway, now that's settled, Trevor, I want to talk to you about those loans. I'm getting more bothered about them by the hour. How can a manager lend so much to so many, without having met any of them? Never mind not having seen any of the properties involved."

"Putting it that way, sir, it does seem rather odd. Even though everything else looks okay."

"You mean the introductions and the professional valuations?"

Trevor nodded. "And we've got a good solicitor's undertaking over each set of deeds."

"And, Trevor, it's profitable for the bank with arrangement fees and good interest rates. The only other box which isn't ticked is the one about repayments."

"But the planned expansion of Gatwick is only just getting underway. That's what I understand, anyway. If that's the case and the pilots aren't yet fully employed, they won't have the income to meet any planned repayment programme."

"It's all so open-ended though. But you're right about Gatwick. That's what we've been told, anyway. But where's the actual evidence? I think I want some independent confirmation of what's going on."

"From where, sir?"

David grinned. "Not only am I going to have to do without you on Friday afternoon, but also tomorrow."

Trevor's eyebrows sought out his hairline. "Tomorrow, sir?"

"Yes, I want you to do a bit of detective work. First thing tomorrow, get on the road to Gatwick. Have a nose around. Ask a few questions. But no getting on a flight, mind you."

Trevor grinned. "I don't think they operate flights from there to Devon. And I certainly don't want to go anywhere else."

"And after Gatwick," David continued, "I want you to do a house-crawl around Crawley and Horley. In a moment, have a look through the securities registers and make a note of the addresses involved. Then, tomorrow, go and seek them out and see what we're lending against."

"But I've never been to these towns," Trevor said. "I wouldn't know where to start."

"Go into a newsagents. Get a street map of the area." David paused and rummaged in his briefcase. He then withdrew a red-covered street atlas of Tunbridge Wells and Tonbridge. "Here, have a look at this. I got it when we were house hunting three years ago. There's bound to be something like this covering Crawley and Horley." He then turned to the back cover. " See, it's produced by Estate Publications in Ashford. I reckon they must print them for most towns in the south-east."

Trevor now looked rather pleased at the prospect of having a day out in his Austin A30. A bit of police work would certainly make a nice change from ticking off items against bank registers. He then left the room to get the addresses of the properties he needed to check out.

David was not sure what comfort such an investigation might give him. Trevor certainly did not have the skills to make comparative valuations of the properties, but just seeing them would aid David's peace of mind. And it would also be good to know what was actually happening at Gatwick airport.

It was now mid-afternoon and David was contemplating what to do next when the telephone rang. He picked up the receiver and recognized the voice of Frank Windsor's secretary who must be dealing with the switchboard this afternoon.

"There's a lady on the phone for you, Mr Goodhart. But she refuses to give her name. I tried to insist, but she was adamant."

That was odd. A lady? Not Sarah, surely? "You better put her through, then."

"Mr Goodhart?" a voice then asked, not one that David recognized. "I desperately need to see you. As soon as possible."

Chapter 20

David took a deep breath. This was not something he had wanted to hear. Someone ringing him up? He was a bank inspector, for goodness' sake. He was not at the branch to service the needs of customers. They should speak to the manager or his staff for that. In any case, customers, or anyone else for that matter, should be unaware that he was even here at the branch.

"Speaking," he answered, guardedly.

"Mr Goodhart, I must see you," the woman repeated.

"And you are?"

"If I say, I must have your assurance that you will tell no one that I've rung."

Oh dear. In no way did he want to get drawn into a conspiracy like this.

"I don't think I can give you that assurance. I'm working here with my assistant. I share everything with him. We don't have secrets. It's the only way a team can work."

"I have no problem with that, Mr Goodhart. When I say no one, I wouldn't count your assistant. Of course I accept that. No, I don't want you to let the people in the bank know. Especially the manager."

Definitely a conspiracy, then. But curiosity was now setting in. Ever since that Crowborough Collective lunch, David had been harbouring forebodings of possible goings-on in Crowborough. Was this phone call linked in some way?

He decided to take a chance and give this woman the assurance she sought. "Very well, then. But I'm not sure why you want to speak to a bank inspector."

"Thank you," the woman said. Even at David's end of the line, the relief emanating from those two words was palpable. "I'm Barbara Callard. Ted's widow. And it's because of your role that I want to see you."

On hearing her reply, David expected to taste blood from the lip he had involuntarily bitten. This was the last person he might have expected to ring, never mind wanting to meet him."

"But why, Mrs Callard?"

"I can't say on the phone. But, please, can we meet?"

"I'm not sure about that . . ."

"But please," came Mrs Callard's heartfelt interruption. "Not in Crowborough, though. I don't want anyone here to see us."

"Mrs Callard," David replied, now feeling like a schoolmaster dealing with a recalcitrant pupil, "this all sounds rather conspiratorial. Quite frankly, I don't think I should get involved in something like this."

"If you promise to meet me, Mr Goodhart, you'll understand my reasons. Please, there's a café in Hartfield. Will you meet me there tomorrow morning for coffee? It's called Hartfield Tea Rooms, on the right hand side of the road as you drive in from Crowborough. I do need your advice. You're the only person I feel I can turn to."

David felt nonplussed. Why? Why him? How come this Mrs Callard even knew anything about him? But his curiosity was now getting the better of him. If he refused to meet her, he might forever kick himself, wondering what this had been all about.

"Very well, Mrs Callard. Shall we say 10.30?"

"Oh thank you so much, Mr Goodhart. You can't know how much this means to me."

David replaced the receiver in its cradle and leaned back in his chair. What on earth was he getting himself into?

Chapter 21

Trevor felt liberated; freed from checking documents and ticking boxes at Crowborough. Savouring, instead, the freedom of the open road in his beloved Austin A30. All right, he was only going to the Gatwick area, no more than an hour away. But it was a change of routine; a time simply to enjoy his own company. He was also feeling more at ease with himself. That brief phone call to Katie had certainly helped. Should he now feel more optimistic about their future together? This coming weekend would provide the answer to that. The only downside today would be not being back at the branch when Mr Goodhart returned from seeing Mrs Callard. Trevor could hardly believe it when he had heard that his boss was having coffee with her this morning. How would he be able to contain his curiosity as to what she might have to say?

As for the weekend, he had already checked the train timetable for Friday and a fast train left Paddington at 2.30. That should get him to Barnmouth by the early evening. Last night he had written to Mum to book his old bedroom. How could she refuse for her ever-loving only child? Father was another matter altogether. He would have a very different view about the return of his prodigal son. Prodigal? On a bank clerk's meagre salary? Reckless might be more appropriate, given his career temptations linked to his saxophone.

Whether he would be able to see Katie on Friday evening was another matter. It might be better to wait until Saturday. She was probably working in the morning, but he could pop into the bank to see her and arrange a time to meet up. He had toyed with the idea of taking her to football. She would love that, surely? Torquay were certainly playing at home this Saturday - against Bradford City. Good that he had been mindful to check that out. It could certainly be a good match. But what would Katie think? Would it stir up romantic memories of their previous date at Plainmoor? In their current circumstances, perhaps not.

His route to Gatwick would be by way of the A264. Leaving Tunbridge Wells, this would take him through the affluent suburb of Langton Green and then on to East Grinstead. He had never been to that particular town, but was well aware of its significance during the war and post-war years. It was the home of Queen Victoria Hospital, specialists in reconstruction surgery for allied air crew who had been badly burned or crushed in their planes during the Battle of Britain. These brave men, known as Guinea Pigs at the hospital, came under the wing of one of Trevor's superheroes, Sir Archibald McIndoe. It was he who had pioneered plastic surgery techniques which would change for the better the lives of so many airmen. Trevor had come to learn about this great man through his interest in Spitfires and Hurricanes and he had even penned a tune in appreciation of what these planes and their pilots had done for their country. It was a bluesy number which he had entitled *The Few for the Many*. But he had not yet had the nerve to perform it in public.

As he approached East Grinstead, he passed the hospital on his off-side and he briefly took his eyes off the road ahead to do a serviceman's 'eyes right' in acknowledgement of the hospital's good works. It was as well that he quickly focussed back on his driving. Even a brief glance had caused his A30 to straddle the white line in the middle of the road.

Ten minutes later, he had reached the airport and found a place in the car park adjacent to what looked like a newly-constructed terminal building. Perhaps, because of it being mid-morning, the concourse was not busy and Trevor found it difficult to believe it was a major London airport. He needed to get some pertinent information to take back to Mr Goodhart and suddenly saw what he needed: an enquiries desk.

It was not only the desk's title which had drawn him to it, but also an attractive young lady, not unlike his darling Katie. As he approached the desk, she looked up and large, lustrous blue eyes fixed on his own like a magnet. Fair hair, slightly curled, framed her round face that needed only a hint of make-up to aid her natural complexion. Her welcoming smile confirmed that she had been well-chosen to staff this particular desk.

"How can I help you?" she said, encompassing this short question with deep-felt sincerity. Trevor immediately believed that this girl would be able to give him all the background information he needed, provided he was able to concentrate on her answers, rather than on the girl herself.

"I'm doing a project," he said, avoiding any reference as to why. Such projects were usually related to schools or colleges and even though he still looked young for his age, he was not that young. "It's about the airports around London and I need some information about Gatwick. Any chance of some help?"

"Of course, sir."

Trevor felt his heart swell. 'Sir?' He was not often so addressed.

"That's good," he said, hoping that the allure of the girl was not going to make him blush or stutter. "I understand that big expansion plans are going ahead."

The girl nodded enthusiastically. "You bet. It all really started about two years ago. The railway station was opened in May '58 and then Transair established a base here. They were the first major airline to do so. Then, in June, the Queen came to do an official opening."

"But it was open well before then wasn't it?"

"Yes, but in a much smaller way. It wasn't until 1958 that this actual terminal was built. It was to attract major airlines to use us. Dan-Air and British United now fly from here." The girl then leant forward and continued more quietly, "And don't put this into your project yet, but it's rumoured that next year we're going to be re-named London (Gatwick). And London Airport is going to become London (Heathrow). Gatwick will then be well and truly on the map."

This obliging girl had now given Trevor all the information he needed. The Crowborough manager had been right when he had told Mr Goodhart that big expansion plans were underway. The need for all those additional pilots certainly looked justified. But Trevor now had a potential problem: if he stopped asking the girl questions, she might think his project was going to be thin on the ground.

"That's been a great help," he said. "Just what I needed. Now I think I'd just like to have a look round. If I've any more questions, can I come back?"

"Of course," the girl said, as if she really meant it. "I'm here all day."

Trevor was tempted to ask her what she was doing for lunch and then remembered two things: he still had more research to do for Mr Goodhart; and it did not say much for his feelings for Katie if he was thinking of chatting up another girl. Perhaps Katie was experiencing the same situation. Was this question of seeing someone else simply a case of her thinking of chatting that person up, when her true feelings were still for him?

He made a detour away from the enquiry desk and then left the terminal for the car park. Once back on the road he immediately saw a signpost for Crawley. Within only a matter of minutes he was on the outskirts of the town. At the first parade of shops he came to he saw exactly what he was looking for: a newsagents.

Once inside he scoured the shelves. The shop seemed to stock every magazine and periodical under the sun, but he could not see what he was looking for. There was no option but to ask the rather surly-looking man behind the counter.

"I'm looking for a street atlas," he said. "If possible I'd like one to cover just the Crawley and Horley areas."

The man said nothing, but simply pointed to a section of the top shelf towards the back of the shop. Trevor had ignored that particular shelf which housed magazines such as Health and Efficiency and Playboy. He had not wanted to appear to be a pervert peeking at such periodicals. But there, alongside them, was the familiar red cover of the street atlas Mr Goodhart had shown him. Why the newsagent had chosen this position for such maps he would never know.

Having bought a copy he returned to sit in his car, taking from his pocket the sheet of addresses he needed to seek out.

Mr Goodhart had suggested that, first of all, he should concentrate on the properties in Crawley; those in Horley could be sought out another time. There were eight in all, but he was surprised to find only one of the roads listed in the atlas's index. He checked the publication date of the atlas which was 1957. Three years ago. It could well be that, in a developing area like Crawley, the rest might well be on a recently-built estate. In which case, how was he going to be able to establish its location? Driving around the whole area might be the only answer, but needle and haystack came readily to mind. He decided that, for a start, he would find the road which was included in the atlas.

The address was that of Mr. Crickhaven whom he had discussed previously with Mr Goodhart. It was Guildhurst Road, number 80. The street atlas showed it to be on the other side of the town. He just hoped that his sense of direction would get him there. He did not want to keep checking with the atlas which now lay beside him on the passenger's seat.

He switched on the ignition, but when he turned the key, the engine refused to start. A flat battery? Yet there had been no problem until now. He had only been stopped outside the newsagents for about twenty minutes, so the battery should not have run down in that time. And all the time he had been driving, it must have been charging up. Had the battery simply given up? It must be some five years old, but Trevor did not know what might be the standard lifetime of a battery. Thank heavens the car had a starting handle. He got out and retrieved it from the boot. After a few abortive swings, the engine suddenly roared into life. The wonders of modern science. But was this an ominous sign? Would he have to make further use of the starting handle as the day went on?

Trevor stowed the handle back into the boot and quickly got behind the steering wheel, relieved that the engine was still ticking over. He moved off, over-revving the engine to thwart any possibility of stalling. He did not want to go through this rigmarole again. The high revs reminded him of a neighbour they had in Barnmouth. Mum had nicknamed him The Vicar, simply because of his excess revving of the car's engine. Trevor smiled at the thought and just hoped that his current battery problem would turn out to be a one-off hiccup.

The roads leading to Mr Crickhaven's property did not inspire confidence. Rows of semi-detached and terraced houses had seen much better days and Trevor was thankful not to be living in this area. But it was like a different world when he turned into Guildhurst Road. Four-bedroom detached houses, built in Georgian style, guarded each side of what was more like an avenue, flanked by cherry blossom trees. Trevor could imagine their splendour and aroma at springtime. The houses were well-spaced, each standing in what must be a quarter of an acre of manicured gardens. These houses could well justify the bank's professional valuation of £8,000 for the Crickhaven property.

The houses on the left hand side of the road displayed odd numbers, with even numbers on the right. Unlike Croft Road in Crowborough, each house clearly showed a number to the side of the front door and Trevor made his way to the far end of the road. He then hit a problem. The last house on the right was numbered 60. Where were numbers 62-80? Although the road curved off to the right, the name changed to Guildhurst Crescent and the house numbers started again at one. How very odd. Unless Trevor had taken the address down wrongly. Perhaps it should have been 30, rather than 80. He turned the car round to have a look at that particular property. Certainly, if this one belonged to Mr Crickhaven, Trevor judged the bank's security to be more than adequate for a loan of £5,000.

Like the other houses in the road, this one looked in pristine condition. Adjacent to the front lawn, several terracotta pots contained a variety of late-flowering red roses, while two six foot conifers stood either side of the front door, as if guarding it like sentries. Being fast-growing plants, Trevor imagined they would need to be replaced in the next year or so.

He then had the problem of trying to find the other properties and he decided to go back to quiz the newsagent who had supplied the street atlas.

"I dunno," the man simply said when Trevor questioned him about the missing addresses in the atlas.

"But they should be listed," Trevor persisted.

"Why?" the man replied, his lip actually curling as he sneered at Trevor. "I wouldn't trust any of these street atlases. Produced by cowboys."

Trevor sighed. Cynical as well as irritable. "But could the streets be on newly-built estates?"

"Could be. Estates are being built up everywhere."

"But where exactly? I don't know the area."

"You'll just have to drive round," the man said, then turning his back on Trevor to tend to his stock of cigarette packets stacked against the back wall. Conversation clearly ended.

Trevor shook his head. Charming. Thanks for nothing and he turned to leave the shop. If this was typical Crawley thank goodness he lived in Tunbridge Wells. But he was now well and truly fed up with this exercise and, with time running on, he decided to give up for the day. He returned to his car and blew out his cheeks when the engine turned over properly. He would, though, get the battery checked out in the near future.

He would be back in Crowborough in time to report back to Mr Goodhart before he packed up for the day. And he could not wait to hear how the meeting went with Mrs Callard.

Chapter 22

David left the branch at 10 o'clock. He had again been able to park his car behind the building and he was soon on his way to Hartfield.

It was unusual for an inspector and his assistant to be out on separate missions during the course of an inspection. In due course, he might well have to justify this to the chief inspector. Branch inspections normally had to be completed within a given timescale: a set number of man-hours being allocated, depending on the size of the branch. It was not within the discretion of an inspector to take as long as he liked. Getting value for money was a prime objective for the bank. The problem David had today was that neither his task, nor Trevor's, was necessarily directly attributable to the actual inspection of Crowborough branch. Depending on the outcomes, the bank might well judge both missions to be wild figments of the imagination of an inspector exceeding his inspectorial brief. Oh, well. It was too late to question his judgement on this now.

He was soon passing the Dorset Arms and he could well-imagine having another lunch there before he finished at Crowborough. There was something about that aromatic log fire crackling away as they supped their pints. Within a couple of minutes, he had reached Hartfield and immediately saw the tea rooms on the right hand side of the road. There was no parking space outside and he had to make do with a spot about a hundred yards up the street.

He was five minutes early when he opened the café's door. There were several couples chatting over cups of coffee and one solitary lady sitting next to the window at the back of the room. A cup of what looked like steaming coffee sat on the table in front of her. She looked up, as if expecting a companion, and actually raised her eyebrows when their eyes met. David nodded and made his way straight to her table.

"Mrs Callard?"

"Mr Goodhart," she replied, standing up and offering her hand.

Her grasp was firm, yet betrayed an underlying softness. David guessed that she was in her early fifties. Before her current woes, however, he could understand people believing that she was much younger. She was about five-foot-six, slim and wore a worsted grey suit which looked to be made-to-measure. Her dress sense complemented a face which must have turned heads in her youth. But, now, her high cheekbones and firm chin created a somewhat severe countenance, emphasized still further by straight hair being pulled back into a tightly-formed bun. And any past sparkle which may have been reflected in her hazel eyes was long gone, replaced by patent sadness. No wonder, having been only recently widowed, never mind having lived for many years with the tragedy of her severely-handicapped son.

"I'm so glad you agreed to see me," she said, sitting down and indicating that David should take the seat opposite.

"And I'm so sorry about your husband," David replied. "I can't imagine what a shock that must have been for you."

David could see tears forming in Mrs Callard's eyes, but they were only fleeting and he had to admire her composure in handling such a delicate subject matter.

"Thank you," she simply said, then asking, almost pleading, "Did you actually meet him at the lunch last Monday?"

David nodded. "I certainly did, albeit briefly. And I really took to him. He seemed like a breath of fresh air among all those other people at the lunch. I simply can't believe that he should have then collapsed like that."

"And neither can I," Mrs Callard replied. "That's why I wanted to see you."

David frowned. "But wait a minute. How did you know I was at the Crowborough Collective lunch? And for that matter, how did you know anything about me to make your phone call?"

"Ted told me you were going to be there. And he said he was going to try and have a word with you."

"But who told him?"

"Frank Windsor. At your bank."

David was not surprised at her answer. It had been as though everyone at the lunch had been aware of his presence. Apart from Mr Windsor, who else could have told them? As for the 'infamous inspector' reference . . . But why would Windsor have told Ted Callard? It was not as if he were a business customer of the bank. It was clear to Mrs Callard what David was thinking, without his actually having to say..

"I might be wrong," she continued, "but I think Frank Windsor told everyone at their previous meeting. That you were going to be a guest. Perhaps all members do that if they want to take guests. To clarify the numbers for the meal?"

That made sense, David supposed. But he was still a little disconcerted to learn that all and sundry knew that he was going to be there for the meal. It hardly accorded with his desire to play a low profile when carrying out his branch inspection.

"But why did Ted want to have a word with me?"

Before answering, Mrs Callard took a sip from her cup of coffee and then looked embarrassed. "I'm so sorry, Mr Goodhart. I never ordered a coffee for you."

"Don't worry," David said, turning towards the café's counter and beckoning to a waitress. "I never thought of it myself. Please. I'll get it. What about you? Ready for another?"

Mrs Callard shook her head. "No thanks. One's enough for me. For the moment, anyhow. But before I answer your question about Ted, I just want to go back a bit. To give you some background information."

She then paused while the waitress set down David's cup of coffee. David thanked the girl and waited for Mrs Callard to continue.

"I first met Ted in 1925. You could say we were childhood sweethearts. I felt so lucky. All the girls were after him. You see, even then, he was so big and strong for his age, never mind good looking. He played all the sports, but loved his boxing most of all. No one else could live with him in the ring. But he was a gentle giant. I know that sounds like a typical cliché, but it was true."

Mrs Callard hesitated to taste her coffee, while David wondered what this was all about. Why was she telling him about their early days together? The boxing bit certainly fitted, though. David remembered Ted's iron grip, also his nose, which had seen better days.

"Anyway," Mrs Callard continued, "we got married in 1935. That's when Ted started his scrap metal business. He worked all the hours of the day to make it successful. And any time off, he boxed. He was so fit and healthy. All his activities saw to that. Then the war came. Because of his work, he went into the Ordnance Corps and did for the services what he did for himself. He was instrumental in acquiring scrap metal to build aeroplanes. It was a flat-out job, all the time. But he could cope with it because he was so fit." She then smiled, for the first time since David's arrival. "He hardly had any time to be with me. Just the occasional leave. Despite that, Peter duly arrived. He was born in 1940."

Mention of the boy's name made Mrs Callard pause and she pulled a handkerchief from her handbag. David feared that tears were imminent, but she simply wiped her lips, having finished her coffee.

"Sorry for having gone on like this," she then said, "But I'm trying to give you a picture of the sort of man Ted was. After the war, he re-started the business and then, five years ago, Peter had his dreadful accident. You see, it wasn't just his physical injuries. It was his brain, as well. It was irrevocably damaged. It makes him so difficult to live with. I must say that when it all happened, I went completely to pieces, but Ted's strength carried us through. At first, it was his mental strength, but then his physical strength became vital. Peter was always big for his age - just like his Dad - but after the accident, he just kept growing. Goodness knows how I'm going to cope with him on my own . . ."

Again she paused, but had no recourse to her handkerchief. David took the opportunity of mentioning his own father's head injury and this certainly seemed to create a bond between them. But it was also Peter's physical injuries which Mrs Callard would now need to cope with without her husband. Frank Windsor had previously expressed his fears about this and it was clearly a problem very much on her mind.

"What I'm trying to get over to you, Mr Goodhart," she then said, "is that all his life, Ted had been big and strong. He was the healthiest person I've ever known. And that's mentally and physically. I simply can't believe he had a heart attack last Monday. In fact, I won't believe it." She then paused and eyeballed David before emphatically adding, " There is no way at all that Ted could possibly have had a heart attack."

The vehemence of her statement shook David. After such a gentle lead up to this moment, he was at a loss as to how to react. What was the alternative to a heart attack? It was not something that he wanted to contemplate. In any case, was Mrs Callard being realistic in her assessment? David could not help but recall that one of his old school chums had recently died of a heart attack - and that man had been the epitome of good health. Why should that not also be the case with Ted Callard?

"Has there been a post-mortem?" he asked, although sure that this would have been a necessity in this particular case.

Mrs Callard nodded. "There was certainly going to be one, but I've not yet been told of any result."

"What about the police? Have you spoken to them about what you think?"

This time Mrs Callard shook her head. "I don't think there's any point. Not until we get the result of the post-mortem."

That was probably true. But all this background information and theorizing might well be pertinent to Mrs Callard, yet in no way did it explain why she wanted to meet up with David.

He took a deep breath before saying, " But why are you telling me all of this, Mrs Callard? It's not as if you know me. We haven't even met before. And I only saw your husband briefly last Monday. I'm certainly not sorry to be having coffee with you this morning and I hope it has helped you just to be able to talk about what's happened. But why did you ring me in the first place?"

Mrs Callard was peering down at her cup and saucer while he was saying all this, but she now looked up at him and raised her eyebrows.

"I think I could now do with another cup of coffee," she said. "Will you join me?"

David smiled at her and nodded. "Of course," he said, getting up to seek out the waitress who had disappeared into a back room. "But these two are on me," he added, turning back to Mrs

Callard who acknowledged his gesture with another smile. She was clearly starting to feel more at ease with him.

"Now, come on Mrs Callard," he said when he returned to the table, having ordered their coffees. "Why did you ring me? And you still haven't answered my question as to why Ted wanted to speak to me."

"He wanted to speak to you because he was worried. He wouldn't tell me exactly why. But I could tell it was financial and he said that someone was up to no good. Yet he said he couldn't speak to anyone in Crowborough about it. So when he knew you were going to be at the lunch, an outsider, he wanted to get your advice. He said he wanted to bend your ear," she added, again smiling, this time rather wistfully

"If his concern was financial, did he have any money worries?"

"No, no, no. That's what's so strange. The business is going great guns. And as a family we're as well off as we need to be. No borrowing. Even the mortgage on the house is paid off. Peter's needs are, of course, demanding, but he received a lump sum compensation package. And that's all properly invested. The interest we get each month from that more than covers Peter's day-to-day requirements. But Ted really thought something bad was going on. Yet he didn't want to go to the police. He said he didn't have enough evidence."

As David mulled this over, their coffees arrived and he passed the sugar bowl towards Mrs Callard.

"No thank you," she said. "Anyway, after what's happened, I decided to ring you. In case you were able to be of any help. I know Ted would have wanted me to do that."

David took a sip from his coffee as he wondered how to respond. If the family had no money worries, how could Ted's concerns have been financial? Unless, somehow, it was linked to their son.

"You say that Peter's day-to-day needs are covered, but what about other possible outgoings? Like capital outlays. Do you need to make changes to your home because of Peter's disabilities? Especially as he's such a big lad. Or changes in his transport requirements? Do you need to call upon lump sum payments in addition to your monthly income from the investments?"

"The house is generally fine," Mrs Callard answered, "but we do need to make some changes, particularly because of Peter's wheelchair. And our car needs up-grading. Perhaps this is what it's all about. We need a much bigger one, to take the wheelchair more easily. We could do with some van-like vehicle. The chair could then be wheeled in through the back doors or tailgate. But that sort of motor is so expensive. And Ted didn't want to take up any borrowing. Having got ourselves debt free, he wanted to keep it like that. The only alternative Ted thought of was to withdraw a lump sum from Peter's compensation monies. He was in the middle of trying to sort that out when he . . ."

Mrs Callard could not finish the sentence. She had both hands round her coffee cup as though wanting to steady herself. It had clearly been a difficult morning for her. In her situation, David felt he would have found it hard to control his emotions. It was only eight days since she had been widowed. Would she ever get over it? In the meantime, she had to cope with Peter. On her own. Even with the proposed new vehicle, would she have the strength to load the wheelchair into it on her own? No chance. She would definitely need help. Possibly a full-time carer would be needed. Perhaps there would be insurance monies to cover this.

"I'm still not sure what I can do to help," David said, when Mrs Callard recovered some of her composure. "I'd certainly like to. But how?"

"I just thought that, as a bank inspector, you might be able to learn what might have been troubling Ted. You might come across things in your line of work. I suppose it's a long shot, but

I needed to talk to someone. And there's no one in Crowborough I'd want to go to instead. I know that must sound strange to you, but I hope you understand. So if anything crops up, I do hope you'll get in touch with me. I really need a shoulder to lean on."

Probably without realizing it, Mrs Callard was now misjudging David's position. It was not the first time that his role as a bank inspector had been deemed synonymous to a police inspector. He had always previously denied any possible similarity in the two jobs. On the other hand, he was now getting the feeling that, in this respect, things might be becoming a bit different here in Crowborough.

Chapter 23

It was just after 3.30 when Trevor entered the rest room. He found Mr Goodhart leaning back in his chair, hands clasped behind his head, staring up at the ceiling.

"Sir?"

Mr Goodhart's eyes now focussed on him and he smiled. "Just thinking, Trevor."

Trevor took off his coat, draped it over the back of his chair and sat down. "About anything in particular, sir? Football? Jazz? Circuses? Or could it simply be about work?"

Oh dear. Had he gone too far? Mr Goodhart looked askance at him. However, he then smiled again and had clearly not been offended. "Don't be cheeky, Trevor. It doesn't become you. But before I deign to share my thoughts with you, how did you get on?"

Trevor pursed his lips and tried to decide where he should start. On the drive back from Crawley, his mind had been working overtime on what he had established on his trip away from the branch. Yet his main problem related to what he had not established. It would certainly be good to share his thoughts with his boss and reap the wisdom of his experience.

"I'm afraid it's a question of good news and possible bad news."

"I could do with being uplifted, Trevor, so let's have the good news first."

The most uplifting part of the day for Trevor had been his chat with the gorgeous girl at the airport's enquiry desk. But best not to mention this to Mr Goodhart, especially after being given time off on Friday to sort out his relationship with Katie.

"Gatwick's definitely expanding," he said, his words getting Mr Goodhart's full attention. "In a couple of years I reckon it'll be as busy as London Airport. In fact I was tipped the wink that it'll soon be called London (Gatwick)."

"That'll certainly be good for the Crawley area," Mr Goodhart replied. "Especially for the housing market. But I have a feeling this is where your bad news comes in. Housing I mean."

Trevor nodded. "Not because of houses being built, though. There's lots of that going on. And there are plenty of expensive houses. Four bedroom detached, that sort of thing. The only problem was that I couldn't find the ones I wanted to see."

"But I told you to get a street atlas."

"I did, sir. Just as you said. But it hardly helped."

For some reason Mr Goodhart did not look really surprised and simply said, "Go on, Trevor."

"Take Mr Crickhaven's house. It might well be my mistake, but I'd written down the number of his house as 80. Yet the houses in his road stopped at 60. But I could have misread 30 for 80. So it could've been my fault. But number 30 would certainly fit in with our valuation. Anyway, I must go and check with the ledger. If it really is number 80, I won't know what to think."

"I know what I'm thinking," Mr Goodhart replied, pausing, yet apparently deciding not to elaborate. "But what about the other properties?"

Trevor shook his head. "That's the problem. I couldn't find any of them. None of the addresses was in the atlas. They could be on newly-built housing estates. The street atlas is three years old. I did ask the newsagent where I bought it, but he was a fat lot of use."

Mr Goodhart leant back in his chair and again placed his hands on the back of his head. This time he gave Trevor his full attention. "I think we should try again, Trevor. Nothing against what you've done so far, but perhaps we should go and have a look together. Two heads better than one, eh?"

"What about simply talking to Mr Windsor?"

"Not at the moment. It's just that . . . put it this way, it has the makings of a case I heard about a couple of years ago. Phantom loans. To be more precise, phantom properties. The actual loans were real enough. In fact there were two such cases, but with different scenarios. The first was all down to a crooked manager. He created loans for fictitious customers against non-existent properties. It only became known about when he took early retirement to spend his final years in the Caribbean. In the event he only had twelve months there before the forces of law and order caught up with him."

"And this was one of our managers?"

David shook his head. "Fortunately not. That one was Lloyds and the next one was the Midland. This time the manager was simply naïve and incompetent. Not corrupt. He simply lent money against a property which he failed to check actually existed."

"You're saying something like those examples might be happening here, sir?"

Mr Goodhart shrugged and raised his eyebrows. "What do you think, Trevor?"

Trevor slumped back in his chair. Surely Mr Goodhart could not be serious. Mr Windsor was hardly a senior manager, but in this small town he was probably a pillar of the community.

How could he possibly be corrupt? But naïve? His lending to GB Builders was certainly questionable, but these property loans were different. He may not have seen the houses themselves, but he had certainly obtained professional valuations over them. Trevor now sat up to answer his boss.

"I can't see either of these scenarios applying here, sir. We're dealing with highly respectable people in a small community. That sort of thing simply wouldn't happen here."

"I hope you're right, Trevor. But something odd is going on in your so-called small community. Take my morning. I was shocked to hear that Mrs Callard doesn't think her husband had a heart attack."

"What? But how else could he have died? A stroke? But that's effectively the same thing."

"She didn't say in as many words. But the implication was there. She's still awaiting the results of the post-mortem. One way or the other, that will certainly reveal the actual cause of death."

"Is this why she wanted to see you?"

Mr Goodhart nodded. "And also because she didn't want to talk about it to anyone locally. Now why should that be?"

"Goodness knows, sir. But it's a bit odd, isn't it? Hang on, though, didn't Mr Callard tell you that Crowborough Collective had been very supportive of them? That's why he joined, wasn't it?"

Mr Goodhart clearly agreed. "It certainly was. So why doesn't Mrs Callard want to talk about his death to any of those people?"

"This isn't turning out to be a normal inspection is it, sir?"

"No, Trevor. But where do we go from here?"

"See what Mr Windsor thinks?"

"But he's one of the people Mrs Callard didn't want to speak with. She made it clear that she didn't even want him to know she was talking to me."

"What about the police, then? Especially if she's worried about the cause of her husband's death."

"She says she hasn't any evidence for that. Not until she gets the result of the post-mortem."

Trevor was now getting conflicting messages. " But her situation is nothing to do with the property loans here. What are you going to do about those? Surely, you've got to see Mr Windsor?"

"Possibly. But as I said before, not at the moment. First of all, I want you to check out that address for Mr Crickhaven. While you're doing that I'll try and work out what's best to do."

Trevor got up and went out into the general office. For such a small branch it was a hive of activity as the staff strove to balance the books before going home. It was now four o'clock and they would certainly hope to be finished before five. It was all about how accurately they had dealt with the transactions during the day. It ought to be simple enough: every debit must have a credit of an equal amount. But if items had been incorrectly recorded, even a difference of only a penny had to be resolved before accounts could be ruled off. Trevor often thought it incongruous that the cost of time and effort spent in finding such a small difference could far exceed the value of the difference itself.

Poor handwriting was one harbinger of differences. Carelessly-written sevens could easily be interpreted as ones, while eights and threes were not always properly defined. This could easily be the case with the Crickhaven address and he made his way to the Securities section to scrutinize the register. Sure enough, the clarity of the number was questionable. Trevor had quite justifiably read it as 80, but, on reflection, it could also be taken as 30. He certainly hoped this would be the case. He would then at least have properly identified one particular property.

He would need to check the professional valuation and solicitor's undertaking over the deeds to clarify matters. But these would be locked away in the strongroom. With the staff being so busy he was reluctant to drag them away from their book-balancing to open up and he decided to await the morning before exploring further.

He made his way back to the rest room and hoped that Mr Goodhart would agree with his decision. Not all inspectors would. Some would go out of their way to make things as difficult as possible for branch staff. They were the ones who created a 'them and us' mentality, but Mr Goodhart was not like that. He believed that close harmony always brought out the best in people. At the end of his inspections branch staff never seemed overtly pleased to see his team's departure.

Trevor certainly counted himself lucky to be Mr Goodhart's assistant. There was one particular inspector he would abhor working with. That man boasted that he needed a brandy at breakfast time to get him going. Then, at lunch, he downed a minimum of four pints of bitter, insisting that his assistants kept him company. His particular team endeavoured to work flat out in the mornings; an alcoholic haze encompassed much of the afternoon. Mr Goodhart might well like his pint, but his consumption was always within reason. He and Trevor were able to work mornings and afternoons.

As expected Mr Goodhart agreed that Mr Crickhaven's address should be investigated further in the morning. Trevor then asked him what action he proposed to take after today's forays into the outside world.

"Nothing at the moment," he said. "I'm going to sleep on it all for now. My mind's being pulled one way and then the other. I hope a good night's sleep will pave the way forward tomorrow."

Chapter 24

B arbara Callard returned to her house just before one. It was empty and she was glad of that. All she wanted to do was to sit down with a nice cup of tea and think about her morning. Peter was at his day centre and would not be back until three. Two hours respite at home meant so much to her these days.

As she went to put the kettle on, she contemplated on how their world had been turned upside down five years ago. A head-on car crash had seen to that. The official verdict said that no one was to blame. But how could that be? Someone must have been on the wrong side of the road. And, in her heart of hearts, Barbara knew it was Peter's driver. But he was a volunteer, often taking Peter and others to school football matches. How could she blame someone for carrying out such regular good deeds? But where was his responsibility? It should have been part and parcel of the job. In his profession he knew that well enough. And, ever since then, she could see the guilt in his eyes; every time they met. Which was not often these days. He was one of the Crowborough lot she tried to avoid at all costs. Especially with the suspicions she now harboured over poor Ted's death.

She made the tea and slumped down in her favourite easy chair. That was better. She thought back to the Hartfield tea room and was relieved that her meeting with Mr Goodhart had gone so well. It had been awkward to start with; for both of them. But she had soon felt their growing rapport and she suspected this was also the case with Mr Goodhart. He seemed to display such empathy when they talked about Peter, particularly about his head injury. That was so unusual. Most people showed little understanding of brain damage. Though that was understandable; such injury was largely unseen.

People could easily relate to some physical disability, like a broken arm or leg. But a head-injured person often looked perfectly normal. It was what went on unseen in the brain which was so devastating. Peter's case was different in that he had physical and brain disabilities. A double whammy. Yet friends, and even doctors, could only relate to what they could see. Their sympathy and understanding was restricted to Peter's inability to walk, or look after himself. His head injury was effectively swept under the carpet.

Barbara did not have this option. She lived with it constantly. And it could be so wearing. She loved Peter dearly, but sometimes she felt like screaming in frustration. She hated herself for that. But his short-term memory loss was a major problem. As she, herself, got older, Barbara knew how her own memory could play tricks. She might not be able to remember the name of someone she met yesterday, yet the names of people she knew 40 years ago were indelibly printed on her brain. But it was different with Peter. When he got home today he would ask where she had been. After being told, he would ask the same question again ten minutes later. Then again. And again. In the early days after his accident she had been able to exercise commendable patience, but after five years, this had stretched to breaking point. She always cajoled herself when impatience got the better of her. He was the one with the problem; not her. Far better if she could turn a deaf ear to Peter's infuriating repetitions. But it was never easy.

She had also learnt that most head-injured people suffered from a lack of concentration and an inability to organize themselves. They had difficulty in planning their days and performing simple procedures. Yet this was not a problem for Peter; being wheelchair bound saw to that. In a way it was almost a godsend in that it prevented him from carrying out irrational activities, so typical of the head-injured. Barbara knew of one car owning head-injured young man who would give lifts to strangers to wherever they wanted to go. He ended up in Bristol one day, much to the consternation of his parents who had no idea of where he had got to. At least Barbara did not have this particular head-injured trait to deal with.

And now she had to cope with Peter alone. Fortunately she had been able to get him enrolled in his day centre for five days a week. What a help that had been. It had meant that she could get all her jobs done during the day, giving Peter her full attention in the evenings.

As for Ted, he had been a superman with Peter. His physical strength had been instrumental in handling the lad who had grown almost as big as his father. But, just as important, Ted had given Barbara such moral support during her many times of deep depression. And now he was gone. She still could not believe it.

She drained her cup of tea, refilled it from the pot and immediately worried about the stressful times ahead. Not just with Peter having no Dad to support him, but with the scrap metal business. Without Ted at the helm it could never continue as before. And how would that affect their finances? There should be some insurance money to come, but what about day-to-day finances? At least from a legal point of view the business could continue without Ted. A year ago he had converted everything from his sole ownership into a limited company. Barbara was made a director and so was Frank Endacott, their loyal and long-serving foreman. Frank would now be in charge of running the business, with Barbara handling the accounts and paperwork. She had been doing this part-time recently, so she knew what was needed. Ted had taken the decision to make the change and Barbara now wondered if he had a premonition that something might happen to him. Yet that could not be so. It was only during the last couple of weeks before he died that something had started to trouble him. And she knew this had nothing to do with the business. He had not mentioned anything specifically, saying that he did not want to worry her. That, in itself, was enough to make her worry. But she was convinced it had something to do with Crowborough Collective, or at least one of its members. Why could he not have told her?

How could she ever forget last Monday when she was given the news? Ted, dead? He was the last person to have a premature death. He was the fittest person she knew. She simply could not believe that he had suffered a heart attack. She was certain the post-mortem would confirm her view. But if so, what would happen then? What would she do when the police came knocking on her door? She only had suspicions that Ted, himself, had suspicions of possible wrongdoings. He had never given her any clarity of his feelings. So what good would she be to the police? They would want facts, not suspicions.

But it had been good to talk to Mr Goodhart. She felt sure that Ted would have wanted her to do this. Would it be possible for him to put some flesh on the bones of her suspicions? Yet he was a bank inspector, not a police inspector. And she knew that bank inspectors were principally auditors of the bank's books. Yes, he would also be concerned about security arrangements within the bank, but it was hardly feasible that his role might encompass goings-on in the town itself. How could he possibly glean any information which might confirm her suspicions over Ted's death?

Yet it had been good to talk to him, something she was not prepared to do with anyone else. Crowborough was such a small community and, to her mind, such a closed one. Especially as far as Crowborough Collective was concerned. Yes, they had given support to Peter and she hoped this would continue with Ted now gone. But that help had only come from some of them. She just thought there was something incestuous about the rest. It was not just about the one person she would have no truck with; the fact was that he had so many confidants within the group. Talk to one and you effectively talk to them all. And, in her heart, could she really trust any of them?

That was exactly why she must hold her tongue; why she had turned to Mr Goodhart without anyone else knowing. Please, God, let him be of assistance in some way.

Chapter 25

"**C**an we have a quick game of Monopoly?"

David stared at Sarah. Sarah stared at Mark. Was the boy mad?

David now rounded on him. "A quick game? That's never happened before."

"But if I'm banker, I'll force you to mortgage all your properties. That'll make it quick."

Coals to Newcastle? "Don't talk to me about mortgaged properties. I'm having my fill of those at the moment. No, let's have a game of Sevens."

"But Dad . . ."

"Mark, what's that delicious aroma coming out of the kitchen? They call it dinner. And if I'm not mistaken it won't be long before it's served. So just enough time for a couple of games of Sevens."

Uttering a theatrical sigh, somehow breathed through pursed lips, Mark rose from his chair and went to the bureau, home to various board games, dice, a chess set and a pack of cards.

But David and Sarah well-knew that any dissent would only be transient. The routine of game-playing before dinner had been part and parcel of their lives for eight years now. The worst punishment Mark could ever be given was the abandonment of their nightly ritual. And it did not really matter if this was Monopoly, Sevens or anything else. Provided it was a game of some sort. On those rare occasions when such activity had been banned, David, himself, also felt as if he had been punished. He always found these family games therapeutic after a stressful day at work. And it was always good for the three of them to do something together. He liked to think of it as family harmony - except when Mark's losing led to his storming up to his bedroom in a paddy.

The next part of their routine after the ending of any game was to raid the drinks cupboard. And now, feeling euphoric after winning two hands of Sevens, and with Mark having duly retreated to his room, David asked Sarah what she would like to drink.

"How about a Babycham?" she replied. "I've not had one of those for ages. If I close my eyes I might even think it's the real thing."

David grinned. "Just as well because we haven't got the real thing. But it sounds as if you want to celebrate something."

"Not really. But I'm feeling more relaxed now. I think I've somehow put the raid behind me."

That was good to hear. The last few days had certainly been difficult for Sarah. He was not sure how he would have coped with being faced with a raider - apparently armed. When he opened the cupboard he was relieved to find one bottle of Babycham waiting to be consumed. He opened it, together with a bottle of Double Diamond, and brought the drinks and glasses to the coffee table in front of their settee and easy chairs.

"Cheers," he said as they touched their glasses. "That's really good news - about how you're feeling, I mean."

Sarah nodded. "Yes, but I still keep seeing that man's eyes. I just feel I've seen him before."

"You thought it might have been one of those travellers."

"I know, but I've gone off that idea."

"But who else? You're hardly likely to have met someone who then turns out to be a bank robber."

"That's true. But I'll keep my thinking cap on. Anyway what about your day? How did you get on with that lady?"

David had told Sarah the night before about his forthcoming meeting with Mrs Callard. She had been rather sceptical. Why would someone so recently widowed want to talk to a complete stranger about her husband's death? Last night David could only share her feelings. But now? Actually meeting Mrs Callard had been rather illuminating. And he really wanted to share his feelings with Sarah; to gauge her response. But not until after their meal, with a brandy glass in his hand.

"Later," he said. "After the meal. And it's not just Mrs Callard I want to talk about. Trevor also had an interesting excursion today."

"Oh?" Sarah said, giving him her full attention. This always seemed to be the case when they started talking about Trevor. "Tell me more."

"Later, I said. I'm getting impatient about this meal you've cooked up. Let me guess. Not hot-pot again?"

Sarah shook her head vigorously. "I think I'm going to take that off the menu - full stop."

David winced. "What then?"

"Steak and kidney pie."

"With mashed potatoes?"

"Of course. And carrots and parsnips."

And what could be better than that? Apart from hot-pot.

An hour later, satisfyingly replete, David slumped back on their saffron Greaves and Thomas settee, stretched his legs out to rest his feet on the coffee table, and swirled his brandy around its goblet. Now, with Mark up in his room working on his homework, he was ready to talk.

But where to begin? Sarah was still tidying up in the kitchen. Their normal routine was for her to wash the dishes, leaving him to dry. But she always insisted on doing the final clearing up herself. Yet he was not too bad at doing that. Not everything went into the wrong places. Oh well . . . At least it gave him a few moments to gather his thoughts on what had happened today.

"All right, then, where's mine?" Sarah had left the kitchen much quicker than he had thought. He had deliberately not poured out a brandy for her, expecting to do that when he was ready to refill his own glass. He got up, mumbled an apology and filled a second goblet with what he would have preferred to be the finest cognac. Instead they would have to make do with the supermarket's own brand.

"Now, what about this widow of yours?" Sarah asked, when they were both settled on the settee, having had their first sips of their golden brandy.

"Of mine?"

"You know what I mean. But seriously, why did she want to see you? It's not as if you'd ever met before. How did she know anything about you?"

"Those were the first questions I asked her," David replied, marvelling, yet again, at how he had managed to marry such a perspicacious wife. They really had become a team. Fifteen years of blissful marriage had seen to that and Sarah always proved to be a great sounding board if he needed to chew over a problem.

Like now.

"She doesn't think her husband died of a heart attack."

Sarah started, almost upsetting her glass. "What?"

"She reckoned he was the fittest person she knew. Never had a health problem. So why should he suddenly peg out?"

"But anyone could have a sudden heart attack. What about that friend of yours?"

David nodded. "A bit unusual, though."

"But if it wasn't a heart attack . . ."

"Quite."

"Suicide?"

"Not from what I've gleaned about the man."

"Oh, David. Only last April you became embroiled in a murder here in Tunbridge Wells. Not another one, surely?"

"I certainly hope not. The post-mortem will provide the answer, one way or the other. But if it is murder, there's no reason why the bank should be involved, let alone me. He only had a private account with us. And I only met him because I was a guest at that lunch."

"But Mrs Callard seems to be getting you involved - whether you like it or not."

David pursed his lips, sighed and took a much-needed swig from his glass. Too much; the liquor burned the back of his throat. "I know, but I'm getting curious now. And I'd really like to support her if I can. But if her husband has been murdered, I don't see how it could have been done. Especially with so many people at the lunch. In any case, why would someone want to do it? It sounded as if he was such a popular man."

"Who told you that, David?"

"Frank Windsor."

"Anyone else?"

David shook his head.

"One man's opinion, then - as far as you know. So he might not have been popular with others."

"You reckon Windsor got it wrong?"

"No. But is he a good judge of character?"

Oh, dear. Was this another question mark over our man in Crowborough? His judgement concerning GB Builders was certainly suspect. And he blatantly fawned over so many people at the Crowborough Collective lunch. Why was that? He was also a mite patronizing when he referred to Ted Callard as 'our Ted'. And what about these property loans? What was going on there? If there was something untoward, and this certainly looked to be the case, was he complicit in some way? Trust Sarah to put all these doubts in his mind.

"I'm not sure about Frank Windsor," he replied, draining his glass and wondering if he should refill it. That had certainly been his intention earlier. But now? Better not, unless he wanted a thick head in the morning. And he had the feeling that he needed to be clear-headed for the remainder of his inspection of Crowborough branch.

"But there was something else Mrs Callard said," he continued. "A few days before Ted died he was clearly worried about something. She thought it was financial. But they aren't hard up. It sounded as though he needed a sizeable lump sum to buy a new vehicle. Something much bigger - to help their son get in and out with his wheelchair. That would certainly not come cheap."

"Was he trying to get a bank loan? From Frank Windsor? Had he been turned down? Was that why he was so worried?"

Surely not. A loan request like that could have proved to be an opening for Frank Windsor to try and get Ted Callard's business accounts from Barclays. No. David decided that Sarah was wide of the mark this time. For the first time?

"I don't think so," he replied. "I just wonder if it might be something to with their investments. Mrs Callard did say something about that, but . . ."

"David?" Sarah was clearly disconcerted as he suddenly became distracted.

"Just thinking," he eventually replied. "I told you that Frank Windsor seemed to fawn over everyone at the lunch. Well, one person in particular was an investment consultant. An odd character, to say the least. Derek Herretson. Windsor said he was the most successful investment consultant in town, not that there's probably much competition in Crowborough. Anyway, he even boasted of putting business Herretson's way. I've never heard anything like it. Introducing customers to the competition? He said it's because Herretson manages to offer interest rates far higher than the bank. Windsor has even lent money to a builder customer because Herretson's interest was more that the rate he was being charged on the overdraft. The mind boggles."

"Doesn't sound very banking-like to me," Sarah said, stifling a yawn. Was it all getting too boring for her? Or was it that second helping of steak and kidney pie? Or the brandy? Whatever, perhaps it was nearly time for bed.

But David still wanted to talk to her about Trevor's discoveries. The mention of Trevor's name would surely waken her up. Gone would be any thought of somnolence. As soon as he raised the topic, he knew his judgement had been sound.

"Ah, my lovely Trevor," Sarah said, sitting upright and then feigning to swoon. Her eyes then became as bright as the spotlights at Robert's circus. David just hoped that she was winding him up and that any apparent infatuation with Trevor was not something he should be worried about. No, there was no chance of that. After all, she could give him some 20 years. Old enough to be his mother, for goodness' sake.

"Never mind his being lovely," he said, "it's what he got up to today that I want to sound you out about."

"He's not been two-timing me?"

It could only be the brandy. Or was it simply a case of her teasing him gently, rather than allowing National Counties Bank to dominate their conversation late into the evening?

"Sorry," Sarah then said. "You want to be serious, don't you?" She then snuggled up to him and kissed him on the forehead. " But I'll only give you five minutes. Then it's bedtime."

"I reckon there's some dodgy lending going on," David said, responding to Sarah by wrapping his arm around her shoulder. "But it's not straightforward."

"Your Mr Windsor again? Everything seems to be coming back to him."

"I know. It's a bit disconcerting. But as far as Trevor's concerned, I asked him to look at some houses in Crawley. Ones that Windsor has lent against. But Trevor couldn't actually find them."

"Crawley's a big place."

"Granted, but I did get him to buy a street atlas. He thinks he might have found one, but there's a question mark over the house number. As for the others, there must be a good reason for not finding them. They've all been professionally valued for the bank."

"What does Mr Windsor have to say about it?"

"I haven't asked him yet. I only got all this from Trevor late this afternoon. And I haven't yet checked on the valuations in the files. I'm going to do that in the morning. Then I'll talk to Windsor. Depending on what I find and what he says, I might have to go and see the valuer."

"And who's that?"

David grinned. "The Honourable Charlie Spencer O'Hara, would you believe?" He's the local land agent the bank uses."

"The Honourable? And is he?"

"I certainly hope so. He was another one I met at the Crowborough Collective lunch. Supercilious so-and-so. But that hardly means he doesn't know what he's doing."

"Anyway, you're going to see Mr Windsor first. That's what you'd normally do if you think there's some dodgy lending going on."

David nodded and gave Sarah a squeeze. "But, as I said, I don't think it's that straightforward. There seem to be so many odd things going on at the moment. I just need to clear my mind. I told Trevor I was going to sleep on it."

"Come on, then," Sarah said, getting up. "I'll eventually let you do that."

Chapter 26

The next morning the car failed to start. Surely he was not going to suffer Trevor's travails of yesterday? David had owned the Consul for three years; not actually owned the car, because the bank had provided it for him. During that time it had never let him down. Now, as he tried to turn the engine over, it just whirred. He was on the point of thinking that they would have to use Trevor's A30, when the engine suddenly fired. But was this episode an omen of some sort?

After three years, he was due to have the car changed by the bank and perhaps he should now start thinking seriously about a replacement. The bank's scheme allowed him to make his own choice up to a certain limit. But would it be his own choice? Sarah would not be interested, provided he got a car which would get them from A to B, but Mark was bound to want to have his say. No, Mark, the bank will not run to an Aston Martin DB4, or a Jaguar XK120. Mark's say would, then, be only theoretical, not practical.

But what make should he, himself, look for? A Vauxhall Victor or Cresta would be possibilities, or he could up-grade to a Ford Zephyr. On the other hand, Rover had just produced an

80 version to replace the 75 and that looked particularly classy. A light green and olive two-tone would do nicely. But would the bank run to it?

In the meantime, as he made his way to pick up Trevor, he hoped that this morning's episode would only be a one-off blip. He needed to count on the Consul's usual reliability until he could make a change.

Trevor's first task that morning was to seek out the professional valuations and solicitor's undertakings for the property loans, particularly the ones for Mr Crickhaven's house. Unlike last night, this would not be an inconvenient time for the branch staff. Day-to-day requirements from the strongroom, such as cash, securities registers and ledger sheets, were locked away each evening and withdrawn the next morning. Deeds and other securities, including property valuations and solicitor's undertakings, remained locked up all day, unless specific items were needed. While the strongroom was open Trevor would arrange for the items he wanted to be got out for him.

David had decided that, first of all, Trevor should restrict himself to the documentation relating to the properties he had tried to find yesterday. That would give them a good idea of what was going on. In particular, they needed to establish the correct number of Mr Crickhaven's house.

"It's number 30, sir," Trevor said when he returned to the rest room. "I'm sorry, but I got it wrong. Not really my fault, though," he added, reminding David of Mark's usual response when accused of some wrongdoing. "The writing in the securities register was appalling. I'm sure you'd also have taken it down as 80."

There was no need for David to respond to such a challenge. The main thing was that it was definitely Mr Crickhaven's house which Trevor had actually seen. And the Honourable Charlie's valuation duly confirmed this by attaching a photograph.

David immediately noticed two tall potted conifers standing to attention like guardsmen on either side of the front door; Trevor duly confirmed that they were there when he saw the house.

So far so good. Now for the solicitor's undertaking. David extracted it from Mr Crickhaven's folder and saw that it had been provided by Walsgrove and Lithgow, the solicitors who were properly authorized to act for the bank. The undertaking had been signed by the senior partner, Julian Palfrow, and properly described the property as 30 Guildhurst Road, Crawley. Mr Palfrow also confirmed that the deeds were being held by his firm to the order of the bank. The bank's standard form of mortgage had been completed by Mr Crickhaven and Mr Palfrow expected to be able to despatch this, plus the deeds, to the bank in the near future.

David blew out his cheeks, turned to Trevor, and smiled in relief. "Nothing wrong with any of this, then. A good solicitor's undertaking and a professional valuation of the property you actually saw yesterday. But the whole situation is still a bit odd. Mr Windsor hasn't yet met the customer, nor has he set up a repayment programme."

"You can't have everything, sir."

David accepted that Trevor was being facetious; the lad knew as well as he that all boxes had to be ticked for any lending proposition. And knowing the customer was one of the most important.

Leaving that aside for the moment, David then asked, "Now, what about those other undertakings and valuations you've got there?"

Trevor spread them out on David's desk and they each picked up a couple to examine. It took about five minutes for them to skim through all of them and David could tell that they had both come to the same conclusion.

"Mine seem fine, sir," Trevor confirmed. "Just the same as Mr Crickhaven's. And each valuation has a photo."

"But of a house you couldn't find, Trevor."

"I know, sir. But these do seem as though they're on some newly-built estate. The actual road names are different, but the houses look as if they've been built by the same developer."

"If that's the case, it explains why these addresses weren't included in your street atlas."

Trevor nodded and looked enquiringly at David. "So what are you going to do now, sir? You said you were going to sleep on it."

"The trouble was that I slept too well last night. When I woke up, the only things going on in my mind related to some lurid dreams I'd had. And they had nothing to do with banking."

"Palace weren't going to be relegated?"

"No, no. Nothing as lurid as that. In fact I can't remember a thing about the dreams now. But having checked out these undertakings and valuations, I think I must now go and see Mr Windsor. While I'm doing that, I'd like you to go into the general office. Have a word with Mr Scrivens and the other staff. Get a feel about the office routines and make sure all security measures are properly in place."

"Just one thing, sir," Trevor said as they both rose from their chairs, "will you tell Mr Windsor that I went to Crawley yesterday? To try to find the houses?"

"No. Better not. Without speaking to him first, he'd think we'd been going behind his back."

"Which we were, sir."

"Yes, Trevor, but he doesn't need to know that. Not yet, anyway."

Five minutes later, David was sitting across the desk from Mr Windsor, admiring the wall paintings while the manager finished a telephone conversation. David had already learnt that a customer was due in half an hour, so this telephone call was eating into the time available to him.

"Sorry about that," Frank Windsor said when he eventually put down the receiver, then smiling wistfully. "This job would be much easier without customers."

David smiled at the comment he had heard many times before. Managers in most organizations probably felt the same. No doubt doctors would also prefer life without any patients.

"I know you haven't much time this morning," he said, "but I do need to speak to you again about the loans to all these airline pilots."

Frank Windsor nodded and again exhibited the rather self-satisfied demeanour he had shown before. He was still clearly delighted with this chunk of business he had acquired for the bank.

"The first one I came across," David continued, "was the loan you agreed for Mr Crickhaven . . ."

"Yes," the manager interrupted, "he was my first one. Introduced by Julian Palfrow. I told you that before."

"But you've not actually met Mr Crickhaven."

"No, he's not down here yet. Still lives up in Cheshire. Most of his flying is done out of Manchester."

"But Mr Palfrow must have seen him. To deal with all the paperwork."

"Actually, I don't think so. He's certainly handled all the legal work, but he arranged for all the signing to be done at a firm of solicitors he knows in Cheshire."

"Including our mortgage?"

"Yes, everything. And it's all now back at Julian's firm."

David frowned. "But all this was months ago. Why haven't the deeds come to the bank yet? We're still just relying on his undertaking."

"Julian said there'd been some hiccup at the land registry. But it should be cleared up this week. We should have everything here by Friday."

That was something, then. "But when will you be meeting Mr Crickhaven? And setting up the repayment programme?"

"Should be this month. He's expecting to transfer down from Manchester to Gatwick. He told me that on the telephone."

At last, some positive information. There had actually been some customer contact. Why could Windsor not have mentioned this before? And it seemed that Julian Palfrow was at last getting a move on.

"You seem to have got a good relationship going on with Julian Palfrow," David then said, deciding that it might be an idea to learn a little more about the solicitor, one who had chosen to introduce so much business to the bank. What did he get back in return? He was hardly doing it through the goodness of his heart. On the other hand, it was a small town; the sort of place where businesses should thrive through good personal relationships. Despite this, David smelt a whiff of ulterior motive in the air.

"I certainly have," Windsor replied, rather too smugly for David's liking. It made him feel, still more, that having a good working relationship with the solicitor was one thing, but this one was looking to have something almost incestuous about it. If this was, in fact, the case, the ominous undertones he was feeling might well develop into overtones.

"And because of all the new business I've been getting," Windsor continued, "it's improving my stock with Regional Office. Julian's a great friend of Angus McPhoebe . . ."

David felt proud that this bombshell was not reflected in his demeanour as he sat there aghast in front of Frank Windsor. To his mind, this was the kiss of death over Mr Palfrow. How could anyone, never mind Julian Palfrow, be a great friend of Angus McPhoebe? He was so taken up by this revelation that he had switched off from what the manager was saying . But having missed some of it, he soon picked up the gist.

". . . and he's always getting invitations to regional lunches. In fact I'm taking him there next month, not to a lunch, but to a cocktail party. You've heard about the new regional manager?" David nodded and imagined that Julian Palfrow would soon become a great friend of Mr Threadgold. But he was now getting very wary about where this conversation was heading. "Well," Windsor continued, "Angus is arranging a cocktail party to introduce Mr Threadgold to prominent people in the region. I'm taking Julian and Charlie O'Hara."

David was already starting to think of these two as the terrible twins and was finding it difficult to reconcile Windsor's utter enthusiasm for two people whom he, himself, had not taken to at all at the Crowborough Collective lunch.

"However," Windsor then said, frowning, making David's ears prick up for the possibility of a rider in the air. Could this conjunction have something to do with his concerns about all those housing loans? "I'm just a bit worried about the two of them. Julian's not been the same in recent times." Windsor then paused, almost as though he was having second thoughts about making such a comment about the branch's authorized solicitor. David eyed him and could almost visualize Windsor's brain ticking over. He said nothing and the manager then clearly made the decision to continue his train of thought. "I think he's been working too hard. He seems to have so much on his mind these days. And Charlie's got big family problems. He lives with his father in their ancestral castle near Lewes and there's been a big falling out. For some reason, his father has donated the whole place to the National Trust. Very commendable, I'm sure, but not as far as Charlie's concerned. He was expecting to inherit the lot. He had grand plans to convert it into luxurious holiday accommodation. He reckoned he'd make a fortune out of it. Now that's all dead and buried. All his inheritance gone, just like that."

If Windsor thought that David might feel sorry for these two in their hours of need, he would be disappointed. Neither man had appealed to him when they had met, both having exuded an arrogance which had yet to be proved justified. At least, their respective undertakings and valuations appeared to be in order.

Before David could respond about the apparent plights of Messrs Palfrow and O'Hara, the manager's telephone rang. Windsor picked up the receiver, acknowledged what he had been told, and replaced the telephone on its cradle.

"My appointment's arrived," he said, moving papers to one side of his desk and brushing the surface with his hands to remove what David could only believe were imaginary fragments of dust. "I can continue in the afternoon, if you like."

"No," David replied, "I think that's all for now." He was still concerned about the whereabouts of the remaining houses in Crawley, but could not tackle Windsor about this without admitting that Trevor had been out and about trying to find them. And he was certainly not going to say that he and Trevor would be making a second trip to Crawley.

"Just one further thing, though," he continued. "How's George Bathurst getting on with redeeming his investments with Derek Herretson?"

"No news about that at the moment," Windsor admitted, looking a little sheepish, as if he had not actually followed this up. But when he saw David's raised eyebrows, he hurriedly added, "George has certainly tried to contact Derek. He left a message, but Derek hasn't got back to him yet. Of course he's a very busy man."

David could not help but think that there was always time to do the things you want to do. He wondered if this Herretson creature was one of those who has all the time in the world to relieve you of your money, but suddenly finds himself extremely busy when you might want some of it back. It was like ordering not-immediately-available goods from a store. Paying in full up-front could result in the store's complete lack of interest in responding to follow-up calls. But withholding payment until delivery kept everybody on their toes.

"I think you better keep a close eye on that one," he replied, looking as sternly as he could. "Let me know when you get some news."

David felt sceptical that any good news would be quickly forthcoming - if at all. In fact he was becoming increasingly distrustful of Mr 'stick-insect' Herretson. Questionable aspects of the man and his business seemed to be growing. And David's reservations had nothing to do with the fact that the man could afford to run a DB4. But he decided that further investigation into his activities would definitely not go amiss. Oh dear, it did seem that, despite what he had thought when he saw Mrs Callard, he was now confusing his banking role with that of a police inspector.

Chapter 27

I t was the Nevill Crest and Gun's turn to enjoy David and Trevor's custom for lunch. They both liked to share their favours around the local hostelries, but a repeat visit to a hospitable pub was no bad thing. David had been planning to try out one of the Rotherfield inns today. The generous spaces between the tables at the Eridge pub would, however, better facilitate their discussion of this morning's events. He was always conscious of sharp-eared occupants at neighbouring tables.

The village of Rotherfield was also a little further away. It might be a better bet for imbibing there on another day. As far as he was aware there would be two choices: the Catt's Inn or the King's Arms. Someone had told him that the Catt's Inn was a pub for hardened beer drinkers, whereas the King's Arms might be better for food. Perhaps they should try both while they were working in Crowborough. If they were there long enough. He was certainly getting concerned about the increasing length of this inspection. If he, himself, was concerned, the chief inspector in London might be getting even more agitated about his apparent dilatoriness. But the chief was not to know what was going on. He was unaware of the extramural activities which were hampering progress. When matters were resolved, eventually(?), the chief should be understanding of the extra hours they were putting in at this particular branch.

They both chose pints of Harvey's again. For food, instead of their usual sandwiches, they opted for chicken and chips in the basket. They were both hungry. Whatever Sarah had planned for their evening meal tonight, David was sure he would do it justice, despite this additional lunchtime nourishment.

As they awaited their food, David asked, "How did you get on around the branch this morning? Everything in order?"

After sipping his beer, Trevor nodded and wiped his lips with a rose-pink serviette which lay on the table with accompanying cutlery. "Everything seems fine, sir. Mr Scrivens might be a bit old-school, but he's got the branch working properly."

"Perhaps that's because he is, indeed, old-school," David replied, well pleased with the quality of the beer today. "It's a question of maintaining well-practised standards. We seem to be seeing a slapdash tendency these days. Old-school discipline is getting to be a thing of the past."

"You mean by young people, like me?"

"Not you, personally, Trevor. Heaven forbid. And I'm not just thinking of misplaced apostrophes. Take restaurants, for instance, or even this pub. Let's say we've finished our meal. A waiter could then go past this table empty-handed several times on his way to and from the kitchen, yet never think of picking up our dirty crockery on the way. It would be as though he had tunnel vision - only being able to deal with one table at a time. Someone studying time and motion would have a field day with that kind of attitude."

"Now," David continued, as their food arrived. Rather too quickly? But it looked hot and ready to eat, "tell me what you found out this morning."

"When I wasn't talking to anyone, I attempted to be as inconspicuous as possible. Not easy in such a small branch. But I tried to look as though my mind was elsewhere when I was, actually, alert to what was happening around me. On that basis, I reckoned the staff would act normally. They'd carry out their duties with no fear that they were being spied on."

David could understand Trevor's theory but he was a little sceptical as to its effectiveness.

"Take the pass door, for example," Trevor continued. "Without realizing I was watching, they were meticulous about getting proper identification of anyone wanting to enter the back of the branch. Admittedly that didn't happen very often, apart from branch staff who had been outside for some reason. But a couple of electricians arrived to do some work within the branch and they were certainly properly identified."

"I'm pleased to hear that," David replied, thinking back to a case he had heard about in London. "There's one particular story I could tell you when that didn't happen."

"Go on, sir."

"It was in a much larger branch and they had decorators in. Different workers always seemed to be milling around. And if someone was carrying a step-ladder, or even a clipboard, he could become part of the furniture. It bred complacency among the staff - particularly in the use of the pass door. Anyway, one familiar so-called worker had been biding his time. He was seeking to take advantage of any opportunity which might open up to him. Then he pounced. He was last seen fleeing from the branch carrying a cash box. A cashier had carelessly left it unattended within his vicinity."

"I bet heads rolled for that."

"They certainly did. And when the inspectors went in to investigate - not me, I hasten to add - they had a field day. They discovered a multitude of other security misdemeanours going on."

"It's often the way, isn't it, sir? Laxity of the rules in one area can become infectious. At least this doesn't appear to be the case in Crowborough. And I had a long talk with Mr Scrivens. He really is pernickety in the way he's running the branch. A good thing, too. And I do like his wing-collar. It seems to give him an aura of authority when dealing with the staff."

"And you really think he's the one running the branch? Not Mr Windsor?"

Trevor put down his cutlery on his plate, bit his lip and steepled his hands, as if in prayer. "I think he probably is," he said, after a few moments thought. "Mr Windsor seems to be ensconced in his room all the time. Even yesterday afternoon, when everyone was struggling to balance the day's work, there was no sign of him. You'd think he might help out some time."

Yes, David certainly agreed with that. It was not necessary all the time. But every now and again it was good to see a manager mucking in with the staff.

"Not like a manager I knew down in Devon," he replied. "The St Marychurch branch in Torquay to be precise. The manager lived in the flat above the branch. Each morning he would go downstairs before breakfast and open the post. He then distributed it to the various sections in the branch by about 8.30. After that he went upstairs for breakfast. It meant the staff always got off to a quick start. Then, after the branch closed at three o'clock, he rolled up his sleeves and got stuck into the clerical work. It meant everyone got to leave the branch by four o'clock and the manager could get on with his real passion in life - sailing."

"I can't see Mr Windsor doing that, sir."

"No, and he doesn't seem to share Mr Scrivens's fastidiousness when it comes down to lending."

Before Trevor could respond, a waiter stopped at their table and picked up their empty baskets and cutlery. David hardly had time to put down his knife and fork before everything was whisked away."

Trevor grinned. "The exception that proves the rule?" he said, when the waiter had gone. He had clearly remembered David's interpretation of this saying from a few days ago.

"You're learning quickly, Trevor. What it must be to have such a learned boss."

"Fishing for compliments, sir?"

"On the contrary, I was complimenting you."

Trevor then frowned and raised his eyebrows. "But getting back to Mr Windsor's lending, has something else happened?"

"Nothing really new. Any problems are still basically down to those housing loans. And, of course, what I'm sure is a terrible misjudgement with GB Builders. Apart from that, I reckon his lending is generally all right. But why would he lend George Bathurst money simply to invest in some schemes run by that Herretson man? It just doesn't make sense. I've now got serious doubts as to whether that borrowing will ever get repaid."

"But Bathurst just has to withdraw his money from Herretson's schemes."

"In theory, yes. But I simply don't think it's going to happen."

"That nose of yours, sir?"

David nodded, but sincerely hoped he was wrong. "I'm getting serious reservations about Derek Herretson. There's something about what he's doing which doesn't ring true. How can he offer interest rates so much higher than us? And you saw his property. Just like a private house. Why no mention of his companies? Normal business premises wouldn't be like that. And from what Windsor told me this morning, I reckon he's ignoring George Bathurst's request for his funds to be repaid. There may be good reasons for this, of course. Maybe the money has been invested on a strict term basis. But Windsor seemed to wriggle when I pressed him on what was going on. I'm not sure he's being completely open about it."

"So you've now got a question mark over Mr Windsor?"

David was not sure how to respond to that. As the inspection had progressed, his opinion of the man had changed. At first he had found him to be rather pompous and self-important. Then Ted Callard's death seemed to have caused a pin-prick to burst his pretentious balloon. Since then he had shown unexpected humility, apart from when he exuded pride in his relationship with his solicitor pal, Julian Palfrow. All in all, David was finding him to be a rather complex character. But did that justify a question mark hanging over his head?

"I'm not sure how to answer that, Trevor. When I went to that lunch, he fawned over nearly everyone he introduced me to. Herretson, in particular. At the time, I didn't take to that man at all. I certainly wouldn't trust him with any of my own money. Yet Mr Windsor apparently keeps pushing his own customers in his direction."

"I still can't grasp why he should do that."

"Nor can I, Trevor," David replied, finishing his beer and making use of a serviette the waiter had left behind. "Are we going to have another one?"

Trevor shook his head vigorously, as though two pints at lunchtime was unheard of. "Thanks, but not for me, sir. But getting back to Mr Windsor and Herretson, do you think something might be going on between them?"

"Inducements of some sort?" David answered, deciding that he, too, would stick to only one pint.

"That seems a bit like backhanders, sir. No, I was thinking of some kind of introductory commissions."

"Sounds like the same thing to me - particularly if they don't get put through a specific commission account at the bank. And

I haven't yet come across such an account. But, no, I really can't see Mr Windsor getting involved in something like that. As for Herretson, I'd certainly like to know how his systems work. I gather he actually distributes his interest payments on a monthly basis. That must be an attractive feature for his investors."

Trevor frowned, as though he found such a system difficult to contemplate. David certainly knew of no other comparable scheme. "How can you find out how he does it?" he then said. "Better not ask Mr Windsor about it, in case there is something funny going on between them."

It suddenly dawned on David that there was an alternative way to get some information. Frank Windsor had said that Henry Purcell's residents at his residential home were also using Herretson's services.

"I told you before, Trevor, about Henry Purcell. The one who runs a residential home in Crowborough. A good one, according to Frank Windsor. Funny little man. I'd say funny- peculiar, but he'd say funny-ha-ha. Always trying to make a quip. Anyway, I met him again at Palace on Saturday. He was also a guest in the directors' box. A guest of the chairman, would you believe? And you know what, I saw another side of him. I suppose I would with his being a Palace supporter. When we were being entertained at the end of the match, he actually invited me to visit his residential home. It was one of those invitations thrown out which neither party would expect to be taken up. I certainly didn't give it another thought. But now?"

"You know, sir," Trevor said, smiling broadly and leading David to think that he was about to utter something which might be within HP's compass, "when I joined the inspection staff, I thought the job was about inspecting branches - inside those branches. Yet here in Crowborough, you've been out entertaining a widow in Hartfield, I've been exploring the countryside around Gatwick and Crawley and now you're contemplating going out to visit a residential home. As the lyric in that new film goes, "What's it all about, Alfie?"

David really enjoyed working with Trevor. Not only did they have a shared interest in football and jazz, but Trevor had a sense of fun in him. Yet he always knew perfectly well when it was time to be serious. It was a question of judgement which David was not sure that Frank Windsor shared.

"Indeed, Trevor. What's it all about? And to part-paraphrase another well-known saying - that is the question. The answer's really all about these strange things apparently going on in Crowborough . And I might well get an answer or two if I do take up Mr Purcell's offer to visit his residential home. But you also mentioned Gatwick and Crawley. That's another conundrum. We still haven't got answers about those houses you couldn't find. I really do think we've got to try again."

"Another trip away from the branch." Trevor posed this as a statement, but David could feel a follow-up question in the offing. "Can we really justify that, sir? If we carry on like this, we'll never complete the inspection. What on earth would the chief say to that?"

Just what David had been wrestling with. It was good to know that Trevor was also keeping it in mind. "I think that'll all depend on what answers we get. If it turns out to be a wild goose chase, my head could well roll. And it wouldn't be just the chief I should worry about. What about Regional Office? My *bete noire*? Angus McPhoebe? Especially as Frank Windsor has just told me that McPhoebe and Julian Palfrow are great friends. And I wouldn't be at all surprised if that turned out to be a threesome with the Honourable Charlie Spencer O'Hara. Have I got it wrong, Trevor? With all this fawning? Everyone else seems to be at it. Windsor certainly was with Messrs Palfrow and O'Hara at that infamous lunch. Two more people I didn't take to. And I now wonder if McPhoebe is at it as well. But what's really bothering me is that we're relying on documentation from these two for all those housing loans."

Trevor bit his lower lip. "When you put it like that, another trip out looks entirely justified. But should we both go? I could go again on my own. But, remember, I'm going down to Barnmouth on Friday."

"I think we should both go, Trevor. No reflection on your going alone, but, as I said before, I think two heads would be better than one. Even though that street atlas of yours doesn't show the actual addresses, we can use it as a general map of the town. It could give us an idea of likely places for new estates. We can also ask around. We're bound to see a postman or two. As to when we go, Friday's definitely out. So it'll have to be tomorrow. Morning would be best."

Trevor appeared pleased that this trip would not just be down to him. "Your car or mine, sir? They've both got potential battery problems."

"Definitely mine." David had no wish to be cramped up in Trevor's A30.

"But mine's got a starting handle. Has yours?"

David now felt embarrassed. He had always thought of himself as some sort of car buff, but he did not actually know the answer. He had never had cause to use a starting handle, but he ought to know if the car was equipped with one. He chose to ignore Trevor's question by simply saying, "We'll still use mine."

"I'll be navigator, then," Trevor said. "I must say it'll be easier with the two of us - one holding the map and one driving."

"And you'll also be holding the paperwork."

"Sir?"

"The undertakings and the valuations for the houses in Crawley. We'll take them with us. The photos could be particularly useful."

"Take them out of the branch? We shouldn't do that, should we?"

"Needs must, Trevor. No one will know."

"But what if the branch want to refer to one? And we've got it out at Crawley."

"We'll just have to take that risk. But it's unlikely to happen."

"But if it did . . .?"

"Trevor! If I'm prepared to take the risk . . ."

Trevor raised his hands in mock surrender. "And I always thought of you as the perfect role model, sir."

David grinned. That's my boy. And provided Angus McPhoebe did not get to know about it, he was happy about what they were planning to do.

Chapter 28

In the morning the Consul started like a dream. Another good omen for the day? The first had been a rare treat for David: a full-English fry-up. On a Thursday? Saturday was the chosen day on the spasmodic occasions he enjoyed such indulgence. Especially if he was going to football. He could only put this treat down to feelings of guilt on Sarah's part. Last night's meal had not been up to her usual standard.

It had not helped with his getting home late for dinner. He and Trevor had stopped off at the Nevill Crest and Gun for the second pint they had eschewed at lunchtime. They only had one, but once they got talking about football, they had lost track of time. Sarah had not been best pleased.

All right, it was his fault that the casserole had been overcooked. And that Sarah had missed out on her aperitif to obviate the meal turning out even worse. But responsibility for the incinerated apple pie lay firmly with Sarah. How could this paragon of cuisine have left it in the hot oven, completely forgotten about, for over two hours?

Yes, today's fry-up was a most welcome peace offering.

They reached Crowborough just before nine. Trevor immediately made his way to the strongroom to get out the valuations of the houses in Crawley. David had decided that they would restrict their investigations to the properties there. Those in Horley would be left for another time, should this prove necessary. They aimed to leave by 10.30; before then they would carry out some of their delayed inspection work.

At 10.29 precisely the telephone rang. The manager's secretary sounded worried. It was Regional Office; Mr McPhoebe said it was urgent.

David let his eyelids drop and sighed. Angus McPhoebe: the last person he wanted to speak to. On the other hand, thank goodness they were not already on their way to Crawley. Without the branch knowing of their whereabouts, McPhoebe would have gone ballistic. Just one minute had saved their being the recipients of his undoubted chagrin.

"Good morning, Mr McPhoebe," he said, lacing his words with as much bonhomie as he could muster.

"Ah, Goodhart," came the blunt reply. McPhoebe, as usual, shunned any form of salutation. "There's been another raid."

The words shook David. For once, McPhoebe's brusqueness was well-judged. Small talk should never herald such a stark statement. But where? God forbid not Tonbridge again.

"At Battle," McPhoebe continued before David could question him. "Just after the branch opened. I need you to get there straightaway."

"Anyone hurt?" David asked. And he was not just thinking of physical injury.

"No, thank God. And very little was taken. The cashier did everything right. Just like your wife."

David relaxed somewhat. That was good news, as was the implied compliment about Sarah. Was the man becoming human?

"I'm on my way, then," he said. Crawley would have to wait. Could they fit it in tomorrow morning? Before Trevor set off to Barnmouth? It was certainly a possibility.

"Just before you go," McPhoebe said. "How are you getting on at Crowborough?"

David bit his lip. This question had come too soon. He was not yet ready to talk about the things he was getting anxious about. "All right, at the moment," he said, hoping that a non-committal response would suffice.

"Not surprised at that," McPhoebe replied, seemingly satisfied at David's answer. "Windsor's a good man."

David groaned inwardly. McPhoebe was so fond of this 'good man' syndrome. Yet, in the past, so many of his good men had turned out to be anything but that.

"He's also got good connections there," McPhoebe added, before David could reply. "Professional people. Top men."

Top, rather than good? But David had a horrible feeling he knew to whom McPhoebe was referring. He did not need specific names. And he feared trouble in the offing with Angus McPhoebe. It all depended on what was actually going on at Crowborough.

"Anyway," McPhoebe continued, "report back on Battle as soon as you can." He then slammed down the phone. David was all in favour of brevity, but this important call had lasted less than a minute, with David having only uttered about a dozen words.

"Change of plans, sir?" It was clear that Trevor had got the gist of the call, without knowing the specific details.

David nodded and rose to get his coat. "There's been another raid. At Battle. We've got to go."

"You all right, sir?" Trevor asked, genuine concern etching his words.

"I'm fine, Trevor. But thank you. I'm mightily relieved it's not Tonbridge again."

"You think it might be the same person?"

David shrugged. "McPhoebe just said no one was hurt and not much money taken. That part's the same. We'll learn more about the man when we're there. How do we get to Battle, Trevor?"

Trevor frowned and David guessed he hadn't been there, either. It sounded off the beaten track. Was there a direct way from Crowborough? David had a road map in his car and, when they got in, they pored over it.

"The most straightforward way," he decided, "is to go through Rotherfield and then the next village of Mayfield. Cross-country by the looks of it, but probably quicker than the A roads."

He passed the map to Trevor and started up the car. Within about eight minutes, they had reached Rotherfield and immediately saw the Catt's Inn on one side of the village square. The King's Arms was on the next corner and both places looked suitable for a pub lunch.

The historic village of Mayfield made David feel lucky to be living in such a picturesque area. He loved the peg-tiled houses in the villages, together with the oast houses dotted around the fields.

Twenty minutes later they reached the outskirts of Battle. The journey had proved to be far quicker than he had imagined from the atlas.

The branch of National Counties was at the bottom of the High Street, opposite the Abbey. As at Tonbridge, the entrance was sealed off with police tape, a constable standing guard at the door. David flashed his identity card and he and Trevor were allowed into the branch. He immediately asked to be shown to the manager's room.

He soon established that the circumstances of the raid were almost identical to those at Tonbridge. David felt sure that it must have been the same man, despite not being given any specific information to identify him. Once again, his only feature which might be recognizable were his eyes. But, unlike Sarah, the cashier had no recollection of seeing the man before. David was relieved that the cashier seemed unfazed by his experience. He just hoped that the young man would not suffer any setbacks in the coming days.

After only half an hour at the branch, David had all the information he needed to report back to Angus McPhoebe. The manager and staff had acted impeccably. Their training had been spot on and had been carried out to the letter. No one had been hurt and only a few pounds had been stolen. It had been a pleasure to heap praise on all their shoulders. He wondered if Angus McPhoebe would do the same.

They arrived back at Crowborough at 2.30. David immediately contacted Regional Office. Angus McPhoebe was not around, so he gave his assistant the details of what had happened at Battle.

It was now too late to contemplate going to Crawley and David also had doubts about making it tomorrow.

"I'm not sure about our trip to Crawley," he said to Trevor, once they were seated at their desks in the rest room. "There's not enough time this afternoon. I don't think tomorrow's on, either. You'd need to be back by noon to get home and then catch your train. I reckon going to Crawley would be cutting it fine. Especially if we get any hold-ups - delays, I mean, not raids."

Trevor frowned and looked anxious. "I could always cancel my trip to Barnmouth. I could go next weekend. Katie would understand."

David would not have expected anything less from Trevor. He was certainly lucky to have him as an assistant. He knew of many others who would not have responded like that.

"Certainly not, Trevor. The bank isn't the be-all and end-all of everything. A good private life is equally important. If not more so. And I do want you to get things resolved with Katie."

"But we can't keep putting things off here. Not just so that I can sort matters out with my girlfriend. We should have gone to Crawley today. Now it won't be until Monday."

"It can wait. Anyway, instead, I'm going to try and bring forward my visit to HP's residential home. I'll try and go tomorrow afternoon. I'm getting itchy feet to learn more about Derek Herretson. I think HP might be my best bet at doing that."

"But you can't say that's the specific reason you want to go there."

"Of course not, Trevor. I need to be more subtle than that. I'm going to talk about a relative. An aunt of mine might soon need a nursing home. When we get talking about fees, I'll find a way of getting round to Herretson."

Trevor grinned. "Very cunning, sir."

"So, in the morning, we can carry on with our inspection work here. We'll then go our separate ways at lunchtime. Just remember to come in your own car tomorrow. That way you won't need my taxi service to get you back to Tunbridge Wells."

"One other thing, sir. You do realize we haven't had lunch today?"

No, David did not. For some reason lunch had not crossed his mind. And it was too late now. Yet, strangely enough, he did not feel hungry - or thirsty. "Sorry about that, Trevor. Never thought about it. Afternoon tea, instead?"

"On best china, sir?"

"And cucumber sandwiches?"

"You know, sir? I think I'd prefer a pint and chicken in a basket."

"But not today, Trevor. We could go out and get a couple of sandwiches or a packet of biscuits. Have them here with a cup of tea."

Trevor shook his head. "Nah. I'll just hang on for my four-course feast tonight."

David was then spared continuing what he felt was becoming an inane conversation. The telephone rang. "That same lady's on the line again," the manager's secretary said frostily. It was clear she did not approve of Mrs Callard's continued wish for anonymity. David simply asked her to be put through.

"Mr Goodhart?"

"Good afternoon, Mrs Callard. Do you have some news?"

There was an inordinate pause at the other end; no words came forth, just a rasp, as if from the back of the throat. Mrs Callard was clearly struggling with her emotions. David knew the feeling. It happened to him after the death of Dad. Always on the telephone. He had so wanted to speak, but words would never come out. Fortunately, the circumstances alleviated any embarrassment, but . . .

"Don't worry, Mrs Callard," he said gently. "I'm still here. So take your time."

"Thank you," she eventually said, her words being enunciated clearly, making David feel she was over the worst. "The police have just rung me. They've had the result of the post-mortem." Another pause; then she cleared her throat. "They said that Ted was murdered."

David was shocked at the news, though not really surprised. The clues had been there all along. But he was still shocked. Particularly shocked that something like this could happen in Crowborough. And to a man he had been speaking to shortly before he died.

"I'm so sorry," he said, hoping his words bore the sincerity he felt and intended. "Do you want to talk about it?"

"Yes, please, Mr Goodhart. I need to talk. And I'm so pleased I've got you. I daren't speak to anyone else." She paused again, before adding, "Anyone else, anyone at all, could be his murderer."

What a terrible predicament to be in. She was right, of course. The murderer must have been at the lunch. And Mrs Callard must know most members of Crowborough Collective.

David let her words sink in and then asked, "Did the police say how?"

He actually heard her deep breath on the end of the line before she spoke. "Yes," she then said, "He was poisoned. They think it was potassium cyanide. In his coffee. The amount he ingested would have made his death instantaneous. He might have realized something was happening, but probably thought it was a stroke or heart attack. My poor darling Ted. How could anyone do such a thing?"

David heard sobbing at the other end. He could well understand such emotion. Mrs Callard had never believed that her husband could have had a heart attack. Yet the alternative was unimaginable. Now it was a reality. No wonder she was so upset. And he had no answer as to why someone chose to have done it. But he had the feeling that this might change over the coming days. There could now be no doubt that there was one definite villain in Crowborough. And someone with the wherewithal to know what he was doing. David would not have a clue as to where to get potassium cyanide. The killing was also clearly premeditated; planned and carried out with precision. What sort of man were they dealing with?

"I really can't believe it," he replied, then repeating, "I'm so sorry."

"Could you possibly spare the time to see me again," Mrs Callard positively pleaded, her composure returning. "I do need to talk to you. And not just over the phone."

Another trip out of the branch? What would Trevor say? The lad had been looking askance at David throughout this conversation. But David could never turn down such a heartfelt request. Mrs Callard clearly needed him. And bearing in mind all the things that had arisen during their inspection, she might well have a salient piece to insert into their ever-growing Crowborough jigsaw. But that was very much an afterthought; his prime consideration now was for Mrs Callard's well-being. Yet should she be speaking to him?

"Of course," he said, " if that's really the way forward. I'd certainly like to help if I can. But if something specific's concerning you, you should go to the police. In any case, they must be coming to see you. They'll need to go through Ted's things. To look for clues?"

"I know. They're actually coming tomorrow afternoon. But I really wanted to see you first."

This was now starting to look a bit murky. Should he really get involved? On the other hand, he was feeling intrigued. And he had just said he would see her. He could not go back on his word.

"What about tomorrow morning, then," he said, still unsure as to whether he should be doing this. "Same time and place?"

"That would be perfect," Mrs Callard replied, exuding a sense of relief. "Thank you so very much."

David put the phone down and stared at Trevor. "I imagine you got the essence of that," he said, his finger and thumb stroking his chin as he turned over the conversation in his mind. "A murder, though. In Crowborough, of all places. Mrs Callard actually pleaded with me to see her again. Says she can't talk to anyone else. Just as well we put off going to Crawley until Monday."

Trevor frowned. "You really think you should go and see her, sir? It's not as if it's to do with the inspection here. She should be going to the police."

"I know. They're actually going to see her tomorrow afternoon. She wants to see me first. As for it not being to do with our inspection, I'm not so sure. Anyway, I've agreed to see her. Tomorrow morning. While I'm doing that, you get your head down here. If I'm not back by twelve, get our bags locked away in the strongroom. Then off you go and get your train. And make sure you give my very best wishes to your lovely Katie."

Chapter 29

By noon on Friday there was no sign of Mr Goodhart. He had left at 10.15 to see Mrs Callard at half past. Why was his meeting taking so long? But Trevor now needed to leave the branch in order not to miss his train. It meant that he would not know until Monday how Mr Goodhart had got on. Could he wait that long? It took him back to his childhood: ticking off the days and hours before Christmas or a forthcoming birthday. At least being with Katie meant that his mind would be on other things.

He arranged for the strongroom to be opened to deposit their bags until Mr Goodhart returned. He then sought out Mr Scrivens.

"I'm now off for the rest of the day," he said, having got the chief clerk's attention after a lengthy telephone conversation with a customer. "I'll be back on Monday, but Mr Goodhart will be here this afternoon."

"I've never known such comings and goings," Mr Scrivens replied. Was that a rare twinkle in his eye, or was there a veiled criticism lurking behind his pointed words?

"Needs must," Trevor replied, immediately realizing that he had borrowed one of Mr Goodhart's stock phrases. "We like to spread our wings," he added, grinning. "But, seriously, it's all legitimate inspection work. Until now, that is. But not for me this afternoon. I'm off down to South Devon."

"My, my!" Mr Scrivens exclaimed, raising a hand towards his mouth, then dropping it, choosing instead to finger the sharp cut of his wing collar. "Just for the weekend?"

Trevor nodded. "More's the pity. It's where I come from. I'm making a rare visit to see my parents."

He deliberately chose not to mention Katie. Far better for Mr Scrivens to think of him as a dutiful son, rather than a wayward boyfriend. Or should his trip be all about a wayward girlfriend?

"And where's Mr Goodhart been off to this morning?" Mr Scrivens then asked, apparently not wishing to pursue the matter of Trevor's role of dutiful son. He had, instead, certainly pitched a loaded question. The whole branch must be aware of the anonymous lady who had twice rung the bank inspector, both times causing him to disappear the following morning to destinations unknown. There was nothing like a piece of office gossip to keep everyone on their toes. Particularly if there was a hint of sensation about it. Trevor braced himself to give a noncommittal reply.

"It's a family thing," he said, quite truthfully. All right, it had nothing to do with Mr Goodhart's own family, but it certainly had everything to do with that of Mrs Callard. Yet he immediately realized that his reply could stoke up the gossip-mongers' boiler. Who was this 'other woman' entering the inspector's life? Was he not a happily married man?

Trevor was still grinning about this when he got in his A30. He had been able to park it in the next street and he would be in Tunbridge Wells within fifteen minutes. He had already packed an overnight bag and, after a quick change of clothes, he would be ready to walk down to the station.

Diesel trains now operated on the Hastings to London line and, as he waited on the platform, he heard his approaching from afar. Not only were they noisy, but they were not the most passenger-friendly trains. They had straight-sided carriages to negotiate the tunnels on the line, thus restricting passenger elbow room inside. He was pleased that the onward journey from Paddington to Barnmouth would be in more comfortable rolling stock. That Great Western train would also have an added bonus: it would be pulled by a steam locomotive.

Having lived most of his life in the West Country, Trevor had grown to love the GWR, now the Great Western division of British Railways. As a boy, he had spent many a happy hour train-spotting on the embankment adjacent to Newton Abbot railway station. The day's highlight was to see the Cornish Riviera Express and the Torbay Express passing through. The Cornish Riviera was always headed by a 'King' class locomotive, the biggest and most powerful in the GWR. The Torbay Express had to settle for the slightly smaller 'Castle' class, because the branch line beyond Torbay was inaccessible for the larger engine. Trevor would not be catching either of these trains today; they would have left earlier. But if, on arrival at Paddington, he had the time, he would certainly walk to the front of the train to see the chosen locomotive.

His train was due to leave Paddington at three o'clock. He would have plenty of time to make his way there, using the Bakerloo underground line from Charing Cross. But when he reached the tube station, it was closed. Strike action of all things. What should he do now? How else would he get to Paddington? It was too far to walk and taking a taxi was far too extravagant. The only alternative was to go by bus, but what number? He could not see any that displayed Paddington as a destination. But if he got one to Marble Arch, he could walk from there. He felt quite proud that, as a west countryman, he had been able to work that one out.

He arrived at Paddington with two minutes to spare. No time to check out the engine and he took his seat straightaway. How different from his last time in Paddington. Demob day, five years ago and he had waited two hours for a train.

After a year at RAF Aldergrove, he had been posted to Pitreavie Castle in Scotland. Not an aerodrome this time, but a small headquarters station, just outside Rosyth. As a fireman, he seemed to spend most of his time painting fire extinguishers and hydrants. The nearest he got to putting out a fire was being called to a chip pan blaze in the kitchen of the officers' mess. When demob day arrived, he could not leave the camp until five o'clock. It meant having to fill in seven hours before catching the night train from Edinburgh to London and then experiencing a likely long wait in the morning at Paddington.

As luck would have it, the Ted Heath Orchestra was playing that night at Edinburgh's Usher Hall. What a treat for an aspiring jazz musician. Trevor deposited his kitbag in the left luggage office at Waverley station, wallowed in two hours of wonderful music, then caught his night train. Despite good timings and connections, he still had two hours to wait at Paddington before catching an express to Devon.

Today, a compromise between two minutes and two hours would have been welcome. But he had obtained a window seat, facing the engine. Far better to see what was coming towards him; it was a relic from his train-spotting days.

The busy outskirts of London were soon behind them. Once past Reading, he was on the lookout for the famous Westbury White Horse, built on the escarpment of Salisbury Plain. Katie had told him to look out for it. She had been fascinated to see it when she had come up to London to see him play at Ronnie's.

He must then have nodded off, almost missing his stop at Barnmouth. He had not felt tired getting on the train. It must have been the rhythm of the wheels on the rails. Or their busy week had unwittingly taken its toll. But he felt rather guilty. Mr Goodhart must have been hard at it that afternoon. And Trevor was already getting anxious to know the outcome of his meeting with Mrs Callard. He also wondered if his boss had got to the residential home and learnt anything about Derek Herretson. He was starting to feel that there were snags in having an afternoon off like this.

Mum and Father lived on a bus route and a red Devon General double-decker soon arrived at the station. Within ten minutes, he was at their front door, but he could not bring himself to use the knocker.

He had never acknowledged to anyone the problems of his home life. He could barely acknowledge them to himself. Far better to rid them from his mind completely. But it was a fact: Father had been a root cause of his decision to further his career over 200 miles away. Mum and Father. Why could it not have been like everyone else? Mum and Dad? Why had Father insisted on such a formal parental appellation? It was a wonder he had not demanded to be called 'sir'.

Now, more composed, he rapped the knocker.

He heard bolts being drawn back and the key turned in the lock. The door was then pulled open.

"Ah, the prodigal son has returned. Back at last to see your ageing parents?"

Trevor managed to retain his demeanour. The absence of any salutation was straight out of the Angus McPhoebe text book.

"Oh, enough of that, Father," Mum said, emerging from her husband's shadow. Her eyes, unlike his, positively sparkled as they rested on Trevor and she squeezed past to embrace him. "It's so good to see you, son."

"You, too, Mum," Trevor replied, planting a kiss on her cheek. What a contrast. Not even the offer of a hand from Father.

They went inside and Trevor followed Mum into the kitchen. Father took to his paternal armchair next to the fire in the living room.

"Have you had anything to eat, love?" Mum asked, putting on the kettle.

Trevor shook his head. "Didn't fancy anything on the journey. And I couldn't get anything before. There was a tube strike. I only just caught the train."

"I've got some sausages. Fancy that? And chips?"

"Smashing," Trevor replied. He then put his arms round Mum and flicked his head towards the lounge. "How's it been? Are you okay?"

Mum turned round and faced him. She had missed his head movement, but his words needed no interpretation. She smiled wistfully. "You know how it is, love. I can't really complain. But I do miss having you here. Now, you go into the lounge. Try and have a word with him. In his own way, I think he's also missed you."

Trevor pursed his lips. Chance would be a fine thing. But he had better try. He would only be here for two days. Far better that they be spent in harmony. Acrimony was to no one's benefit.

"How are you, Father?" he asked, taking the armchair on the other side of the fireplace. Father remained head down in his newspaper, but then looked up.

"How long are you going to be here?"

What sort of answer was that? The art of conversation? It was hardly alive and kicking.

"I'm going back on Sunday. But I won't get in your way. I'll be spending time with Katie."

"Not come back just to see us, then. What about your mother? For some reason, she misses you."

"And you, Father?"

"How could she miss me? We're stuck with each other."

Trevor sighed. How obtuse was that? Why was he always so deliberately provocative? The kitchen clearly beckoned. Especially as the aroma of frying sausages was already wafting through the house.

"I didn't mean that, Father. I just wondered if you, yourself, might have missed me. Anyway," he added as he got up from his chair, "I'd come back more often if I could. But I've got a job of work to do. And it's over 200 miles away."

"You didn't have to go away. You could have stayed down here and looked after us. I reckon you think more of that sousaphone of yours than us."

"It's a saxophone, Father. And that's only a hobby." Goodness knows what Father would think if he knew his son was tempted to take up music as a career.

"Your supper's ready," Mum called out from the kitchen. A merciful release, if ever there was one. And he was then pleased to see that his cutlery - one set only - was set out on the kitchen table. He would just have Mum's company as he ate his meal. In any case, there was no way that Father would move out of his precious armchair.

"He's not getting any better," Trevor said, in between bites of sausage. "I don't know how you can put up with it."

"What else can I do?" Mum replied. "But it helps that I do see something of Katie. She often pops in after work. It helps make up for you not being here."

Now, that was good news. Katie would surely not come round and see Mum if she had her eye on someone else.

"Is she all right? I haven't seen her in months. And it's difficult to tell in letters." Especially that last letter, but he would keep quiet about that one.

"More fool you for not coming down to see her," Mum replied, but with a grin. "Yes, she's fine."

"I was going to wait until tomorrow morning before seeing her. As she's not on the phone at home, I thought I'd pop in to see her at the bank. We could then have the afternoon and evening together. I thought we might go to football and then have a Chinese."

"What? Football? You men! You really have no idea, have you? Katie needs to be wooed. And you can't do that at football. And you better get a move on. If not, I'll never be able to use that new hat I've just bought."

Trevor grinned. "I can't think what you're talking about, Mum. But I suppose I could walk round to her place tonight." He then looked at his watch. "Eight's not too late, is it?"

"How old are you? Twenty-five, isn't it? And you still need your old Mum's advice. 'Course it's not too late. Unless you want to spend the rest of your evening in that front lounge."

That was certainly not a valid option. Katie's house was a couple of miles away by road, but only half that distance by way of back lanes and across a couple of fields. Trevor just prayed that the cows had been bedded down for the night. Some years ago, he had been chased by an angry Friesian. He did not relish a repeat of that.

With not a cow in sight, he reached Katie's house in less than half an hour. But the house was in darkness; not a light to be seen. Katie had told him when he rang from the branch that her parents were away; a major reason for his wanting to come this weekend. Thank goodness Mr Goodhart had dismissed any question of his visit being postponed. To be on his own with Katie would be just perfect. But why was the house in darkness?

He knocked on the door, but knew this gesture would be futile. Where was she? Talking to Mum, he had been so uplifted. It had been great to hear that the two of them had been meeting up. But now? Where on earth could she be? All his previous doubts now flooded back. Would his coming back this weekend prove to be a huge mistake?

Chapter 30

David arrived at the Hartfield tea rooms just before half past ten. He had always been a stickler for punctuality. Sarah was the same. If they received an invitation to a party, they always arrived at the appointed time: neither before, nor after. They were often the only ones to do so. It could be difficult to know whether the hosts were pleased or not.

But, unlike the last time, he entered the tea room to find that Mrs Callard had not yet arrived. The café was, in fact, devoid of other customers. He wondered if there might be a worried bank manager behind the scenes. He decided to sit at the same table and ordered a coffee. The waitress seemed delighted to have someone to serve.

As he waited, he reflected on what he and Trevor had encountered since arriving at Crowborough. It was certainly turning out to be an unusual inspection. Such visits were normally straightforward affairs. They could certainly reveal matters of concern, such as security misdemeanours, usually through carelessness, rather than design. And a manager's lending might highlight examples where the bank could be put at risk. Yet here in Crowborough, so many other question marks had been raised. It may well be that, in due course, these would be resolved satisfactorily. But the one categorical matter that had arisen was Ted Callard's murder. Although, on the face of it, this had no relevance to the branch inspection, David was, nevertheless, being drawn into it by Mrs Callard. Just as he was dwelling on this, the door opened and Mrs Callard stepped into the café.

David stood up as she reached his table and shook her proffered hand. Although she appeared to be a little flustered after having arrived late, her overall appearance seemed less severe than on Monday. Perhaps it was because her hair was no longer pulled back into a tightly-formed bun. A neat fringe now softened her previous stark forehead. And having removed her coat, she was more casually dressed in a lime-green twin-set and knee-length tartan skirt.

"I'm so sorry," she said, draping her coat on the back of her chair. "Peter had a funny turn this morning and it delayed his going off to the day centre. I'm never normally late. Please forgive me."

David smiled in understanding and they both sat down. He beckoned to the waitress to bring over another coffee.

"Don't worry," he said. "I've only just arrived myself. And, to be frank, it was nice just to be on my own for a bit of quiet contemplation."

"About me, I suppose," Mrs Callard said, genuine concern reflected in her hazel eyes. David had noticed their colour before and, this morning, they gazed at him with undisguised directness. Perhaps they reflected Mrs Callard's learning of the cause of her husband's death. She must have welcomed such knowledge, even though it was loaded with unimaginable horror. The resolution of a vexed question must, in some way, be beneficial. As far as his inspection was concerned, David knew that he would feel more settled when he learnt the answers to their many 'Crowborough' questions.

"Not really," he replied, smiling and hoping, in some small way, to assuage Mrs Callard's concern. "We've had quite a week in Crowborough. Plenty to get our teeth into. Much to contemplate. But nothing to compare with what you must be going through."

"You know," Mrs Callard said, taking a sip from her coffee which had just arrived, "I feel a little better now I know what's happened. That must seem strange to you. I mean, how can you possibly feel better after being told your husband's been murdered? It doesn't make sense. I suppose feeling better is the wrong expression. But the not knowing beforehand was simply horrible."

David remained quiet, restricting his response to a slight nod of acknowledgement of what she had said. He felt sure that they must both feel that knowing or not knowing the actual cause of death still left questions to be answered: why, in particular? But this was a matter for the police. So why had Mrs Callard called for this meeting with him?

"I suppose you're wondering why I wanted to see you," Mrs Callard continued, as if reading his thoughts.

David now nodded purposely, though at the same time smiling to lessen any chance that Mrs Callard might be offended by his response.

"You've every right to," she added, returning his smile. In relief that she was talking to him? "I'm asking an awful lot of you. Until a few days ago, you'd never heard of me. As for myself, never before could I have contemplated picking up a telephone to ring a bank inspector. Especially someone I'd never even met. Yet it's happened. And I'm glad. You can't imagine what it's like for me to have your shoulder to lean on."

As she spoke, those hazel eyes were unwavering. In other circumstances, David might have found it disconcerting. But behind her unrelenting gaze, he discerned a strength of character which could only help her in these trying circumstances. But would he, himself, be able to be of any help? It would appear that Mrs Callard certainly thought so.

"But why me, Mrs Callard?"

Mrs Callard paused before replying and used the time to finish her coffee. She then raised her eyebrows. "Would you like another one, Mr Goodhart?"

David nodded and with no waitress in sight, stood up to go to the counter. "It's on me today, Mrs Callard. Or would you like something stronger?"

Mrs Callard actually grinned. "In a tea room? At this time of the day?"

"Just checking," David replied, wondering if he had been too flippant with someone he hardly knew. The waitress then appeared and he ordered two more cups. He then resumed his seat.

"Now, to answer your question," Mrs Callard said, "it's what I said on the telephone. I can't help but be suspicious of everyone I know in Crowborough. Putting it bluntly, someone at the lunch must have killed Ted. What makes it worse is that I actually know most of those who were there. And, until now, with one particular reservation, I had no reason to doubt any of them. So, who could it have been? How could I talk to even one of them? Not even Inspector Saunders." Mrs Callard paused and shook her head. "It's a fine thing when I can't bring myself to speak to a policeman, of all people. That's why I approached you. An outsider. How could I talk to anyone else in such circumstances?"

David had to admit it was a conundrum. Made worse if the murder had been done in league with others. But that was hardly feasible. That would imply a Mafia-style organization operating in Crowborough. In this sleepy quarter of South East England? No, whoever killed Ted Callard must have had a personal reason for doing it. There had to have been a drastic falling out. But this was not something for him to get involved in. Despite Mrs Callard's reservations, this was a job for the police.

"But, Mrs Callard, it must surely be the police you should be talking to, not me."

"And they're coming to see me this afternoon. I just hope it won't be Inspector Saunders. But I wanted to show you something first. It's because I think Ted's death is tied up with something financial. In other words, your line of business. And there's something else important to me. I already feel I can trust you implicitly."

David certainly appreciated the compliment, but he was feeling disquieted about what Mrs Callard wanted to show him. On Monday, she thought that the financial aspect might have been to do with their need for a new vehicle. This could have necessitated withdrawing a lump sum from their investments linked to Peter's compensation monies. No mention had been made as to where these investments had been lodged. David was now unnerved that his fears on this might soon be confirmed.

Mrs Callard delved into her brown leather handbag and withdrew several pieces of paper. She selected one sheet and passed it across the table to David.

"This particular letter doesn't say anything concrete," she said, "but it's clear that Ted was not getting anywhere with what he was trying to do."

David took hold of the letter and was immediately taken aback: it had been written on National Counties headed paper. It was a 'Dear Ted' letter signed by Frank Windsor. All it said was that Windsor would like to help if he could. He was not, though, able to comment on the affairs of another professional person.

"Do you have a copy of Ted's original letter?" he asked, looking at the other papers in Mrs Callard's hand.

"No," she replied, shaking her head, "Ted didn't always take copies of the letters he wrote. But he might not have actually written one this time. He could have just met up with Mr Windsor. Asked him something face to face. Perhaps Mr Windsor then prevaricated. He might not have wanted to answer the question straightaway. So he then sent Ted a letter instead."

David supposed that was possible. But why was Frank Windsor involved anyway? Surely he had not got himself mixed up in something untoward? "So what else have you got there?" he asked, putting forward his hand in the hope that Mrs Callard would pass over the remaining papers.

"I wanted to show you a couple of recent investment statements," she said, handing over two pieces of paper. "We get one every month. They show the amount of monthly interest which gets paid into the bank account. That's the account we have at your bank. Ted's business accounts are at Barclays in Tunbridge Wells. As well as showing the interest payments, the statements always state the capital value of the investment. You'll see it's £100,000. That hasn't changed since the original investment was made. So there's plenty of capital to draw on to finance a new car."

Although David was listening to what Mrs Callard was saying, he was mesmerized by the name of the investment company shown on the statements: DH Investments. It was just what he had been fearing.

"And those final letters you've got there?" he asked, pointing to Mrs Callard's hand.

"These are copies of letters Ted did actually make. The first was to Derek Herretson a month ago. It clearly wasn't answered, so Ted wrote again. He was simply asking if it was feasible to make a withdrawal from the investment. He didn't know if it would be possible. He hoped it would be an option to cover the cost of the car. It was Peter's compensation monies, so the new car would be for his benefit. In fact it was now essential to have such a different vehicle. And his second letter wasn't answered, either. That must be why he contacted Mr Windsor. He probably just wanted to know what was going on."

David was now feeling distinctly uneasy. What was going on? Or, more importantly, not going on? And he could not get out of his mind what Frank Windsor had previously told him: that George Bathurst's request for repayment of his investment (the bank's investment?) had also apparently been ignored. Was this down to Derek Herretson? Or was Windsor not being straight with him? No, he could not possibly place such an accusation at the door of one of their own managers. Especially one whom Angus McPhoebe held in such high esteem. On the other hand . . .

"I'm not sure what all these letters demonstrate," he eventually replied. "There could be innocent explanations here. Holidays, for instance. I don't know how many people Derek Herretson employs. He could be a one-man band. If he's away, there could easily be delays in answering letters."

David knew that this was not a satisfactory argument at all. But he was not sure how to play out this scenario with Mrs Callard. He certainly did not want to share the concerns which were now dominating his mind.

"But we're talking about over a month," Mrs Callard replied, effectively agreeing that David's words were not satisfactory. "That's no way to run a business."

"You're right, of course," David said, then smiled, as he added, "and if he's that dilatory, I wouldn't want to be his bank manager. Anyway, we still don't have an answer to Ted's concerns. And that is a concern. My advice is to show all these items to the police. When they come to see you, they'll ask lots of questions. These letters might answer some of them. They'll also want to know if Ted had any enemies. So they'll certainly be interested to hear about any suspicions of his. And any you might have. I hope you'll agree that this really is now a matter for the police."

"Mrs Callard nodded. "But I'm still so glad you found the time to see me. It's been a great help just talking about it. I really am grateful."

They got up to leave and David settled the bill. The only constructive way he had been able to help Mrs Callard was to encourage her to open up to the police. And, surely, any reservations she might have about Inspector Saunders must be unfounded. But underlying matters were another thing for him There certainly seemed to be another question mark over Derek Heretson's operations, quite apart from his being able to pay such high interest rates. And how come, Frank Windsor's name had again cropped up?

Chapter 31

David left the tea rooms at a quarter to twelve. That should get him back to the branch in time to see Trevor off. He just hoped that the lad's trip to Barnmouth would prove worthwhile. David had so much time for Katie; she was a girl in a million; just the one for Trevor. But who was he to matchmake? Only the individuals concerned could decide upon a meaningful relationship. They might well have views and feelings contrary to outsiders looking on. Even so, David felt that only one factor could set back their burgeoning bond: the distance between Barnmouth and Tunbridge Wells.

His planned route to Crowborough was then thwarted. Just beyond the Dorset Arms, he encountered a crashed Austin Devon straddling the road. It was at a dangerous junction on the brow of a hill. He had been wary of this spot when returning from their pub lunch at that particular inn. Despite the apparent absence of on-coming traffic, he had virtually stopped when making the turning. Just in case. It was clear that one driver, on this occasion, had not been so careful.

There was no option but to turn round and find an alternative route. He was fortunate in having a good sense of direction:

unlike Sarah. His darling wife could not leave a shop without turning the opposite way to where she needed to go. But the accident eventually added fifteen minutes to his journey and Trevor had left by the time he arrived at the branch.

Before leaving for Hartfield, he had spoken to Henry Purcell who would be delighted to welcome David to his residential home. They arranged for the visit to be at two o'clock that afternoon. The home was situated in the Warren area of Crowborough, the more salubrious part of town. It would only take David a few minutes to get there. It meant having about an hour and a half to fill in beforehand. This also included the time to have some lunch, but he would not go to a pub. He had always abhorred drinking on his own; he liked to think it was his way of knowing that he was not an alcoholic. How sad to sit alone on a bar stool with only a pint of best bitter for company.

Instead of visiting a pub, David chose a Cornish pasty from the butcher in the High Street and ate it at his desk with a brew of National Counties tea. Rather than retrieve their bags from the strongroom, he decided to spend the time available by writing a couple of reports. He had all the information he needed in his head, without recourse to any of their files or documents.

After setting off for the residential home, he found it without difficulty. It was a large Edwardian property, just adjacent to the main road to the south coast. It could easily have been a hotel in previous years. If so, conversion to a residential home would have been simple for the Arthur Waits of this world. The property stood in several acres of manicured gardens and the lawns appeared to be free of weeds and moss, unlike his own. Separate beds had been set out for red and yellow roses which were still in bloom, as were clumps of pink and white Michaelmas daisies which were dotted around the grounds. He could imagine this setting being much appreciated by those residents wanting temporary escape from the confines of their rooms.

He left his Consul in a large parking area in front of the property. Two flagpoles stood on either side of the entrance, one flying the Union Jack, the other the flag of St George. David was of an age to admire such overt patriotism.

The front door was locked and he rang the bell. He certainly approved of the security measure of having a locked entrance. It could, otherwise, prove to be a field day for visitors of ill repute. Gone were the days when even private front doors could be left unlocked. It was the same with cars, although some drivers seemed to think that the absence of a key in the ignition was enough to deter would-be thieves. Had they never heard of Kirby-grips? Or a cracksman's ability to short-circuit a car's starter system?

A smartly-attired woman of about forty opened the door and greeted him with a warm smile. She wore a well-cut tweed suit which perfectly befitted this autumnal day. He had half-expected the staff here to wear nurse-styled uniforms, but then realized that this was a residential, not nursing, home. In some respects, it might be thought of as more like a hotel, than a form of care home.

"You must be Mr Goodhart," the lady said, extending her hand. David found this gesture unexpected from a member of the staff until she added, "I'm Cynthia Purcell . . . Henry's wife."

"I'm very pleased to meet you, Mrs Purcell," David replied, shaking her hand and then following her into the reception area. This was as impressive as the welcome she had given him. If it was an indication of the quality of the business, there would not be a worried bank manager in the background.

Before he had a chance to have a good look round, HP arrived and gave him an equally warm welcome.

"You found us all right, then?" he asked. "Not really difficult, what? In a place like Crowborough, I mean." Then adding, with a grin, "But it might have helped if I'd flown Palace's flag outside,"

Was this his first quip of David's visit? Or was it simply a sincere acknowledgement of their shared interest in Crystal Palace football club?

"Anyway," HP continued, ushering David to one of the doors leading to rooms away from reception, "let me show you around."

As David was led on a tour of the ground floor, Mrs Purcell remained where she was. The first thing he noticed was the absence of an antiseptic aroma, so prevalent in fully fledged nursing homes. The main corridor was wide enough for wheelchairs to pass each other comfortably and the walls were decorated in soothing shades of lemon and lilac. The first room they entered was a large lounge, with the inevitable easy chairs flanking each wall. But the few residents in the room all looked reasonably able-bodied, unlike those David had seen in out-and-out cheerless nursing homes. This room was not at all depressing.

Nor was the next door dining room. About a dozen tables were set out to accommodate two to four people. Lunch was now over and a member of staff was re-laying the tables for the evening meal. David was impressed that the tables were covered by spotless white linen cloths. No easy-to-wipe-down surfaces here.

Upstairs there were some twenty bedrooms, with about twelve more in a recently-built adjoining annex. HP took David into an unoccupied room. It was spacious and boasted a picture window overlooking the grounds to the rear. All the other bedrooms were occupied. David was not surprised. The overall standard of this residential home was of the highest quality.

"Very impressive," he said when HP ushered him into his office at the end of the tour. It would be a pleasure to work in this room. Windows on two walls would make the room bright, even on the dullest days. Tea and biscuits were already laid out for them on a round coffee table. This sat easily between three comfortable-looking Ercol chairs. HP's working desk and chair, together with three filing cabinets, occupied a windowless wall to the side.

Henry Purcell smiled at the compliment. As at last week's lunch, he was extravagantly dressed in his primrose and tan check suit, though, this time, minus his yellow and blue waistcoat. But today's flamboyance was not accompanied by his previous attempts at *joire de vivre*. During the tour of the home, he had resisted making any further quips and David was actually getting to like the man. This contrasted starkly with the severe reservations he had formed when they had first met.

"What sort of place is your aunt actually looking for?" HP then asked, reminding David of his alleged reason for looking over the place. "You can see we're just a residential home. No nursing facilities, at all. Would this suit her? Or does she need some nursing care?"

"That's a difficult one," David replied, needing to get off this subject as soon as possible. A little white lie was in danger of developing into a whopper. "She probably does need a little nursing care. But what about your fees? Are they competitive?" he added, smiling quizzically.

"We're not the cheapest," HP replied, getting up and going to one of the filing cabinets. "But we're virtually full. I reckon our residents get what they pay for."

He then returned to his chair and handed David a sheet which detailed room rates and other charges which might be incurred. The figures looked reasonable and they led David nicely on to the subject which was his real reason for coming.

"And the fees are paid monthly?" he asked. "I imagine that would suit your residents. No doubt they all get their pensions paid that way."

Henry Purcell nodded. "And many of them also get interest on their investments paid monthly."

Bingo! David could not have expected it to be so easy to get on to his chosen subject. "Really?" he said. "But bank interest is only paid half-yearly. Not to mention dividends on stocks and shares."

HP's eyes now glowed. Was it through smugness? Was he back to his previous self? David hoped not, now having seen another side to the man.

"We've got an excellent investment consultant in town," HP then said. "I think you met him at the Crowborough Collective lunch. Derek Herretson. He manages to offer huge returns on money put his way. Far better than anywhere else. And, I'm sorry to say, that also includes your bank."

David frowned. "That's not good to hear . . . from our point of view. How does he do it?"

"I've no idea. But it's all above board. A couple of years ago, I put a chunk of my own money with him. I soon learnt how meticulous he is. Each month I get an investment statement. It details the amount of capital in my name, plus the amount of monthly interest paid into my bank account. It's such an efficient system. I had no hesitation in recommending Derek to one or two of our residents. They were so pleased that they then recommended him to others. Most of our residents are now using him."

HP had just said that it was all above board; David somehow doubted this. And it was beginning to look as if most of Crowborough might be using Derek Herretson. No doubt his tentacles stretched out still further. To Tunbridge Wells? Uckfield? Even to Charlie Spencer O'Hara's territory around Lewes? Goodness knows how much Herretson's investment fund must be worth. And how was he able to manage his investors' deposits so well to be able to offer such high rates of interest? Never mind paying this out monthly.

But how could David get the conversation around to requests to withdraw capital? Had any of HP's residents had difficulty with this? It would certainly seem that Ted Callard and George Bathurst might have encountered problems. A thought then struck him: a reason why there might be protracted delays in arranging repayments.

"I'm just thinking about these higher rates of interest," he said, then smiling as he added, "I have to confess to being rather envious. I agree it's not a thing National Counties can compete with. Nor other banks, I imagine. But is it because deposits are placed with him on a fixed-term basis? That's something the banks don't do. It could be why Herretson's returns are so much higher."

"I don't think so," Henry Purcell replied. "Not in my case, anyway. And a year ago, one resident needed her investment repaid and she got it within a week. The only other case recently would have been Mrs Collier. She had the room I just showed you. She died a month ago and I know she had a substantial sum invested with Derek. But repayment of that must be in the hands of her executors. I certainly haven't heard anything about it. But there's no reason why I should."

David decided to leave it at that. It did not seem that he was likely to acquire any further information. It was comforting to know that one resident had managed to get her investment repaid. But that was a year ago. Circumstances might have changed since then. He would certainly be interested to learn of the outcome with Mrs Collier. But that could take weeks, depending on the executors.

It was now time for him to go.

"Thank you so much for sparing the time to show me around," he said, standing up. "I must say I'm mightily impressed. If my aunt decides to come, I'm sure she'd settle in well. It's just that she does probably need more care than you can provide. But I'll certainly talk it over with her."

"Just let me know if she'd like a look round," HP replied, also rising. "We're here to help if we possibly can."

They made their way to the front door. As they shook hands, HP said, "No football at home this weekend. We're away to Northampton. Do you go to away games?"

David shook his head. "No. I always think it's a long way back home if we lose. But it'll be nice to win tomorrow and stay top of the league."

After spending an hour back at the branch, David made his way home to Tunbridge Wells. Throughout the day the car had started perfectly. That was good. He had thought it might have meant a trip to a garage in the morning. He would now be able to have a lie-in, instead.

On opening the front door, he was immediately disconcerted: no aroma was wafting through the house. But he could hear Sarah in the kitchen. If she was not cooking, she would be drooling over her new toy: an Electromatic twin-tub. A couple of months ago, she had seen an advertisement in the Daily Mirror. It described a new wonder product and she had decided that she must have one. David had mounted steadfast opposition: the machine now had pride of place in the kitchen.

Perhaps she was right. Maybe direct selling from a factory would take over from normal High Street retailing. There certainly seemed to be a cost saving over traditional products made by Hoover and Hotpoint. But David was always a mite suspicious of entrepreneurs suddenly arriving on the scene with a new product. The man behind the Electromatic name was someone called John Bloom. Who was he? Would he be successful? The fact that he put the name Rolls on his machines struck David as being pretentious in the extreme. Not for Sarah, though; she loved the idea and now proudly proclaimed that she was the only one in the family to own a Rolls.

He kissed her on the forehead and then overtly sniffed the air. He then put his arm around her and said, "I hope this new machine of yours isn't taking over from your culinary tasks. I can't smell a thing."

"That's because nothing's being cooked," she replied. "It's Friday night and I've downed tools. I reckon I deserve a break from cooking. So I decided we'd have fish and chips. In fact, I tell a lie. It was Mark's choice. And if I agreed, he actually said he'd go down the road and get them himself."

"He must have an ulterior motive," David replied, knowing how Mark's mind could occasionally work in devious ways. "But it means we can have a snifter while he does it. First, though, I'll just go upstairs and get changed."

While he was donning his favourite navy Guernsey sweater and corduroy slacks, he heard the telephone ring downstairs. A few moments later, Sarah called up to him from the hall.

"David, will you come down. It's that brother of yours. And he doesn't sound best pleased."

Chapter 32

Trevor dunked a toasted soldier into his softly-boiled egg. He never enjoyed such hedonism in Tunbridge Wells. Mum was a star. She had offered him a blanket choice: fried, poached, scrambled or boiled. It had been a no-brainer. He, himself, had never achieved a perfectly-boiled egg; Mum had never failed. Sheer bliss. And a second egg lay on his plate, the top of its shell begging to be cracked open.

He was in such a good mood; a far cry from last night. Retreating from Katie's dark and empty house, he could not face returning straight home. He decided to walk into central Barnmouth, then taking solace from the calming stream which divided both sides of the town. During the day, a variety of water fowl ducked and dived in the clear water, supervised by the black swans, unique to Barnmouth in this part of the country. But all was quiet at night time, the stream's inhabitants duly tucked up in their nests. Just as Trevor should be at this time of night. Instead, he slumped on a wooden bench, wallowing in self-imposed misery. Should he have come all this way, after all? Returning to Crawley to seek out those phantom houses ought to have taken precedence. Why had Mr Goodhart not insisted on that? It might have been good man-management on his part, but any over-running of the Crowborough inspection might have serious repercussions. And the involvement of Mrs Callard could cause still further delays, never mind what that investment consultant might be up to.

He dragged his mind back to Katie. Where was she? How could Katie have left him so high and dry? It was nearly twelve before he made his way home, ready to face another darkened building. But, on this occasion, he knew it was occupied; Mum and Father would be tucked up in bed. Thank goodness he had foreseen such a situation; the spare front door key nestled in his pocket.

He tossed and turned throughout the night, but was spared bad dreams as to what Katie might have been up to. He could not have abided that. Such dreams always spawned synthetic realism which begged legitimacy. And he could never understand how he could awaken from a bad dream and fail to rid it from his mind. Even worse, was to fall asleep again, only for the dream to continue from where it had left off. At least, on this Saturday morning, he had been spared that.

He rose from his bed, not bothering to shave and found Mum bustling away in the kitchen. Father, thank goodness, was apparently having a Saturday morning lie-in.

"'Morning, dearie," Mum said, drawing him close, but then reeling back over-dramatically, her cheek having briefly caressed his stubbly chin. "You make sure you shave before meeting up with your Katie."

My Katie? If only . . .

Mum then glared at him. "But why didn't you come back here when you found her house empty?"

"Mum? How did you . . ."

"You're the end," she interrupted. "Katie waited here until ten and then gave up."

"Waited here? What are you talking about?"

"She came round. Your Katie. Decided she couldn't wait until tomorrow to see you. She cycled over. How did you miss her?"

Damn it! Why did he have to take the route across the fields?

"I didn't go along the main road. I took the short cut."

"And you didn't think she might have come here? You men! Your father was just the same. Had no idea how to court a girl. Just like you last night when you talked of taking her to football." She then turned back to her oven, muttering ,"Men!", just loud enough for Trevor to hear.

The finality of her words shook him. Especially the comparison Mum had made between himself and Father. Like father, like son? Heaven forbid. But how could he have known that Katie would come round? If only they could both have had telephones in their homes. U2 spy planes were flying all over the world, while getting a man on the moon was, surely, in the offing. Yet, unless you were rich, home telephones in this country were still the exception in so many places. Harold Macmillan might say that we've never had it so good, but not having a telephone did its best to distil that particular notion.

Anyway, last night's gloom was now well and truly banished. Katie had actually come round to see him. How good was that? Everything between them must still be all right.

"How was she, Mum?" he asked, as he cracked open his second egg. "What did you talk about? She must have been here a couple of hours."

"Never you mind," she replied, with what could only be feigned indignation. She still had her back to him, but he could imagine her eyes twinkling. "Let's just say it was girls' talk."

"Girls? In the plural?"

"Cheeky. Remember you're a guest here this weekend."

Trevor got up, wiped his lips clear of any runny yoke, and gave Mum a hug. "Best Mum in the world."

"Oh, it's like that, is it? Trying to get round me."

"Only because I want to know how Katie was last night. I haven't told you, but her last letter got me a bit worried. Has she been seeing somebody else?"

"Of course not, Trevor," Mum replied, turning round to face him and placing her hands on each of his cheeks, this time, apparently, not minding his stubble. "Katie told me about her letter. About her so-called other person. There never was anyone else. Never has been. She deliberately wanted to get you thinking. She wasn't meaning to be devious. That's not in her character. She just wanted to get you down here. And you'd not given her any indication that you were planning another visit yet. Anyway, it's clearly worked. But there was no malice intended. No mischief. For some reason, she's potty about you. She just needs to be courted."

Mum could not have stressed that last word more. And her pale blue eyes, normally so serene, now blazed with uncommon intensity.

Trevor nodded and took hold of her hands, giving them a squeeze. "You're right, Mum, of course. As usual. What would I do without you? The trouble is that it's not just Katie I'm too far away from. It's also you."

"Get away with you. That's how it should be, son. I know Father doesn't think so, but you did the right thing to get away from Barnmouth. It's too parochial here. Especially if you're keen to get on with your career. And you needed to get away from my apron strings. But it's not been good for Katie. She's twenty-three now. She should be thinking of settling down with someone. And that someone should be you. So, come on, Trevor. Do the decent thing."

With those last words ringing in his ears, he left the house for the walk into town. He could take the bus, but he needed time to think. He always did this best when walking, particular when dwelling on musical compositions. But do the decent thing? People said that when an unplanned child might be on the way. That was certainly not the case with him and Katie. Chance would be a fine thing. For someone so extrovert and vivacious, Katie's scruples about pre-marital hanky-panky knew no bounds. Putting a ring on her finger was the only way to unlock that particular door. But was he ready for that?

He reached the bank at ten-thirty. It seemed strange to stand outside the branch where he had first started work. Sixteen at the time and he had felt very much like a new boy at school. Everyone else had seemed so worldly-wise. It was not until after he had returned from his two year stint of National Service that he was able to speak to people without turning crimson.

The branch imposed itself on a corner, a trio of stone steps leading up to the entrance. Too bad if someone had a mobility problem. Many a time he had helped the infirm in and out of the branch. There was certainly room for a ramp to be installed. One day, perhaps? In the meantime, handrails were now in place for customers who were not too incapacitated.

The first person he saw inside was the first cashier, Bernard Groves. He was standing behind the counter sorting out some pound notes and fivers. He looked up and smiled. With no customer at his till, he thrust his hand across the counter. Trevor grasped it and they greeted each other like long lost friends. Yet Trevor had only left the branch a year ago. It seemed like an eternity. So much had happened in the last twelve months.

Bernard was some thirty years older than Trevor and must be approaching retirement. Initially, he had been frustrating to work alongside. So old school. Somewhat like Mr Scrivens at Crowborough, but without the wing collar. The trouble was that he was ultra-slow at cashiering. Trevor could deal with six customers in the time it took Bernard to serve one. And until three years ago, Bernard and his wife, Celia, had been so arrogant. They had lauded it around Barnmouth as though they were mayor and mayoress, not just a humble bank cashier with wife in tow. That all changed after Bernard had exercised uncommon carelessness. £2,500 was stolen from his till. He had left it lying around unattended and the resultant admonition caused him massive humiliation. Since then, Bernard had been a pleasure to work alongside and, today, Trevor was genuinely pleased to see him.

"Is Katie around?" he asked, causing Bernard to look behind him.

"She's not at her desk," he replied, turning back to Trevor. "But she can't be far away. I saw her a few moments ago." He then grinned, something he rarely did years ago and added, "Or should I say, heard her."

That's my Katie. Still the life and soul of the party.

"Perhaps she's taking the manager's dictation," Trevor suggested.

Bernard nodded in agreement. "But she's not likely to be long. There wasn't much in-coming post this morning. And it's been our quietest Saturday for a long time. Why don't you come into the back office? You can wait at her desk . . . and meet some of the others."

Within five minutes, Katie bounded out of the manager's office, almost being sent flying by Trevor's outstretched leg. He had taken possession of her typing stool and was sprawled out as he waited for her to appear.

"Trevor!" she squealed, then clapping a hand over her delicately-painted pink lips as she realized that she had turned customers' heads in the banking hall. But this did not inhibit her from then throwing her arms around him, oblivious to the austere branch environment. "Where were you last night?"

"That's exactly what I'd been thinking about you," Trevor replied, releasing himself from her grasp. "Until Mum told me this morning."

His mind was now being pulled in two directions: he was finding this situation embarrassing, to say the least; yet Katie would not have greeted him like this if she had any doubts about their relationship. And that would certainly seem to confirm Mum's reading of the situation.

"Anyway," he continued, "let's talk about that after work. You'll be finished by twelve-thirty?"

Katie nodded vigorously. "I'll be outside the front door by then. Not a minute later."

Trevor almost floated out of the branch. Could Katie's greeting have been any better? Apart from causing him acute embarrassment. He made his way to the seafront, passing through the tunnel under the railway lines. This must be the most picturesque railway route in the whole country and there would be no passengers with heads buried in books while the line passed so close to several miles of shoreline. But they should be wary of major storms. Giant waves could engulf the tracks and even threaten the carriages themselves. Today, though, was a fine day and he found an unoccupied wooden bench adjacent to the shingle beach. The sea was calm and Trevor felt almost mesmerized as the gentle waves ebbed and flowed below his feet.

Thank goodness he had, indeed, come down this weekend. It had also reminded him of Mr Goodhart's attributes when manager of Barnmouth branch, something that did not seem to be echoed back in Crowborough. Mr Windsor was an experienced manager, yet question marks were starting to hang down from him like a paper chain. He should be demonstrating to banking apprentices like Trevor the art of good lending; instead, he seemed to be providing an insight into how not to do it.

But this was something to be pursued on Monday with Mr Goodhart. Katie was now his number one priority and last night had clearly been a hiccup; this morning could not have turned out better, first his chat with Mum and then with Katie. They now had the whole afternoon and evening before them.

He arrived back at the branch at just before twelve-thirty; Katie burst through the front door exactly on time. Once again, she flung her arms around him, but this time, any embarrassment was mitigated; they were on their own with no immediate passers-by. She then slipped her hand in his as they walked away from the bank.

"Isn't this great?" Katie cooed, then breaking away from him as she added, "But why didn't you come back to your Mum's last night? I waited until ten. Where did you get to?"

"How did I know you'd gone to our place?" Trevor replied, being bold enough to take back Katie's hand as they were about to reach a café, a few shops away from the bank. "I didn't know where you were. I couldn't believe your house was empty. I knew your parents were away, but I thought I'd find you there. That's why I went to see you. So that we could be on our own."

"That sounds a bit naughty," Katie said, attempting to feign shock and horror, but then squeezing his hand. "But we're on our own now."

"Going into a crowded café?"

"You'll just have to be patient," Katie said, her blue eyes twinkling as she rose to give him a kiss. Trevor almost wilted; the first of the day. Why had she waited so long? Why had he, for that matter?

Sitting side by side in the café, mugs of coffee on the table, Trevor could hardly contain his feelings. But he knew his natural inhibition would do just that. In the meantime, though, this was far better than he had expected. Especially when he had been back in Crowborough. After what Mum had said, there was no need for him to hark back to Katie's letter. But Mum's words still rang in his ears: "She just needs to be courted." But how? To court someone sounded so old-fashioned. He really had no idea. For that reason, he had usually allowed Katie to take the lead. That was why, just now, he had felt rather proud of taking her hand in his. From now on, he would just play it by ear.

"So, what are we going to do?" Katie said, as if reading his mind. She then leant against him and put her arm around his shoulder.

The intimacy of the moment made Trevor shiver involuntarily. He tried to reply, but words failed him. Not that he really had an answer. That business of courting again?

"Are you feeling cold?" Katie asked, real concern lacing her words. "Here, put your hands round your mug. It's piping hot. Anyway, I've got an idea."

"Go on, then," Trevor urged, still perfectly happy to play second fiddle to Katie's enthusiasm.

"Remember our first dates?"

Trevor nodded. How could he forget. If only for one reason: that Katie had actually agreed to go out with him. And, for once, she had responded to him, rather than the other way round. Unlike now?

"Let's do the same things again," Katie enthused, before he could reply. "Let's go to Torquay . . . to football, first of all, and then walk down to the Strand for a drink. Then we could finish off at the Walnut Grove."

Trevor could not believe his ears. Go to football? What would Mum say? She had made it clear that football was off-limits. Would she now tell Katie that this was no way for her to court her son? Trevor could not help but burst out laughing.

"What's wrong?" Katie asked, a rare frown wrinkling her brow. "Football, drinks, jazz . . . I thought you'd be pleased."

"I am, I am," Trevor managed to say, trying to curb his mirth. "It's just that Mum . . ."

"Your Mum?" Katie interrupted, her eyebrows now straining up to her forehead. "What's your Mum got to do with it?"

Trevor turned to Katie and took hold of both her hands in his, appreciating how soft and warm they felt. "I actually suggested that to her. Football, I mean. That I might take you to football. She thought I was mad. She said it was no way for me to court you."

"Is that what you're trying to do now?" Katie said, squeezing his hands. "Court me?"

Trevor felt himself reddening. At twenty-five? With the love of his life at his side? And he was actually blushing? He could only nod in answer to her question.

He suddenly felt her soft lips on his flushed cheek. "That's so lovely, Trevor," she said, then whispering in his ear, "You can court me until the cows come home."

When they had sat down at their table, Trevor had been glad that no one was sitting on either side. Now, he simply did not care. The whole world could have been there. At that precise moment, he knew what he must do. He also knew why. Just not how or when. But first things first.

"It's Bradford City," he simply said, having done his homework. "That's the match today. You really want to go?"

Katie nodded enthusiastically. "Of course. But I haven't got my scarf."

That hardly mattered and at a quarter-to-five, they made their way out of the ground. A good game; a 2-1 win; and the first goal scored by one of Trevor's favourite players: Ernie Pym.

Stage one of their mission duly completed.

The weather was still fine for their stroll down to the Strand. The Queen's Hotel had been the venue for their first date; so why not go there again? Trevor remembered that he had sunk a rare pint that night, lemonade being his normal tipple. Tonight, the beer would have no rarity value; Mr Goodhart had seen to that 'on the road', as inspection work was called.

They left the bar at eight, each of them stumbling slightly, despite the pavements being anything but uneven. It would take half an hour or so to reach the Walnut Grove, situated in the suburb of Chelston. Most of the route would be via the seafront, taking in the length of Abbey Sands, before turning off at the Grand Hotel, alongside the railway station which they would use to get home to Barnmouth.

With the waves gently lapping the shore and the water reflecting the adjacent street lighting, Trevor deliberately slowed their pace. He had never before experienced such romance in the air. Katie's head nestled against his shoulder as they sauntered along, hand in hand. Each time she looked up into his eyes, she gently squeezed his hand. How could he have failed to come back to see her for so long? Houses in Crawley were now the last thing on his mind.

"You should have brought your sax with you," Katie said, as they settled at their table in the club.

"That would mean having to leave you on your own when I played," Trevor replied, now taking the initiative and taking both her hands in his. "I just want us to be sitting here together."

It was when the pianist launched into the first bars of *Polka Dots and Moonbeams*, an all-time favourite of them both, that Trevor knew this was the moment. He must take the plunge. He had been nervous when he had played his first gig and when he took his driving test. But those times were nothing like this. He forced himself to lean across to Katie and whispered in her ear, " I'm not sure how I should be going about this, but . . . but will you marry me? Please?"

Chapter 33

S arah was not often able to drive the Consul. David offered various excuses: it was the bank's car; it was for the use of a bank inspector; or, worst of all, it was too big for a woman. What? Too big? For a woman? How dare he! How could he expect to get away with such a sexist view? But Sarah had to admit that he had said it with a smile. No malice intended. Just as well, otherwise she would have downed tools in so many ways. There would only be one loser then.

But Sarah had not admitted to David one salient factor: she did not like driving the car. It was too long . . . and too wide. Was that the same as being too big? Probably. She had much preferred to drive their previous Hillman Minx. But what she would really like was a little car of her own. She had spotted the exact one: a Mini. She had never habitually read car magazines or, even, car write-ups in the papers, but everyone had become aware of this particular new model: Morris's latest vehicle, aptly name the Mini. It had been launched last year and Sarah loved it being so small and cute. People were already raving about it. As well as being tiny, it had something called front-wheel drive, not that she knew what that meant. David had said that when the roads were wet or icy, it would make driving safer. So be it, but there was one major snag with this new car: the cost. £500 was far too much. And with it being such a new model, the second-hand market was non-existent. For now, then, they would remain a one-car family. If she wanted to drive, she would have to content herself with the Consul.

As she was doing now.

It was just after noon and they were on their way to Bexhill-on Sea, on the south coast. Just the two of them; Mark had a school football match this Saturday afternoon. It was an away game in Orpington and he would get back by about six. Sarah had promised that they would be home in Tunbridge Wells in good time before then.

This day trip had been at the invitation of Robert. When he telephoned last night, he had certainly not sounded pleased and David had picked up the phone with some trepidation. His brother had kept up the pretence for a full minute. Sarah had not been able to follow the full conversation from this end only, but David had recounted it to her when he eventually put the phone down.

"What day is it today?" Robert had immediately said, dispensing with any opening salutation - just like Angus McPhoebe.

"It's Friday," David had replied, though feeling that this could not be the answer Robert was seeking.

"Don't be obtuse, David," Robert had snapped, confirming David's prognosis. "The date, I mean."

"The date?" David queried. "You've really rung me up just to find out the date?"

"No, David, I'm perfectly aware of the date. It's you who doesn't seem to know."

"Oh, my God," David had then gasped, putting his free hand to his mouth and closing his eyes. "It's the 28th."

"Exactly. And what should that date convey to you, my dear little brother?"

"All right, all right," David had replied, wondering if he could blame his social secretary for his omission, "don't rub it in. I'm so sorry, but many happy returns, anyway. How could I have forgotten?"

"That's exactly what I've been saying to myself all day. How could you have possibly forgotten your big brother's birthday?"

Their birthdays had never been a big thing between them. They only rarely celebrated them together, especially since Robert had been with Bertram Mills Circus. But they never failed to send each other a birthday card.

Until now.

Robert had soon returned to his normal self. And to show that he held no hard feelings, he had invited them to go to the circus again and share a bottle of champagne in celebration. After leaving Tunbridge Wells, the show had spent a few days in Eastbourne, before moving on to Bexhill-on-Sea, its last venue before closing down for the winter.

Hence Sarah being behind the wheel of the Consul. To enable David to share Robert's celebratory bottle, she had agreed to drive home afterwards. But she never liked driving on unfamiliar roads, so she offered to take the wheel on both journeys to get used to the route. David had looked askance. For some unknown reason, unless it enabled him to have a tipple or two, he never liked sitting next to her when she drove. Perhaps it was because he felt she was for ever in the wrong gear. It was infuriating that he always seemed to know best. It was like when he had been teaching her to drive; it had been a nightmare for both of them. Sarah had never forgotten how David had pointedly said that it was perfectly safe for her to overtake a preceding cyclist. But why should she not exercise due caution? She was sure that the drivers of the stream of cars behind them would not blame her for that.

Anyway, driving to the circus would certainly help her to familiarize herself with the road. And, provided they both remained cool, calm and collected, the arrangement should work well.

They had warned Robert that they must be back for Mark at six and he suggested that they sup their champagne at lunchtime. They could then see the first half of the matinee performance, before returning to Tunbridge Wells.

"You realize that you won't see the lions and tigers," Robert said, as they were imbibing in his caravan - he and David, that is; Sarah was sticking to water. She would make use of the drink's cabinet when they got home. "They're always the last act at matinees. That way, the cage can stay erected between shows. The big cats will then be the first act at the evening performance."

"It doesn't matter," David said, offering his flute to Robert for a re-fill. "We saw them in Tunbridge Wells. But I hope we can see the horses again."

Sarah was not sure about that. More sawdust being kicked up in their faces? Then, looking at David, she said, "Don't forget you've got some news for Robert."

"Ah, yes, of course," David said, smiling enigmatically at Robert. "Guess who's now in charge at Regional Office?"

"How could I possibly guess that?" Robert replied, as he topped up their glasses. "I don't know anyone at National Counties."

"Maybe not now, but way back you did. How about your old *bete noire?*"

Robert frowned, but then it suddenly seemed to dawn on him. "At Wiveliscombe?"

David nodded. "The dreaded Mr Threadgold."

"Lucky you," Robert said, actually rubbing his hands together. "Does that mean my past will be coming back to haunt you? Not that he'd ever remember me."

"He certainly did a few years ago. I had to see him in Head Office and your name came up. He wanted to know how you were doing. When I told him you were now general manager of the circus, he said he knew you'd always do well."

"He didn't say that to me at the time. He wouldn't even speak to me while I saw out my month's notice."

"The power of hindsight?" David suggested. "But you're not to worry. You won't be the cause of my downfall in the bank. I've got another *bete noire* on my back. Threadgold's deputy."

"Two *bete noires* in one office? That sounds a bit selfish to me."

David grinned. "But more like too much of a bad thing for me."

Sarah was getting a little concerned at the way this conversation was developing. They may be talking in jest, but knowing David, she could imagine his getting under the skins of these two men at Regional Office. In which case, David would be the fall guy. Yet he was so good at his job and he deserved support, rather than attrition.

"It's time you moved into the big top," Robert then said, urging them to empty their glasses. "I can hear the overture starting up. I've got good seats for you again. Right at the ringside."

Sarah could not stop her eyes rolling, glad that Robert had turned his back. She would not want to hurt his feelings after he had spoiled them with the champagne. But those horses. She would just have to close her eyes when the sawdust started flying.

They reached their seats just as the overture finished. Sarah's next concern was whether they would prove to be butts for the clowns. But, as before in Tunbridge Wells, they chose others in the audience as their victims. Phew! The clowns were followed by acrobats, jugglers and an extraordinary low-wire walker, who, somehow on his wire, included all the tricks performed by the previous artistes on the ground.

The ring was then cleared and plunged into darkness. Sarah sensed movement in front of them and the gradual introduction of subdued lighting revealed twelve magnificent Palomino liberty horses standing stationary, nose to tail, around the ring edge. No one had seen them come in and, suddenly there they were, proudly resplendent, before a mesmerized audience. There was now only one problem: they were on the move and Sarah prepared to take cover. Multi-coloured spotlights cleverly picked out individual horses, together with the ring boys who were overseeing the complicated routines in the ring. David and Sarah had not seen this particular act at Tunbridge Wells. Perhaps it was a rehearsal for next year's tour.

Sarah's heart then missed a beat. She felt herself going pale and, wide-eyed, she put a hand to her mouth in horror. Her heart then started pounding, as if it wanted to break out from her chest.

At her side, David evidently sensed her consternation and turned to her, putting his hand on her arm. "Don't worry, love," he said, " it's only sawdust. It'll soon brush off."

Sarah shook her head, but could not speak. Thank goodness this liberty horse act was the last before the interval. They had then arranged to go to Robert's caravan to say their farewells, before heading home. She could not get to the caravan quickly enough.

"It's not that," she said, at last finding her voice. "I can't say anything now. It's too noisy. Let's get to the caravan first. I can't believe what I've just seen. And heaven knows what Robert will say."

David was patently disturbed as they made for the caravan. "Well?" he said, urging her to tell him what was wrong.

"In a moment," Sarah replied, squeezing his hand which she had been so glad to cling on to.

Robert opened the door as they reached his caravan and immediately frowned when he saw their faces. Gone was the jovial air when they had last been with him.

"Something's happened," David said, "but Sarah hasn't told me what. Come on, love, what's wrong?"

"Can we all sit down," Sarah said, suddenly feeling more composed in the security of the caravan. "Robert, we hadn't told you before, but my branch was raided last week. Someone pointed a gun at me. I assumed it was a gun, because it was in his pocket." She then raised her hands at Robert who was about to interrupt, no doubt to express his concern. "No, Robert, I'm fine. Really. I'd virtually got over it. Until just now. But I can hardly believe it. I've just seen the gunman."

It was now David's turn to looked shocked and he took hold of Sarah's hand. "How come, love? How's that possible? You said he had a mask over his face and he was wearing a Balaclava. How could you recognise him now?"

"Don't you remember, David? I said it was his eyes. I'd seen those eyes somewhere before. And now I know where. It was at the circus in Tunbridge Wells. And I've just seen those eyes again. In the ring. It's one of the ring-boys."

David turned to look at Robert, who was wide-eyed.

"That can't be possible," Robert then said. "Surely, it's too much of a coincidence?"

"I reckon it's definitely possible," David replied, stroking his chin with forefinger and thumb. "Tonbridge was one of four recent raids on the bank. The latest one was at Battle on Thursday. Probably all done by the same man. The cashier at Battle certainly shared Sarah's description of him. And being so covered up, there wasn't much for the police to go on. So Sarah's eye thing could be really pertinent. I don't have any details of the other two raids, but after what Sarah's just seen . . ." David paused and looked pointedly at Robert . He then asked, "What other towns have you been to recently?"

Robert pursed his lips as he clearly cast his mind back. "We'd been to Reading and then gone down to Winchester. After that, we were in Portsmouth and Guildford. Then Tunbridge Wells."

"That's exactly why I asked," David replied. "The other two raids were at branches a few miles from both Portsmouth and Guildford. Then came Tonbridge. That's also only a few miles from Tunbridge Wells. And Battle's not that far from Bexhill. It's the same pattern in each case. We originally thought the man might be a traveller . . . in the gypsy sense of the word. But your ring-boy is also effectively a traveller, but with the circus. And his target branches are far enough away from your sites to lessen any suspicion linked to the circus."

"I still can't believe it," Robert said, then looking at Sarah who had remained quiet during these exchanges, though now certain that David's evaluation was correct. "Which ring-boy are you talking about?"

"He's the one with long, jet-black hair, slicked back with Brylcreem," Sarah replied. "I couldn't see his hair at the branch because of his Balaclava. But I recognized his eyes. I couldn't forget them. It was the way he smirked at us in Tunbridge Wells . . . when the horses kicked up sawdust in our faces. It seemed to give him great pleasure. You know, well-dressed people getting treated like that. And another thing . . . he didn't say a word when he confronted me at the branch. I wondered if he might be foreign. Especially as the note he handed across to me was hardly in the Queen's English."

As Sarah described the man, Robert nodded repeatedly and then said, "I know who you mean. It's Antonio. Comes from Spain. Only been with us for four months. He does his job well enough, but he does have attitude. That smirking, for instance.

It'll be ironic if it now comes back to haunt him. Yet I can't believe that he, or anyone else here, would be up to robbing banks."

"The thing is," David then said, "what do we do now? Call the police?"

Robert frowned. "Despite what we might be thinking, do we have enough evidence?"

"What do you mean?" Sarah retorted, unable to hide her scorn. "Don't you believe me? It's definitely him. No question about it. I'd swear to it in court."

"You might just have to do that," David said, putting his arm around her and giving her a squeeze. "Of course we believe you. But do we call the police now? On a Saturday? Or should I speak to Regional Office first . . . on Monday?"

"I don't think we can wait until then," Robert said, smiling at Sarah, as if to show that he had not been offended by her outburst. "If we're sure, we need to move quickly. This is our last day here. We're then packing up for the season. Everything's going to our winter quarters in Ascot. All the ring-boys will then be laid off."

"That settles it then, "David said, drawing away from Sarah and looking around, as if to seek out Robert's telephone. "We better try to speak to Inspector Whitehouse in Tonbridge. He was the one handling the Tonbridge raid. I imagine Battle is under his watch, as well."

Mention of the word watch made Sarah look at her own. It was approaching four o'clock and there was no way that they could hang around here for the police to turn up. "David," she said, grabbing his hand, "we can't stay here any longer. We've got to get back for Mark. I couldn't bear him getting back from football to an empty house."

"And it could be a couple of hours before the police get here," Robert said, clearly agreeing with Sarah's sentiments. "Leave it to me to give Inspector Whitehouse a ring. I can handle everything here. He can then speak to you later. More likely, he'll want to see you, so he could call in tonight or tomorrow."

"I suppose Sarah's formal identification could come later," David acknowledged. "The police have got the note the man wrote. If Antonio's our man, a fresh specimen of his handwriting should confirm it. And they must have fingerprints on the note. Is there any chance that he'll scarper before the police get here?"

Robert shook his head. "Why should he? He doesn't know he's under suspicion."

"Do you think there's a chance he's still kept hold of the money?" Sarah asked, thinking that there could be another way of proving his guilt.

"Every chance," Robert replied. "On a travelling show like this, he wouldn't get many opportunities to spend a significant sum. These ring-boys have long hours of work. I'm surprised he'd had time to go out and rob banks, especially in towns where we're not actually performing. I reckon he'll be keeping the money until we finish our tenting season. All the more reason for speaking to the police straightaway."

"Where would he keep the money?" Sarah asked. "Does he have a caravan?"

Robert shook his head again. "No, the ring-boys share a long trailer. It's partitioned off inside, so they have there own sleeping areas and lockers. If he's still got the cash, it's probably in his locker. But why do you ask?"

Sarah smiled at what was now tickling her. "You know, in films, stolen money always seems to be identified by the serial numbers on the notes. I don't see how that can happen in reality. Most of our notes are well-worn. But the notes I gave him could certainly be identified. I'd just taken in a large credit from Mac Fisheries. As usual, most of their notes were soiled with fish scales and reeked to high heaven. If he's still got those in his locker, it will be proof enough that he's the culprit."

Both David and Robert laughed. Sarah's suggestion had certainly lightened the mood. "Sounds like a case of the Scales of Justice," David suggested to the groans of the other two.

A few moments later, David and Sarah made their exit, leaving Robert to telephone the police. It had certainly been a birthday celebration to remember. But they had better go easy on the contents of their drink's cupboard that evening. They would need to be on full alert if the police were to descend on them.

Chapter 34

"A ring-boy? In a circus? What on earth is going on?"

David remained poker-faced as Angus McPhoebe's incredulity seemed to know no bounds. It was as if he had never heard of a circus, let alone ring-boys. David stayed quiet, always his way of riding out a verbal storm. It would, eventually, blow itself out, without any intervention from him. But why the storm in the first place? What did it matter whom the villain was and what he did, provided he had been apprehended? As for 'what is going on' . . . the raider of four of our branches had been caught - that's what's been going on.

That Monday morning, David had arrived at the Regional Office car park, just as Angus McPhoebe stepped out of his gleaming Rover. He must have spent all his weekend giving it the polishes of all polish. McPhoebe was clearly nonplussed at David's presence. Arriving again without a prior appointment? Matters were made worse when David had refused to reveal why he had turned up unannounced.

"I needed to see you and speak to you urgently," he had simply said. "But not here in the car park. It's a matter for both you and Mr Threadgold."

McPhoebe had harrumphed and stormed into the building, leaving David trailing in his wake. His mood had clearly not improved by the time the three of them had sat down around Mr Threadgold's imposing regional manager's mahogany desk. After introductions had been made for David's first meeting with Mr Threadgold, all David had said, so far, was that the raider had been caught and that he was a ring-boy in a circus. The regional manager's response was muted, compared to that of McPhoebe.

"A circus?" he queried, holding up his hand, palm pointed forward in McPhoebe's direction. It seemed to have the desired effect: McPhoebe slumped back in his chair, possibly deflated, unless he was gathering himself to launch his next tirade. David was quietly impressed with the regional manager's intervention. Had he and Robert got it wrong about the man? Was he carrying out a litmus test to counteract McPhoebe's apparent acerbity?

David nodded. "Bertram Mills."

Threadgold also nodded. "Thought as such. Has this anything to do with your brother?"

McPhoebe now leant forward, back on full alert. "Your brother, Goodhart? What's going on?"

"Calm down, Angus," Threadgold said, impressing David again. How many times in the past had he longed to say that? "I knew David's brother many years ago. He was in the bank then. But he then decided to run away to the circus, so to speak. Wasn't that right, David?"

David smiled and shook is head, as though he could not believe what Robert had done. He remained quiet, his mind in turmoil at this 'David' business. McPhoebe had never called him David, yet they were more of similar rank than that of the regional manager. Was Threadgold softening him up for some forthcoming rapier thrust, or was he genuinely being amicable?

"I always knew he'd do well," Threadgold continued, his words actually sounding genuine this time. "I wasn't surprised when you told me some time ago that he'd become general manager of the circus."

"And still is," David said. But it was strange that Robert was dominating the conversation, as opposed to the arrest of Antonio. He decided it was time to move on. " But let me tell you exactly what's happened."

And he did just that - from beginning to end, leaving out nothing. As he recounted Sarah's role in it all, his heart swelled with pride at her bravery and perspicacity. Mr Threadgold clearly felt the same way.

"Your wife deserves a medal," he said, when David had finished, then adding, "and so do you, David. Without the pair of you - and your brother's involvement - these raids could have gone unsolved for some time, if not for ever. As for those scaly bank notes ... I do admire your wife for having such foresight. The police must have been impressed. Very well done, indeed. Now, I have another appointment. I must leave you in the hands of Angus. I know he wants to be up-dated on how things are going along at Crowborough."

David groaned inwardly. From elation to despair? Mr Threadgold's commendation had made him feel like he had scaled Everest. Now, it was likely that he would feel as though he had been pushed over a cliff edge. And when, in McPhoebe's room, seated across from him at his more common or garden teak desk, the omens were not good.

"Why are you taking so long at Crowborough?" McPhoebe snapped, clearly banishing any thoughts of echoing his boss's words of praise. It was as if the arrest of Antonio had been a figment of David's imagination. But David was sure that McPhoebe would claim some share of the credit - probably at his next one-to-one meeting with Mr Threadgold.

"There's been a lot to do," David simply replied, determined not to give McPhoebe any breakdown of his tasks. He was not carrying out the inspection at the behest of Regional Office. All inspections were instigated by Head Office. Regional Office would be one of the recipients of his eventual report and would take action, if so required. At this stage, he had no need to be beholden to McPhoebe in any way whatsoever.

"But you're now into your third week," McPhoebe persisted, it seemed through gritted teeth. "You should have been finished in two."

"As I said, there's been a lot to do."

The answer clearly did not satisfy McPhoebe. He scowled and took out a pen from his pocket, then scoured his desk, as though for a piece of paper to write on. Was he proposing to compile a derogatory report on this infuriating inspector? But, as usual, his desk was devoid of paper, or anything else. David had wondered before if this meant he was a naturally tidy worker, or, perhaps, he did no work at all.

"Does that mean you've been encountering problems?" McPhoebe asked, putting the pen back in his pocket. Presumably, the derogatory report could be completed later.

"As well as the raids?" David decided to keep his answers brief. Force McPhoebe to probe if he wanted further information.

"Don't be obtuse," McPhoebe snapped. "You know what I mean."

David was not sure that he did, but why should he discuss any aspects of his inspection with McPhoebe, prior to submitting his eventual report? Instead, he decided to point out that McPhoebe had been instrumental in extending the length of his inspection. "Remember, you did interrupt my inspection by sending me off to both Tonbridge and Battle."

"Even so," McPhoebe said, letting out a world-weary sigh, "what else is taking your time at Crowborough? I'm not aware of any problems there. And Frank Windsor's a good man."

That 'good man' again. But David was resolute in not revealing anything to McPhoebe at this stage. He was also a little disconcerted that McPhoebe should be probing like this. Had he an ulterior motive? In most things, that seemed to be the case with him. And why should he persist in referring to Frank Windsor as a good man? Was the manager a prodigy of his?

"Anyway," David said, getting up, having decided there was no point in extending this conversation, "there's still much to do. And I better get back to Crowborough to do it."

He omitted to say that once he got back to the branch, he and Trevor would be off to Crawley. He certainly did not want to give McPhoebe any inkling of that particular problem which was exercising his mind.

As he set off in his car, his thoughts immediately transferred to Trevor. At eight o'clock that morning, he had called at the lad's flat, asking him to use his own car to get to the branch. He also gave him a brief rundown about Antonio's arrest. In turn, he wanted to hear how Trevor had got on with Katie. But Regional Office had beckoned and Trevor's thumbs up and broad smile had to suffice. That was all David needed to know at the time; he would hear the full works on their trip to Crawley.

Chapter 35

D avid had hardly put one foot inside the branch before the manager's secretary rushed up to him. For an older woman, she could move quickly when needs must; this appeared to be one such occasion.

"I've had an urgent call for you," she actually gasped, as if her exertions had caught up with her. "It was from Mrs Callard."

"Mrs Callard?" David repeated. What had happened to her previous secrecy? Before, she had not wanted anyone to know of their meeting up.

"Yes, yes," the secretary said. "I told her you weren't here. I didn't know where you were. Trevor didn't say, but he thought you'd be back late morning." She then glanced at her watch, as if to confirm whether Trevor's prediction had been accurate.

David did the same. It was eleven-thirty.

"Anyway," she continued, "Mrs Callard said she'd be over the road at the Crowborough Cross pub. She'd get there at twelve and wait as long as it takes."

Not only had Mrs Callard now shunned any previous anonymity, but she had also chosen the nearest possible venue to the branch. At least it would mean David not having to get back in his car - should he decide to take up her invitation.

"Thank you," he simply said, moving off and leaving the secretary somewhat agog. He saw no reason to elaborate and made his way to the rest room to find Trevor. The rumour mill in the branch would now be spinning like a Catherine wheel. Everyone had probably become aware that Ted had been murdered. So why would his widow want to see the bank inspector?

It was a question David was also asking himself.

"Hello, sir," Trevor said, looking up as David entered the room. "Have you heard the latest?"

David nodded. "Mrs Callard, you mean? What's this all about, Trevor?"

"Goodness knows, sir. I said you should be back before lunch. Are you going to see her?"

David was being pulled two ways. He and Trevor could not delay their trip to Crawley much longer. It had been postponed twice already. But why did Mrs Callard want to see him? It could be important. Seeing her across the road would, though, be quicker than another trip to Hartfield. But was this pub the most suitable place? Having said that, he had not yet set foot inside. But it did not strike him as a likely spot for an intimate conversation. That was, surely, likely to be the case if he chose to meet Mrs Callard.

"I gather she's going to be there at noon," he said. "If I go and keep the meeting brief, we could then get on our way to Crawley. Say, by one o'clock?"

"That seems fair enough," Trevor replied. "First of all, though, how did you get on at Regional Office?"

"That can wait for a moment," David said, sitting down, having thrown his coat over the coat stand, his normal orderliness eschewed. "More important, how did you get on with Katie?"

Trevor's grin was widespread. He raised his left hand and waggled his fingers. "If this was Katie's hand, you'd see a ring of soldering wire around her third finger. The shops were closed and that's all I could find. She's going to have to wait for the real thing."

David stood up and thrust his hand at Trevor. "Many, many congratulations. I'm so pleased for you both."

"You'll never guess where I proposed," Trevor said, still grinning.

"Go on."

"At the Walnut Grove. It was a bit embarrassing, though. When I found the courage to ask her to marry me, I actually followed it up with a heartfelt 'please'. And, you know what? Katie's answer was actually 'yes, please'."

"My, what a polite pair you both are. Any thoughts yet about a date?"

Trevor shook his head. "No, it's all been a bit of a rush with my having to get back here. But we don't want to wait long. Katie'll have to leave Barnmouth, of course. What do you think her chances are of getting a job up here?"

David's held his hand to his forehead as he thought about possible options. "Might be difficult around Tunbridge Wells - unless she goes part-time, like Sarah. But I should think London would cry out for her secretarial skills. Would she mind commuting?"

"Don't know," Trevor replied. "At least the trains from Tunbridge Wells aren't too bad. But enough about us. What, happened with you this morning? And with Mrs Callard on Friday?"

"It's not just this morning, Trevor. More like the whole weekend." And for the second time that morning, he recounted 'the capture of Antonio', as he now liked to think of it. He also briefed Trevor on his meeting with Mrs Callard, although what happened then looked likely to be superseded if he joined her at the Crowborough Cross.

When he had finished and Trevor had stopped looking agog, he looked at his watch. Just before twelve. "Now, Trevor, do I go across the road, or not? Or should we both go? She's clearly keen to have another meeting."

Trevor frowned, thought for a moment and then said, "Maybe something's changed. Why else would she be happy for the branch to know that she wants to see you? You reckon it's because of her visit from the police?"

That was certainly going through David's mind. Even unwittingly, she could well have given the police information which could lead to Ted's murderer. She had been appalled that she probably knew who it was. It had to be someone at the Crowborough Collective lunch and she knew most of those members. Unless the perpetrator was a guest, like David.

"It must be something to do with the police," he replied. "But why would this make her want to see me again? Unless she thinks it might be linked to the bank . . . and what we're doing here. If that's the case, I think we should both go and see her."

As David rose from his chair to get his coat, there was a knock on the door.

"Come in," he called out.

The door opened to reveal Frank Windsor - a concerned-looking Frank Windsor.

"I've just heard," he said, closing the door behind him, "that Barbara Callard wants to see you."

"Aha," David said, nodding and waiting for Windsor's response.

"What can that be about?" the manager asked, his concern not abating. "Not about Ted, surely? There's a terrible rumour going around that he was murdered. Have you heard about that."

David nodded again as he put on his coat. "It's not just a rumour. It's a fact. Mrs Callard told me."

Windsor now looked bemused. "You've already seen her?"

"Not yet today. It was last week. She wanted to talk it over with me."

Windsor's bemusement multiplied. "With you? Why you?"

David had no intention of elaborating. Especially with another meeting in the offing. The whole point before was that Mrs Callard did not want anyone to know that she was meeting him. Including Frank Windsor. Something had certainly now changed her mind. But this was not something to involve the manager with at this stage.

"I think she just wanted to bend my ear. Someone who wasn't involved in the town. Especially as Ted was murdered at the Crowborough Collective lunch. It didn't take much for her to put two and two together."

Windsor put his hand to his mouth, as if in horror. Yet if he accepted that Ted Callard had been murdered, he must have recognized that it had happened at the lunch. And that the killer was well-known to him - one of his Collective chums. But what about Windsor himself? No, that was not on. But what if there was some sort of conspiracy involved? Could that involve Windsor? David's original assessment of Crowborough Collective had been that it was a self-serving clique of local businessmen, formed for the benefit of its members. Was that not conspiratorial, in itself?

"Anyway," David continued, beckoning Trevor to join him, "We're off to meet Mrs Callard in the Crowborough Cross. If anything pertinent arises, I'll brief you later. But that'll be late afternoon. After we've seen Mrs Callard, we're taking a trip out to Crawley."

Having dropped that little teaser into Windsor's ear, they made their way out of the branch, crossed the busy junction and entered the pub.

Being much larger than the Dorset Arms, it did not have the same ambience. The bar area was crammed with tables and chairs and David was immediately concerned that it would not be conducive for a confidential meeting. But he then spotted a part which was sectioned off into private cubicles. That was more like it. And in the end such cubicle, he saw Mrs Callard waiting, then looking surprised to see Trevor with him.

She rose when they reached her and David immediately introduced Trevor.

"I hope you don't mind my bringing Trevor," he then said, taking the seat next to Mrs Callard. He indicated that Trevor should take the chair opposite. He did not want Mrs Callard to feel ill at ease in having to face them both in a possible two against one arrangement. "Trevor's my trusted assistant . . . keeps me on the straight and narrow," he added, smiling. "We've worked with each other for twelve months now and do everything together. I've brought him along because I have a feeling that our meeting with you might just have a bearing on our work here."

Mrs Callard nodded and Trevor's warm smile seemed to overcome any initial reservations she might have felt. "I think that may well be possible," she said, turning towards David at her side.

"First of all," David said, picking up a menu card from the table, "it's lunchtime. Let's have a bite of something."

"I must say, I'm not very hungry," Mrs Callard said, while, nevertheless, picking up a menu herself. "I've hardly eaten a thing since Ted died."

David was not surprised. The woman beside him seemed far more gaunt than when he had first met her. Sitting so close to her, he could not really judge any change in her body weight, but her skin now stretched over her cheek bones and dark rings were doing their best to support her sunken eyes.

"What about just a sandwich, then? And coffee? Or would you prefer a cold drink?"

"A sandwich and a coffee would be fine. Would that suit you and Trevor?" As both men nodded, she then said, attempting to get up, "But, please, let me get them. After all, I'm the one who asked you to come here."

David put his hand on her arm, which did, indeed, feel emaciated, and eased her back on to her chair. "No, let me. But I'm sure Trevor won't mind doing the donkey work."

Trevor grinned. "Of course, sir," he said, stressing that last word. They all decided on cheese and pickle and Trevor then made his way to the bar to place their order.

"I hope you didn't mind coming to meet me again," Mrs Callard said, when they were alone. "I just wanted to talk to someone about my visit from the police. Like I said before, I simply can't do that with anyone living in Crowborough."

"But when you rang the bank this time, you decided to say who you were."

"I had to," Mrs Callard replied, shaking her head. "I didn't want to, but you were out. And I desperately wanted to see you. I had no choice but to leave a message."

David was glad to see Trevor returning. He had the feeling that both of them were going to need to hear what Mrs Callard had to say. Trevor took his seat and said the sandwiches and coffee would be brought to them in about ten minutes.

"I was just saying to Mr Goodhart," Mrs Callard said, looking across at Trevor, "that I wanted to talk about the visit I had from the police. I really would like to have both of your reactions . . . to what they seemed to be thinking."

This was good. Mrs Callard had immediately drawn Trevor into the fold. David was not surprised. Trevor had that enviable knack of being able to put others immediately at their ease. Yet he had always claimed to be shy where women were concerned. Or was that just when he was trying to establish a personal relationship with someone? Like Katie? Except that Katie's natural ebullience would knock the shyness out of anyone.

"And what were they thinking?" David asked, drawing back Mrs Callard's attention from Trevor to himself. "Do they have a suspect?"

Mrs Callard shook her head. "They didn't say. But I doubt they would have told me if they had. They spent most of their time going through Ted's files."

David could only hope that this had not raised awkward questions over the scrap metal business. Ted had said at the lunch that everything was above board. Yet with it being mainly a cash business, he had been reluctant to go to the police about his suspicions that something bad was going on. Perhaps if he had done just that, he would still be around today. Instead, it was odds-on that his subsequent murder was linked to his fears.

"I told you before that Ted rarely took copies of the letters he wrote," Mrs Callard continued, then pausing as their sandwiches and coffees arrived. When the waiter left them, she continued, "But they were particularly keen to see any copies he did make. And that led them to wanting to know everything about Peter's compensation monies."

"Why would they want to know about that?" David asked, sinking his teeth into his sandwich. "That was years ago."

"I know," Mrs Callard said, "but they discovered something I knew nothing about. I told you before that the driver was never blamed for the accident. On that basis, I thought the insurance company would have dismissed any claim out of hand. But the money eventually came through. £100,000. Ted had said at the time that I shouldn't have worried about it. But, for some reason, he kept the truth from me. The police discovered that the money had not come from the insurance company. It was all in Ted's files. The driver paid the money himself. It seems that it was his way of dealing with his perceived guilt . . . even though he wasn't technically to blame for the accident."

"But that's extraordinary," David blurted out, almost choking on a bit of cheese. "£100,000's a small fortune. Who could afford to do that?"

"I didn't tell you the name of the driver before," Mrs Callard said, "It didn't seem necessary. But now . . . now that I know what he did. Is it possible he could be linked to Ted's murder?"

"And are you now going to tell us his name, Mrs Callard," David asked. "Is this a reason why you asked to see me?"

Mrs Callard nodded, and brushed some crumbs off the navy jacket she was wearing today. "Yes, even though I can't think how it could be relevant. It was the solicitor, Julian Palfrow. He often drove Peter to football. He was always so kind like that. And being such a prominent solicitor, he's probably the only person we knew who could afford to pay out that kind of money. He was a senior partner in Tunbridge Wells at the time. But not long afterwards, he moved to a much smaller practice in Crowborough. I often wondered why. Now it's perfectly clear to me. He must have sold out of his Tunbridge Wells partnership to recoup the money he paid us. Don't you think that's an extraordinary gesture, Mr Goodhart?"

More than extraordinary. Simply unbelievable. From the way Trevor was shaking his head, it would seem that he felt the same. And this generosity of spirit and finance had come from a man whom David had deemed at the lunch to share Charlie Spencer O'Hara's arrogance. Would an arrogant man have done such a thing? Perhaps Angus McPhoebe had been right: Julian Palfrow really was a 'top man'. Yet following their meeting with Mrs Callard, David and Trevor were heading to Crawley, with

Trevor clasping a bunch of undertakings given by this same man over properties which, so far, Trevor had been unable to find.

What was going on, Trevor? David had no need to voice this question. He simply posed it in his eyes, meeting those of Trevor across the table.

He decided to change the subject and turned to Mrs Callard. "When the police looked through Ted's correspondence, did anything else crop up? Or was it just about the compensation monies?"

Mrs Callard pursed her lips and frowned. "They took away various items. I don't know what. The only other thing they discussed with me was what I told you about last time. That Ted was getting exasperated with Derek Herretson. He wasn't getting any answers to his letters. That's why he tried to get Frank Windsor involved. But the police found a copy of a letter I hadn't actually seen. Ted never told me about it. It was the last letter he sent. In it he threatened to withdraw all our investments from Derek. He must have thought that such a threat would have persuaded him to reply to the previous letters. You see, for Peter's sake, he really wanted to get that new car."

"That's understandable enough," David replied, thinking back to how Frank Windsor had eulogized over Derek Herretson at the lunch: 'the most successful investment consultant in town'? He certainly did not deserve such an accolade if he failed to answer letters. But David was suddenly bothered about something else: something he hardly dared to contemplate. So much so that he had to drag his attention back to Mrs Callard, the very least she deserved. "Do you know what the police thought about this? Did they make any comments?"

"Not really," Mrs Callard replied. "They were more interested in the relationship Ted had with all the Crowborough Collective members. It was just that Derek Herretson, as far as I was aware, was the only one featured in Ted's files. Oh, and Julian Palfrow, of course. But I have the feeling they're now going to probe into every one of them."

"I'm not surprised at that," David said, "One of them must have . . . " His words tailed off. The sensitivity of what he was about to say suddenly hitting him.

The point was not lost on Mrs Callard. "That's what's so horrible," she said, her voice breaking. "The not knowing. Someone clearly had it in for Ted. I simply can't think why. He was such a good man . . . "

She then reached into her handbag for a handkerchief and wiped her damp cheeks. "I'm so sorry," she said, looking at David and then across to Trevor. "Before you arrived, I promised myself I wouldn't do this. Typical female," she added, with a wry smile.

"I think you're being very brave," Trevor said, stretching out his arm and taking one of her hands in his. Mrs Callard made no immediate attempt to resist, but then nodded at Trevor in appreciation of his gesture and released his hand. David felt very proud of Trevor. The lad might be of a different generation from Mrs Callard, but, at this moment, mutual empathy abounded.

"Perhaps it's time for another coffee," David said, looking at their empty cups.

Mrs Callard shook her head as she put her handkerchief away. "Not for me, thank you. I've taken up too much of your time already. But I'd like your advice. It's been so good having you to talk to, but I'm sure you'll be moving on soon. What should I do then? I can't really speak to anyone else here in Crowborough. Not with a finger of suspicion being pointed at everyone. Although I can't see that now applying to Inspector Saunders, even though the policeman was at the lunch. Incidentally, he wasn't among the police who called on me. But they said he had given them plenty of background about Crowborough Collective. I suppose he was the one member I could have put my trust in. But, to start with, I was suspicious of everyone. Oh, dear, you can't believe how alone all this makes me feel."

David could not feel more sympathetic to Mrs Callard's predicament and he could see across the table that this view was shared. "You're wrong there, Mrs Callard," he replied. "I'm sure we can both believe that. But, at the moment, I don't think you need to talk to anyone else . . . apart from the police. This situation might not last for very long. As crimes go, I reckon this one's going to be solved very quickly."

Chapter 36

"Do you really think it's going to be solved quickly?" Trevor asked, as they started their journey to Crawley.

David kept his eyes on the road, but he sensed Trevor looking at him enquiringly. He was not surprised. Did he really have any justification in making such a comment to Mrs Callard? Or was he simply trying to console her in what had clearly been her hour of need? She, surely, needed some hope to cling on to. Yet his mind was certainly pointing towards an early conclusion.

"And don't you?" he replied, hoping that Trevor had formed his own thoughts on what had happened and how it might be resolved. He perceived Trevor shrugging next to him.

"I don't know what to think, sir," he replied, after a few moments of reflection. "I certainly hope the killer's apprehended quickly. But without knowing what the police are doing . . ."

His words tailed off and they continued their journey in silence. They were soon passing the Dorset Arms and David reflected on the difference between this pub and the Crowborough Cross. The Dorset Arms won by a country mile.

"Just think about the likely suspects," he then said. "The killer must be a member of the Crowborough Collective."

"But weren't there forty or fifty people at the lunch?"

"Yes, but the vast majority couldn't have done it. Those on my table, for instance."

"That counts out Mr Windsor, then," Trevor said. "And you, sir," he added, grinning.

David frowned. "It's not a time for flippancy, Trevor."

"Sorry, sir. It just sort of came out."

David turned off the road at Hartfield and headed in the direction of East Grinstead. He estimated that they should reach Crawley in half an hour. He took advantage of a straight piece of road with no traffic to glance across at Trevor. "One thing's for sure, Trevor, there's got to be a motive. Yet Frank Windsor told me how popular Ted Callard was. With everyone, it seems. And you just heard how Mrs Callard called him such a good man. I know she must be biased but . . ."

"He can't have been popular with one person, sir."

"And there might have been skeletons in his cupboard which we're not aware of."

Trevor glanced across at him. "Two particular names cropped up just now. Do you think it could be one of them?"

'Stick-insect' and the 'solicitor extraordinaire'? Over the last few days, David had not thought of Derek Herretson and Julian Palfrow by the nicknames he had chosen for them at the Crowborough Collective lunch. But now, 'solicitor extraordinaire' seemed to be particularly apposite. Here was a man who had used £100,000 of his own money when the insurance company had denied the Callards' claim. How many people would have done that?

"It could certainly be one of them," he replied, as they approached the outskirts of East Grinstead. "But there could be others, of course. People we're not aware of. The police must be looking at everyone who was at the lunch. But it's difficult to believe that Julian Paltrow would have a motive. Not after what he did for the family. But it's time we started thinking about him and his undertakings you've got there. And those valuations by Charlie Spencer O'Hara."

Trevor had already taken them out of his briefcase and they now sat on his lap. At David's earlier instruction, he had removed them from the customers' files in the strongroom. The staff knew he had done this as part of their examination of the manager's lending. But they were unaware, and would be appalled to know, that they were now with them in David's Consul. It was highly irregular to remove such documents from the branch, but David was happy to accept responsibility for their actions. They could have left the undertakings behind and just brought with them the professional valuations of the various properties and their respective photographs. But David had decided to keep all the items together, in case any cross-referencing was needed.

"To start with," David then said, "I think we'll just have a general drive round Crawley. We can look out for any recently-built developments. That's where those houses you couldn't find are likely to be. If we don't come up with anything, we can start asking around. Our best bet would be a postman or two. We're bound to see some of them on their rounds."

Trevor clearly agreed and said, " They're likely to be more helpful than the newsagent I asked."

David nodded and it soon became apparent that a likely postman would be their best bet. They had come across several new housing estates, but each one comprised semi-detached or terrace houses, a far cry from the detached, executive properties depicted in their valuations. But the first two postmen they approached had no knowledge of the addresses they were seeking.

"This is starting to look ominous," David said, having parked his car and taken hold of the documents from Trevor. "Look at these photos," he then added, passing several back to Trevor. "They all look the real deal, but we can't find any of them."

"Apart from Mr Crickhaven's, sir."

"And thank God you managed to find his house," David said, becoming increasingly exasperated. "Perhaps we should go and have a look at that one again. Maybe the others are in the same vicinity . . . even if you couldn't find them before."

A few minutes later, Trevor clearly felt quite proud that, without reference to his road atlas, he had been able to find Guildhurst Road and they soon reached Mr Crickhaven's house. David parked the car across the road and a couple of houses past number 30. He did not want possible passers-by to suspect that they were taking undue interest in that particular house.

David checked the photograph attached to O'Hara's valuation and everything was perfectly in order. That was something, he supposed. He then took back all the files from Trevor and looked at each photograph in turn.

"Just have another look at these four, Trevor," he said, still holding the photos, but allowing himself and Trevor to look at them together. "They all look so similar. As if they're all on the same estate. Yet we cannot find such an estate."

Trevor shook his head and then picked out one particular photo from the four. "Look at this one, sir. It's a dead ringer for Mr Crickhaven's. The windows are the same, even the front door." He then peered closely at the photo. "Can't make out any number, though. But it could well be here in Guildhurst Road."

David then flicked through the others. "You're on to something here, Trevor." He then started the car and put it in gear. "Let's drive up and down the road and see what we can find."

There was, fortunately, no other activity in the road and David was able to drive slowly in order to look carefully at each house.

Within a couple of minutes, they had identified each of the houses depicted in the first four photos. All of them were situated in Guildhurst Road. Yet all of them bore a completely different address in their respective professional valuations. And not only had David and Trevor failed to find those such addresses in Crawley, they were also unknown to at least two postmen, as well as the newsagent Trevor had asked previously.

David stopped the car, switched off the engine and turned to Trevor. "Are you thinking what I'm thinking?"

Trevor shook his head, alarm etching his features. "I don't know what to think, sir. But something's very wrong. And one thing's for certain, we don't need to seek out any of these other properties. We've got enough evidence of wrongdoing here in Guildhurst Road." As David remained silent with his thoughts, Trevor then added, "I've never come across anything like this before. Is it really as bad as I'm thinking?"

Oh, yes, Trevor, it certainly is. In addition to the rogue home loans David had previously told Trevor about, David had also heard of another case, almost exactly like what was happening now. It had occurred in a quiet, West Country backwater. The branch manager had ignored basic banking rules and had dispensed with the one golden rule: common sense. He had also failed, utterly, to assess multiple loan requests against the cardinal rules of bank lending. He had chosen, instead, to be swayed by the magnetic power of one influential customer, putting blind faith in whatever that man said. Now, it seemed to be happening again, under David's watch. He could see no alternative to the eventual outcome: Frank Windsor? Guilty as charged?

"After what we've discovered today," David replied, "there are going to be some monumental repercussions. None of them good for the bank. Past reputations will count for nothing. Goodness knows what Angus McPhoebe'll say."

David paused, causing Trevor to press him further. "Go on, sir."

"Just think about this possible scenario, Trevor. The bank's authorized solicitor introduces large numbers of new customers to the branch manager. He offers impeccable references, in this case for respectable airline pilots. These people are moving to the Crawley area because of the expansion of Gatwick airport. They want to buy properties in the £8,000 region, with a loan or mortgage of £5,000 from the bank. In each case, a professional valuation is provided, plus a good solicitor's undertaking. This is to hold the deeds to the bank's order, prior to all documentation being completed. So far, so good?"

Trevor nodded. "That seems to be it, exactly."

"So, Trevor, it's all been done on trust. The manager is dealing with a highly respectable solicitor - Julian Palfrow - and a most honourable land agent, if only because he is, actually, the Honourable Charlie Spencer O'Hara. But what has Frank Windsor actually done, apart from kowtowing to these professional people? More important, what has he not done? For instance, he hasn't met any of these new customers and he hasn't seen any of the properties in question. He hasn't yet seen any deeds for the properties, even though some of the purchases were made months ago. All he has seen are undertakings given by Julian Palfrow."

"But what about Mr Crickhaven? Mr Windsor said he spoke to him on the phone. And his house is there all right. We've actually seen it."

"But the whole point is that Mr Windsor hasn't seen it. I now feel sure that Mr Crickhaven was Julian Palfrow's test case. This pilot was perfectly genuine - job-wise and house-wise. He was the first one. If his loan request went through with no questions asked, it opened the door for others, should Palfrow wish it. And wish it, he did. The floodgates opened. All subsequent cases were a figment of his imagination, aided and abetted by our friend O'Hara."

"But why was Crawley chosen? If Palfrow operates in Crowborough . . ."

"If the houses were in Crowborough, Windsor was bound to know about them, and see them. Crawley was far enough away for him to simply accept the professional valuations for what they were. And it's a fact that Crawley is expanding, because of Gatwick. It would be entirely feasible for there to be an influx of pilots. And if Palfrow could claim that he was representing the pilots' association, the fact that he was domiciled in Crowborough wouldn't matter. And he could also claim to represent them in all their dealings with the bank, simply because they were not local to Crowborough."

"And you really think, sir, that this is what's happened? But why would professional people do such a thing?"

David shrugged. "Greed is the most common reason for anything like this."

"But these people must be well-off."

"You'd think so, but you don't know what else is lurking in the background. Remember what Mrs Callard said? She thought Julian Palfrow had to sell out of his Tunbridge Wells practice. Apparently to recoup the £100,000 compensation monies he paid out. And Frank Windsor told me that O'Hara's expectation of inheriting the family pile had been dashed. His father's giving everything to the National Trust. So, both of them could be harder up than we might think."

"And the money from all the bank loans has gone straight into their pockets?"

David nodded. "And if my scenario is accurate, Mr Windsor has lost the bank £70-80,000."

"Phew!" Trevor exclaimed, putting his hand to his mouth. "That's terrible, sir. What'll happen to him?"

"I don't know. But Angus McPhoebe will have to re-assess his opinion of Windsor being a 'good man'."

"He said the same about Palfrow and O'Hara."

"Yes. The only really good man we seem to have heard of was Ted Callard. And he's dead."

Trevor then gasped and again clasped his hand to his mouth. "You don't think all this business has anything to do with his murder?"

Chapter 37

D avid answered Trevor's question by posing one of his own. "What did you say earlier? About our meeting with Mrs Callard?"

"Sir?"

"Remember? You said that two names had cropped up."

Trevor frowned, then clearly realized to where this was leading. He simply nodded in reply.

"Ah. So you do remember, Trevor. Two names. And we've already dealt with one, not to mention throwing the Honourable Charlie into the mix. And the other?"

"Derek Herretson, sir?"

"Of course. So where does he fit into all of this?"

David knew the answer to that particular question. It had first occurred to him in their meeting with Mrs Callard. At the time, he had hardly dared contemplate what had suddenly bothered him. That was not the case now. And it had nothing to do with Julian Palfrow and his spurious loans. But he would like to bounce his thoughts off Trevor. Two minds were better than one. Though he did not always think thus. There were times when autonomy was his chosen path. But if another opinion was needed, who better to supply this than Trevor? And that time was now.

"He's certainly bothered us for a while, sir," Trevor replied. "Right from the time you asked me to go round to his place."

"And why did we feel that way?"

Trevor pursed his lips, appearing to drag his memory back over what had happened over the last couple of weeks. "What he was doing," he eventually said, "seemed too good to be true. Those interest rates of his. Why could he offer returns far higher than those of the bank?"

They were now well into their journey back to Crowborough. The traffic was heavier than before and David needed to concentrate on the road, especially as they were in unfamiliar territory. It was not the situation to have a meaningful conversation over something of such importance. Yet, because of its importance, he and Trevor needed to get their heads together before they got back to the branch. He then spotted a lay-by, just before reaching East Grinstead. Almost missing it, he braked sharply, ignored the irate tooting behind him, and brought the car to a stop.

"Sir?"

It was a rather desperate 'sir', accompanied by white-knuckled fists grasping his seat.

"Sorry about that, Trevor," David said, realizing that his action fully justified Trevor's consternation. One moment they were toodling along a main road, minding their own business, and then unexpectedly slewing into an unforeseen lay-by. "Needs must," he then added, applying the handbrake and turning off the ignition.

Trevor shook his head, placed his hands back on his lap, but remained quiet.

"If we're going to talk about Derek Herretson in some depth," David said, looking pointedly at Trevor, "I want to be able to give it my full attention. And I can't do that if I'm driving the car. And we need to do this before we get back to the branch. I need to have all my facts right and get my theorizing on the right lines before I see Frank Windsor."

"What do you mean theorizing?"

"Well, we know a lot of the facts. For example, you've just mentioned those high interest rates. You said that they seemed too good to be true. And that expression usually means just that. Yet, according to Windsor, Herretson's reputation is second to none. The result is that so many people are investing with him, most of them probably by way of word of mouth recommendations. I know that's the case with Henry Purcell at his residential home. He was so impressed with Herretson that he recommended him to many of his residents. And he also entrusted the man with some of his own money."

Trevor kept nodding as David made these particular points.

"And then there's George Bathurst, the builder. Frank Windsor actually lent him money to invest with Herretson. The interest he earned from this was higher than that charged by the bank on his overdraft. What a lot of nonsense that is. And, Trevor, might I just say that when you're a manager, don't you dare do anything like that."

Trevor smiled, clearly acknowledging that this was an instruction, not advice.

"And then we have the Callards. It sounds as though most of the other monies put Herretson's way were in the thousands, maybe tens of thousands. But the Callards were in a different league. £100,000, no less."

"Overall, then," Trevor said, "Herretson must be sitting on a huge investment portfolio."

"Yes, Trevor. And with the high interest rates he's paying, more and more funds are likely to flow his way. All by way of personal recommendation. Take Henry Purcell's residents, for instance. Once it becomes known that some are effectively getting significant help with their monthly fees, others would quite naturally want to get a piece of the action. Especially if they know that Henry Purcell is also an investor. What better recommendation would they want than that?"

"Yet when I went round to Herretson's place," Trevor said, " it just seemed like a private house. There were no signs anywhere that it was a business. And the only person I saw was Herretson, himself, when he went to put a case into the boot of his Aston Martin."

"And that particular car indicates he's doing all right for himself."

"Do I detect a touch of envy there, sir?" Trevor said, grinning.

"It depends if it's been acquired all above board. And we're now getting down to the crux of the matter."

"Crux, sir?"

"Yes, Trevor. Is it really all above board? My answer to that is no, it certainly isn't. And another thing is that Herretson's not responding to requests for withdrawals. That appears to be the case with George Bathurst and, possibly with one of Purcell's residents. And it was most definitely the case with Ted Callard. So, Trevor, this is where the theorizing comes in. I reckon we have here a typical Ponzi-type fraud."

"Ponzi, sir?"

"Never heard of Charles Ponzi?"

Trevor shook his head, clearly puzzled by the name.

"He was an Italian," David explained, "but settled in the States early this century. He became known in the 1920s by way of a variety of swindles. One, in particular, will forever bear his name."

"And he's still around?"

"No, he died in 1949. Died, but not forgotten."

"But what's this to do with Derek Herretson?"

"If I'm right, I believe he copied one of Ponzi's scams. Some people call it a case of robbing Peter to pay Paul."

"A Robin Hood?"

"Good heavens, no. Quite the opposite. No good ever comes out of a Ponzi scheme, except for the manipulator, himself . . . in this case, Herretson."

"But how do you know all about this?" Trevor asked, frowning.

David tapped his nose in answer.

Trevor smiled. "You're going to say 'needs must' again, aren't you, sir?"

David grinned, but immediately became serious again. This was no laughing matter. "Let me just suggest what might have happened," he said. "No, I'll do more than that. Let me suggest what actually happened. I'm so confident I'm right."

"Go on, sir. I'm all ears."

"It starts with investors depositing funds with him, on the promise of high returns. He also promises to pay interest monthly, rather than yearly or half-yearly. That's a really popular move, particularly for those with monthly outgoings. But he never actually invests a penny of the money put his way. He stashes most of the cash away for his own benefit."

"But how can he pay those high rates of interest if he hasn't invested the funds?"

"By getting in new investors. He then effectively uses their money to pay interest to his previous ones. And so it goes on. More investors, more interest to pay others. That's where robbing Peter to pay Paul comes in."

"Is much of this sort of thing going on, sir?"

David bit his lower lip as he considered Trevor's question. "I don't think so, Trevor," he eventually replied, "though I might be wrong. But like most things that start in the States, they soon find their way across the pond. I certainly fear this kind of fraud might proliferate in the future. During difficult times, people are always looking for ways to mitigate any hardship. And when an opportunity comes along that looks too good to be true, we both agree that it usually is. And further hardship is then sure to follow."

"But wouldn't people see through a con like this?"

"Not when rational judgement flies out of the window. And these sort of things can look as though people are joining a club. Alongside some of their friends, no doubt. As more and more people join, they are promised more and more of the scheme's profits. It's a bit like the growth of an iceberg. The first punters putting money in start down below at the base and gradually move up as more people sign up to begin at the bottom. Some schemes can offer a commission when existing members recruit new ones and that's where some of the returns come in. As more people join, the old brigade start moving up the iceberg towards the peak. And at the top of the peak sits the instigator . A pyramid would be another good analogy."

"But such a system can't go on for ever."

"It certainly can, provided new recruits keep materializing. And in Herretson's case, investors kept flocking in. Remember all those word-of-mouth recommendations? And it all looks genuine to the investors. Why would they smell a rat? Each month they get a certificate giving details of the interest being paid into their bank accounts. But no mention is made of where their money has been invested. Just the amount. So it all looks above board. But problems can arise when people want to withdraw their money. Small amounts don't cause a problem. Henry Purcell told me of a case when that happened with one of his residents. But large amounts are a different matter altogether."

"Like the Callards' £100,000?"

"Exactly."

"And that's why Herretson procrastinated in not replying to Ted Callard's requests?"

David nodded. "He didn't have that ready money. He'd salted it all away somewhere . . . for his own benefit."

"And then Ted Callard threatened him. And he also told you that something bad was going on. Herretson could well have believed that his whole operation was about to collapse. Especially as we now know from Mrs Callard that Ted had threatened to withdraw all their monies from Herretson. That really would have brought his scam crashing down around him."

"That was Ted Callard's downfall, Trevor. He should have gone to the police. If he had, he'd be alive today."

"But could Herretson really be a murderer? It's all very well conning people out of their money, but murdering someone?"

"He must have panicked. He could see his scheme, as you just said, crashing down around him. And the only threat to it was Ted Callard. Any other requests for repayment would be small in comparison. He could handle those. But £100,000 was quite another matter."

"But it couldn't have been just a panic-reaction. It must have been premeditated, if only to get hold of the poison."

David nodded. "And goodness knows where he got that. Yes, he must have planned it and decided that the lunch was the place to carry it out. He knew Ted would be there and, with so many others present, why should a finger of suspicion be pointed specifically at Herretson?"

"Are you going to the police, sir?"

"Most definitely. But I need to talk to Frank Windsor first. About everything we've established today. But I fear it's all going to be too late."

Trevor looked puzzled, or confused? "Too late, sir? For what?"

"For justice, Trevor. I reckon Herretson's already made a run for it. To Spain, probably. Most likely when you saw him putting a case into the boot of his car. I don't know about the extradition arrangements with Spain, but I fear the worst. And can we be confident that Palfrow and O'Hara are still around?"

"You think they were all involved together?"

"I don't know about that. Unless the other two also put their ill-gotten gains with Herretson. But I don't expect they had anything to do with Ted Callard's murder."

"So it was definitely Herretson on his own?"

David nodded. "I don't see who else. He must have been desperate. And that's bad enough, but remember he's also made off with the life savings of so many people."

"And that money's gone forever? What about Mrs Callard? And George Bathurst? And those at the residential home?"

David shook his head, great sorrow digging deep into his psyche. He could not contemplate the torment which was about to unfold. The bank was likely to lose all the money that Frank Windsor had lent to George Bathurst, but that was dwarfed by the unimaginable hardship to be experienced by all the people who had entrusted their life savings to Derek Herretson.

EPILOGUE

Three months on and David could feel no real satisfaction at being proved right about most of his theorizing in that lay-by outside East Grinstead.

The police were now certain that Derek Herretson had killed Ted Callard to prevent his throwing light on Herretson's nefarious activities. But the man had not been caught. He had certainly fled to Spain, but his exact location was unknown. Even if they caught up with him, they feared extradition problems.

Julian Palfrow and the Honourable Charlie Spencer O'Hara had also disappeared. Vanished into thin air. No one at their respective offices had any idea of their whereabouts. Those people had, in fact, no knowledge of any wrongdoing going on until the police raided their offices and files.

Frank Windsor had been kept equally in the dark. He was now suspended while a thorough investigation continued into his lending activities. So far, over £100,000 had been filched by Messrs Palfrow and O'Hara by way of their rogue houses and the further lending inspection now being carried out threatened more losses. For some reason, Regional Office had insisted upon a different inspector to carry out this task. David had an idea why:

Angus McPhoebe (and Mr Threadgold?) seemed to have taken an exception to the fact that David had found so much going wrong at Crowborough - until then, a highly-thought-of branch. It was almost as though it was a personal affront performed by David. Not only had he not received much credit from Regional Office for discovering so much wrong at his inspection, but, also, little official recognition had been forthcoming for his (and Sarah's) actions in the apprehension of the bank raider. This was despite the praise from Mr Threadgold at the time. Perhaps Angus McPhoebe had discouraged his new boss from lauding this loose cannon of an inspector on their patch. Oh, well . . .

David had also been right about the anguish and hardship caused by Derek Herretson. So many residents at Henry Purcell's residential home had lost a fortune. As had Henry Purcell, himself, and George Bathurst, the builder. Although, in Bathurst's case, the bank was picking up his tab for having lent him the money in the first place.

David felt particularly upset for Mrs Callard. At first, it seemed that their £100,000 had been well and truly lost. But a glimmer of hope had emerged. The police had discovered one of Herretson's bank accounts holding that exact amount, all his other accounts having been cleaned out. They had also found a signed cheque for the same amount in favour of Peter Callard, in whose name the money had been invested. For some reason, it seemed as though Herretson had intended to repay the money, perhaps at the behest of Ted Callard's threats. But this matter was now in legal hands. With so many other victims of the fraud, a successful claim by Mrs Callard, despite Herretson's apparent intentions, was being seriously questioned. David could only hope that, for her sake, she would get some joy.

No other joy had arisen from his inspection of Crowborough branch, but two happy events were likely in the coming months: Trevor and Katie had set a date in June for their wedding; and with Crystal Palace continuing to do well, promotion to the Third Division looked almost certain. In the meantime, Trevor had put on hold any possible career change. David was so pleased about that - as was Sarah.